"[*Death at Pullman*] convincingly recreates a pivotal moment in American labor history...Besides plausibly depicting such historical figures as Eugene Debs and Nellie Bly, McNamara throws in some surprising twists at the end. Laurie King and Rhys Bowen fans will be delighted."
Publishers Weekly

"McNamara...proves, if anyone was asking, that librarians make great historical mystery writers...[In *Death at Woods Hole*] so accurately portrayed is that small-town-in-summer feeling, when towns are overtaken by visitors, who coexist uneasily with locals... I'd follow Emily to any location."
Historical Novels Review

"A well-crafted plot with fascinating period detail... a cracking good mystery."
Publishers Weekly

In [*Death at Pullman*] a "little romance [and] a lot of labor history are artfully combined...Creating a believable mix of historical and fictional characters...is another of the author's prime strengths as a writer...[she] clearly knows, and loves, her setting."
Julie Eakin, *Foreword Reviews*

"The combination of labor unrest, rivalries among local families, and past romantic intrigues is a combustible mix, an edgy scenario that is laid out convincingly...A suspenseful recreation of a critical moment in American social history, as seen from the viewpoint of a strong-willed, engaging fictional heroine."
Reading the Past

Also by Frances McNamara

The Emily Cabot Mysteries

Death at the Fair

Death at Hull House

Death at Pullman

Death at Woods Hole

Death at Chinatown

Death at the Paris Exposition

Death at the Selig Studios

DEATH

on the

HOMEFRONT

Frances McNamara

ALLIUM PRESS OF CHICAGO

Allium Press of Chicago
Forest Park, IL
www.alliumpress.com

This is a work of fiction. Descriptions and portrayals of real people, events, organizations, or establishments are intended to provide background for the story and are used fictitiously. Other characters and situations are drawn from the author's imagination and are not intended to be real.

Book and cover design by E. C. Victorson

Front cover image: Adapted from *Wake up America!* poster by James Montgomery Flagg, 1917. Courtesy of the Library of Congress Prints & Photographs Division

ISBN: 978-0-9996982-7-3

Library of Congress Cataloging-in-Publication Data

Names: McNamara, Frances, author.
Title: Death on the homefront / Frances McNamara.
Description: Forest Park, IL : Allium Press of Chicago, [2020] | Series: Emily Cabot mysteries ; 8
Identifiers: LCCN 2020040087 (print) | LCCN 2020040088 (ebook) | ISBN 9780999698273 (trade paperback) | ISBN 9780999698280 (ebook)
Subjects: GSAFD: Mystery fiction.
Classification: LCC PS3613.C58583 D437 2020 (print) | LCC PS3613.C58583 (ebook) | DDC 813/.6--dc23
LC record available at https://lccn.loc.gov/2020040087
LC ebook record available at https://lccn.loc.gov/2020040088

To Stuart Miller, co-worker and longtime beta reader

ONE

March 1917

I just don't understand how she could be so rude to Mrs. Spofford," my daughter Lizzie hissed into my left ear. It was hard to believe my little girl would turn twenty-one in April. She was a beauty, no thanks to my side of the family. My husband's mother had died when he was very young, but she was supposed to have been very attractive. I could believe it when I looked at my daughter. Her light brown curly hair fell softly around her square face, and the light in her amber eyes was like the sparkle of sequins on her pert little hat.

"I'm sure there's a reason Hazel couldn't come," I whispered back.

"A meeting of the Woman's Peace Party?" Lizzie sniped. She sat back in her chair.

I sighed. Lizzie blamed me for getting her best friend, Hazel Littleton, involved in the pacifist group that had been founded by my friend Jane Addams. But Hazel was already deeply involved with the organization by the time I joined. She'd even traveled to an international peace conference in Europe in 1915. Besides, Lizzie knew full well that if there had been a peace party meeting, I would be there, instead of at the luncheon to raise funds for Belgian relief services we were attending.

"There's a whole table of WPP women over there." I pointed. "I sold them tickets because you asked me to." She had nagged me about it, telling me that protesting the war was a feeble effort compared to raising funds to feed the Belgians.

We sat at one of the round tables in the ballroom of the Blackstone Hotel on Michigan Avenue. The event was sponsored by Lizzie and Hazel's future mother-in-law Regina Spofford. She had seated Lizzie on her right hand. On her left, the chair for Hazel was empty. It was a grand room. Tall windows were darkened by the charcoal smudges of clouds in the dismal sky. Light from electric chandeliers reflected off crystal and mirrors around the room. A dozen tables laid with white linen, and centerpieces of yellow and white roses, warded off the gloom of the March weather outdoors. Most of the stylish ladies who sat in the velvet padded chairs were from more wealth than my modest household could claim, but I'd felt obliged to buy a ticket. Lizzie told me that Regina Spofford was worried she'd disappoint her husband. In any case, I had no problem supporting the Belgian relief effort even if I thought Mr. Spofford was much too gung-ho about getting America into the war that raged in Europe.

Regina was a quiet woman who seemed to be dominated by her gregarious husband. When I first met her, I pictured her as an elegant but limpid vine draped around her husband. I thought she was lucky to have Lizzie as a future daughter-in-law since my girl was determined to prop her up. When Lizzie realized Mr. Spofford had assigned the task of organizing the event to his wife, she had taken up the cause of the older woman's luncheon enthusiastically. Apparently, the man would be harsh in his disappointment if the event were less than a huge success. My daughter was determined to make it a smashing hit that would save her fiancé's mother from disgrace.

Lizzie straightened up and announced, "I believe the donations have already exceeded your goals, Mrs. Spofford. We're going to fund an enormous amount of relief." She'd made it clear to me that she believed the significant money the Spoffords could raise to help the Belgians was far more important than the piddling efforts of the peace groups that were trying to stop the war.

With a timid smile at Lizzie's praise, Regina Spofford rose to introduce the speaker. As she approached the white podium she coughed nervously and fingered a string of pearls. Tall, with soft graying curls, she wore a walking suit of shiny gray silk. Her voice was too soft for the room, but the women quieted as they strained to hear her.

A rustle behind me caught my attention and I saw a busboy hand Lizzie a folded slip of paper. While Regina introduced the English woman who was to be the first speaker, Lizzie grabbed my forearm and showed me the note.

Dearest Lizzie,

I'm sorry to interrupt but I must speak to you very urgently. I am behind the door in the stairway at the back corner of the room.

Hazel

I glanced in that direction. Waiters were still clearing away plates from the luncheon and pouring tea and coffee. The audience clapped politely as an elegant woman in black shook hands with Regina at the podium.

Lizzie's eyes were narrowed, and she pouted.

"Aren't you going to go to her?" I whispered in her ear.

She shrugged and brought up a hand to cover her mouth as she whispered back, "I'm so angry with Hazel for not being here for the luncheon, she'll just have to wait. The speeches have started, and I can't leave till they're all done." She sat back, turning away to hear the speaker.

I started to speak, then closed my mouth firmly. I was at a point with my daughter where too often our relations grated. I was terribly proud of her, but I couldn't help being anxious about some of her choices. I had to be careful what I said because she always took any comment from me as criticism and that only made her do something contrary. I thought she should go and hear what Hazel had to say, but I sat back and listened to the speaker, hoping she'd come to that conclusion herself.

The aristocratic speaker described the woes of poor Belgium. It had been invaded by Germany at the beginning of the European conflict and, for several years after, had been subject to the Germans. I was glad the speaker refrained from repeating some of the most outrageous charges of German atrocities against the civilian population. Stories of chopped off limbs and bayoneted babies had been repeated many times in the press before they were disproved. The truth was grim enough. The country lost soldiers and civilians when they were overrun, and then Germany felt no obligation to feed the people they had conquered.

When the speaker mentioned the recent deportation of Belgians to Germany to work as forced labor, the audience stirred with indignation. I was aware of some of the background to these issues. The current controversy was threatening relief efforts. Money collected from many donors had been used to feed the Belgian people via some very clever diplomacy on the part of a Mr. Herbert Hoover who chaired the international relief committee. Unfortunately, the need to protest the forced deportations and other recent events was leading us toward a complete break with Germany. It was American neutrality that had allowed the supplies to get through. When that ended, the people of Belgium would starve. I wondered how many of the women in the room understood how tenuous the supply line was. Without it, the relief their money bought would never reach the suffering Belgians.

In the wave of murmurs responding to the speaker's description of the situation in Belgium, I heard a sudden yell of "No!" from the back of the room. Looking that way, I saw the women at the farthest table turn from side to side, then shrug. The speaker quickly drew attention back to her plea for donations. Her talk was followed by presentations of checks from several groups before the meeting ended with applause.

"Lizzie, aren't you going to see Hazel now? You've made her wait long enough."

"Oh, Mother." Lizzie threw down her napkin and rose to work her way across the room. I watched her glide through a gold velvet curtain that hung over a doorway in the back. I had turned to Regina Spofford to congratulate her when I heard screaming.

"Help, help!" It was Lizzie's voice.

I ran over, pushing my way through a knot of women gathered uncertainly in the doorway. The curtain and door were both pushed open to a stairway landing. Lizzie crouched, her arm around Hazel's shoulders, trying to sit her up. There was a wound on Hazel's temple and her golden hair was matted with blood. It looked like she had fallen back against the stairs. Her head dropped back on Lizzie's arm. Blue eyes stared blindly at the ceiling and dark blood was dripping down the side of her head onto her clothing and Lizzie's dress. I saw red bruises around her mouth and nose. "Hazel," Lizzie said. "Hazel, please, come back." She rocked her friend gently.

A woman in a dark suit pushed her way through the hovering matrons. "Excuse me. I'm a doctor, please let me through."

Tears blurred my eyes as I watched the doctor feel for a pulse at the girl's neck and wrist. She shook her head. "She's gone."

"No!" Lizzie cried.

The shadow of a tall man fell on us as I huddled over Lizzie and Hazel. "Oh, how awful. The young lady must have fainted and hit her head." It was the head waiter. He tut-tutted, uncertain what to do. "Terrible accident, terrible."

I was uneasy with the assumption that Hazel had fainted. The wound was on the front side of her head, not the back. Someone had hit her.

The doctor stood and faced the man before I could say anything. "No. She didn't faint. I believe she was struck." She pointed to the dead girl's head.

"No!" He was outraged.

"Who could have done such a thing?" someone asked. Suddenly there was a spurt of chatter with an underlying tone of rising hysteria.

I stood up. "You'll need to call the police," I said. "Immediately. And everyone should go back into the ballroom and wait for them. Please."

The head waiter turned on his heel and marched away, shooing women before him. Most of them retreated willingly, leaving Regina Spofford standing helplessly alone. Her face was as white as the table linens. I patted the doctor on the shoulder and pointed. She quickly took Regina's arm and led her to a chair.

Turning back, I stood over a weeping Lizzie. She clutched Hazel to her breast. "Hazel, oh Hazel, please," she cried.

I couldn't take in what had happened. Someone struck down Hazel and now she was gone. Looking down, I saw only a body now, not the girl I'd known, so warm with health and beauty. Closing my eyes, I forced myself to remember her alive to fend off this awful vision. The last time I'd seen her, she was in my husband's study with Lizzie, both with their legs tucked up under them on the sofa, earnestly sharing gossip in whispers. She wore a braid pinned to her head that day, her face flushed from the warmth of the fire. She was brimming with emotion, so alive, and that had been only a few days earlier.

I opened my eyes, turning away. How awful for her parents. Who would tell them their only child was gone…and in such a manner? I doubted her mother, Henrietta Littleton, had attended the luncheon. Like my husband and me, the Littletons were academics. I felt a sharp pain at the thought that their world was about to end.

But who would attack Hazel? Her hat had fallen to the floor beside her and she still wore her coat and gloves. A purse hung from her belt, and I could see that she wore a matching necklace and bracelet. If she'd been attacked by a robber, he must have run away without taking anything. It made no sense that someone would haunt the stairways of the hotel in search of a victim. But why else would *anyone* hurt Hazel? What had she needed to tell Lizzie? Had someone killed her to stop her from speaking? I stared down at my daughter's heaving shoulders. Was Lizzie in danger? If she'd answered Hazel's note immediately, would she have been lying there, too?

TWO

Soon uniformed policemen were tromping around the ballroom. They told the women to return to their seats. The doctor, whose name I still didn't know, came to us with a man she introduced as the coroner. He was a smallish, middle-aged man with sparse hair combed over a balding head and wire-rimmed spectacles. He asked us to return to our table.

I hated to leave poor Hazel with a stranger, but I convinced my daughter there was nothing for us to do but help Regina Spofford. Lizzie stood up, sniffling, and looked down on her childhood friend for one last time, then bit her lip as she let me lead her back to our table. When she saw how blank faced Regina was, she stopped and drew herself up. I knew she would pull herself together to help her future mother-in-law, but first she turned to me. "Mother. We have to find out who did this. You'll get Detective Whitbread to help, won't you?"

I was surprised. It shocked me that Lizzie assumed I could call on Whitbread for help. It had been eight long years since I'd last worked with him. Of course, she'd been busy growing up all those years and paid no attention to my problems. She remembered the times when she was young and I worked closely with the police detective. I felt a sudden rush of desire to see the crusty, lanky old detective. She was right, Whitbread was the only one I could be sure would find the guilty man. Incorruptible as a force of nature, we both knew he could be trusted in a world gone so awry. "I'll certainly ask him," I assured her.

Lizzie went to Regina and knelt beside her, rubbing the woman's cold hands in her own. A waiter approached with a decanter of brandy and glasses. I poured a small amount and handed it to Lizzie to give to the woman. Others at the table eagerly took their portions. Feeling a little weak kneed, I poured myself a small glass and felt the liquor burn down my throat.

A stocky man in a shiny blue suit with a vivid pinstripe stepped to the podium. Wavy brown hair, stiff with hair cream, framed his round face and a brush mustache sprouted under his nose. I didn't recognize him. "Ladies, please. I'm Chief Michael Kelly and I'm in charge here. I'm sorry to have to tell you that a young lady has died." There was a murmur, but he waved his hands to quiet them down. "Now, you can be a big help by following my directions. I'd like all of you on this side of the room, in fact all of you except these two tables—" He pointed to the table in the back corner and our table. "—to gather your things and line up. My detectives will take your names and information, then you may go home. We'll contact you if we need anything further from you. For those of you at the two tables I mentioned, I'd appreciate it if you'd be patient. We'll want to speak with you separately. We'll do it as quickly as we can. Thank you all for your cooperation." He walked away to the doorway where other men in suits and uniforms had gathered. A few officers began wrangling the majority of the women into a line that stopped at a table with two detectives writing in notebooks near the door to the lobby. I noticed Regina Spofford had recovered enough to beckon to one of the busboys.

Lizzie stood up. "Mother."

"Yes, Lizzie, I'll see if I can find Detective Whitbread."

My mind was racing. I looked across the room at the group of officials. I had never met Chief Kelly. Although I didn't see the familiar lanky figure, I was sure Detective Whitbread must be there, somewhere. As the most experienced detective in the city, surely he'd be in charge. Once my good friend and mentor, he'd become a mere acquaintance. Lizzie didn't know the full strength of what had happened to cause the break. She was only twelve at the time. It was my own fault. I was the one who'd broken the trust between us when I lied to him to protect my brother. It was the kind of betrayal Whitbread would neither forgive nor forget. But he would have to put that aside in these circumstances. Any past failure of mine would pale beside the death of young Hazel.

"Mother, please." I could see Lizzie was determined that Whitbread and I were the only ones who could solve the murder of her friend and I was touched that, in such a terrible situation, she believed I could help. I also knew that when Lizzie got an idea in her head nothing would dislodge it. Headstrong and willful, when she believed in something she did so passionately. I'd seen her suffer before when she smashed into a reality she'd never imagined, but I didn't know how to slow her down to soften the blow. I only hoped I wouldn't disappoint her. Asking the detective for help would be embarrassing after all this time, but our past differences were nothing compared to this tragedy. Whoever had killed Hazel had to be found before he attacked someone else. Whitbread would understand that, and I believed that he could help me to keep my daughter safe.

I only hesitated a moment before I plunged across the room to demand to speak to Chief Kelly. Soon he appeared from the stairway, followed by the coroner. He frowned at the interruption. "Excuse me. I am Mrs. Chapman. My daughter, Elizabeth, found Hazel. I wonder if you could tell Detective Whitbread that I wish to speak with him."

The man's dark little eyes darted around the room, taking it all in. They stopped on the group of well-dressed women sitting with Lizzie before raking back to me in my modest walking suit and scuffed boots. He pursed his lips, clearly unsure how to deal with me. I could feel the power centered in the stocky figure. I saw him cock his head at the coroner who looked taken aback. "I'm afraid Whitbread is no longer with the detective bureau," Kelly said. "I'm in charge here. So, tell me, did you know the poor young lady?" He gestured to the partly open door behind curtains.

Surprised, I stared at him for a moment. How could Whitbread no longer be a detective? When Chief Kelly moved impatiently, I replied. "Miss Hazel Littleton was my daughter's dearest friend. Lizzie and Hazel are engaged to young men who are brothers, members of the Spofford family." Instinct told me this man would be impressed by money and power, things that I certainly didn't have but my daughter's future in-laws did. Invoking influence was something both Whitbread and I had spurned in the past. But I was older now, and this was my daughter. "That is Mrs. Richard Spofford with my daughter over there. She organized this luncheon."

Kelly put his hands in his pockets and rolled on his toes for a moment. Contemplating what to do, no doubt. "Yes, we'll need to talk to those ladies. All in due time."

My first thought was that Lizzie would be deeply disappointed to hear that Whitbread's position in the police department had changed and he couldn't help. I doubted Kelly would be an adequate substitute. He certainly wouldn't treat me like a colleague. I didn't know how I would find out what was going on without Whitbread.

My dismay must have shown in my face. "Here, now, do you need to sit down?" Kelly asked. He took me by the elbow and steered me across the ballroom, pulling over a chair and forcing me to sit.

I took a deep breath and sat up straight. "I'm all right."

A uniformed policeman marched across to us, followed by the head waiter. Behind them two other officers held the arms of a thin young man, forcing him toward us. He had straight dark hair parted in the middle and a small mustache. His dull colored shirt and breeches looked dirty, and his worn leather boots were only partially tied with string. I remained quiet in the background. If Kelly forgot my existence, I might be able to learn what the police thought about the crime. I was certain Kelly would never include me in the investigation as Whitbread might have.

The head waiter stuck his chest out, insisting he had important information for the police. "This man was seen hanging around out front. He hid in the men's lavatory when the police came. He's one of the men we fired last week. His name's Johann Hoffman. Management didn't want any Germans on the payroll, the patrons don't like it in these times. We let them go last week. He had no reason to be here." The broad-shouldered head waiter stood tall with indignation. The hotel's actions were unfortunately typical of the rising tide of anti-German sentiment. I hated how irrational people were becoming about such things. We heard about it all the time at Hull House.

"You think he did this?" Kelly asked.

"He was mad about getting fired. And he worked in the ballroom. You know how bloodthirsty Huns can be. He's trying to get back at the hotel by attacking a guest." The head waiter was indignant about the stain on the reputation of his hotel that this crime had created.

Could it be? I looked at the young man who hung between the two patrolmen. If this ex-waiter had killed Hazel to protest anti-German sentiment, he'd made a horrible mistake. Hazel didn't hate Germans; she was a pacifist. She worked with Jane Addams in her campaign to keep America out of the war in Europe. Was he so angry about his dismissal he just struck out at the first hotel guest he saw in a secluded corner? It seemed fantastic to think such a thing. I wondered if Whitbread would believe it.

"No," Hoffman said. "I come to get wages owed me. That is all." He straightened up in an attempt to defend himself.

"Then why did you hide?" Kelly asked him.

"Not hide. I wait for the manager to ask him for money."

"You were paid when you were laid off," the head waiter said. "He had no business being here. Look…there on his boots. That's blood."

We all looked down, including Hoffman. But then he tried to shake himself loose from the policemen. "That is from new work. I have to take job in stockyards to eat. That is from the new job." I remembered a tour I had taken of the stockyards. I was with a group investigating working conditions. Memories of the smell of blood in the place made me shudder.

Kelly glared at the prisoner and motioned to the uniformed officers. "Take him in there. Let's see what he has to say about his handiwork."

They dragged the man through the doorway to confront Hazel's lifeless body. I heard him scream. "No," he shouted. "No, I did not do this. Never." They dragged him back out, white faced and trying to keep from retching. He pulled his hands away from his captors to cover his face.

Kelly was grim. "Take him down to the station. We need to get statements from the ladies. As soon as that's done, we'll go back, and I want to talk to him there."

As they pulled the protesting man away, I asked, "Why would he do that to Hazel? She had nothing to do with his dismissal and she wasn't anti-German, she was a pacifist."

"Quite possibly Mr. Hoffman didn't know that," Kelly said. Then he looked at me closely. "You're the Mrs. Chapman from the university who used to work with Detective Whitbread, aren't you?" I admitted it. "Superintendent Schuettler would be happy to renew the association with the university. You'll have to come talk to me about it." He handed me an engraved card.

Whitbread's interest in the work of academic criminologists and social scientists was unusual. Most police were more concerned with local politics and spurned the academics of the university. I was surprised Kelly knew about our work and wondered if he really had any interest in the kind of sociological studies I'd done with Whitbread.

The officers dragging Hoffman out were only halfway to the lobby door when there was a commotion. Another uniformed man entered followed by an angry looking Richard Spofford, Lizzie's soon to be father-in-law.

THREE

I demand to know what's going on here," Spofford said, stopping in front of the men who held Hoffman.

Kelly hurried over, gesturing to his officers to continue out with their prisoner. "I'm Chief Kelly. And you are?"

"Richard Spofford. My wife sent me a message that there was a death." He turned toward the German ex-waiter who cringed between the two policemen. "I paid for this luncheon and I'm a friend of the mayor. What happened here?"

I saw Kelly eye the businessman. A handsome man, Spofford was of medium height with an athletic build. Lizzie told me he played tennis and golf. He had tight waves of blond hair cut close to his head and a mustache. Very light blue eyes were like those of his son, George, who was engaged to my daughter. Unlike George, who was a sweet, love-smitten young man, Richard Spofford was sharp tongued and quick to anger. He was obviously a prosperous man with important political connections, so Kelly shook his hand and touched his elbow, speaking low and fast to explain the situation.

Kelly's obsequious attitude annoyed me when I thought of how Whitbread would have dealt with the interruption. He would have had Spofford ejected immediately while he pursued the investigation. The fact that he claimed to know the mayor would mean nothing to my old friend. He probably would have advised the man to get out of his crime scene and go consult with City Hall if he had friends there. I couldn't help smiling a little at the thought.

At that moment, two officers appeared with a stretcher carrying Hazel's body, which was covered with a gray blanket. The room went silent. The coroner tried to lead them away, but Spofford stepped in their path. At a look from Kelly they stopped and Spofford stepped beside the stretcher, reaching out to lift the blanket very slightly from the girl's head. His eyes widened and he looked up, wildly searching the room until he found his wife. They held a glance for a long moment of total silence. It was an odd interlude that made me realize how much the commanding Richard Spofford must really depend on his seemingly weak wife. Her look calmed him.

Kelly motioned to the officers to continue and I saw Lizzie start to get up. I put my hands on her shoulders and bent to whisper, "No, Lizzie. She's gone. They have to take her away." I felt the tension in her shoulders release, and she bent her head. It was difficult to know this was the last time we would see Hazel. But the lifeless body wasn't the girl we'd loved in any case. I wiped my own eyes.

Spofford turned on Kelly. "You've got your man. What're you keeping these people for?" He waved a hand.

Kelly took his arm and murmured something but Spofford shook him off. "Nonsense, of course it's him. That's why we have to get rid of these German sympathizers. They're all just waiting to cause trouble. The hotel did the right thing, dismissing them, and that man took out his revenge on that poor, poor girl. Can't you see how upsetting it is for all of these women? I won't allow you to keep my wife and her friends here any longer. She's had a terrible shock and I'm taking her home. Now."

As he marched away, Kelly rolled his eyes, but he called over a subordinate and told him to take the names and addresses of the remaining women and then let them go. Spofford ignored everyone but his wife when he reached our table. Without a glance in Lizzie's direction, he gathered up his wife and rushed her away.

Lizzie collapsed in her chair. "Oh, Mother. Why didn't I go to Hazel when I got her note? Why didn't I go?" She wept.

FOUR

I arranged for a cab to take us all the way back to Hyde Park. It was expensive, but we were too exhausted by the experience to take the train. I needed to get Lizzie home. Wrapping her in her coat, I led her down to the cab. As we drove through the crowded streets, I hugged her to me.

She pulled away and sat huddled in a corner of the cab. "If only I'd gone to Hazel sooner. She wanted to see me, but I waited till the speakers were done."

"Lizzie, dear, there was nothing you could do." I shivered at the thought that my daughter might have interrupted the killer and been killed herself. "I'm just glad you're safe. Hazel wouldn't want you to be hurt."

I felt helpless to console her as she covered her face with her hands. Regret was a natural response, but it wouldn't change what had happened. The sudden death of one so young ripped a hole in the universe. The guilt Lizzie felt would pain her for a long time. Many years ago, a young man died in my arms after stepping between me and a bullet. I still remembered the loss.

I was aware of the dangers of the world, the violence out there. But, until now, I'd worried for my two sons, not my daughter. Lizzie grew up sheltered in our university community, then became engaged to a young man from a prominent family and was drawn into the pampered life of the wealthy in the city. I never dreamed she could be at risk like this. Who could have wanted to hurt Hazel? And did they have a reason to attack Lizzie as well? I was plagued by worries as we rode along.

After a long silence, Lizzie looked at me. "Mother, please, can't you get Detective Whitbread to help?"

"I don't know, Lizzie. He's no longer in the detective bureau. There's a Chief Kelly in charge. He said Detective Whitbread is gone."

She stared at me, her amber eyes dark. "But if you don't get him to help, how will we ever find out who really did this?"

I realized that Lizzie also found it hard to accept that the ex-waiter was responsible for Hazel's death. It made no sense to me either. If that man had attacked Hazel out of anger and revenge for losing his job, then his arrest ended the danger. But, if he hadn't done it, whoever had was still out there and we had no idea why he'd struck.

"This is what you do, Mother, isn't it? You and Detective Whitbread always found out the truth. You have to find out who did this to Hazel. Please, Mother."

I also found it hard to leave the question unanswered. Who would do this to a young girl? And why? I hadn't worked with the police for many years. I was in no position to investigate. But how could I turn away from this if I didn't know who had attacked Hazel Littleton and why? I wished I could accept that it was Hoffman, but I couldn't.

As soon as we reached the doorstep of our townhouse, my husband, Stephen, came out of his study. As always, my heart leapt at the sight of him and I felt the ground firm under my feet again. When he heard what happened, Stephen gave Lizzie a big hug. I called to Delia, our housekeeper, to help me take Lizzie upstairs for a warm bath. After I got her cleaned up, Stephen gave her a sleeping powder. When she fell into a deep sleep, we left her upstairs and went down to the study.

Twelve years my senior, Stephen was nearing sixty. His hair had thinned so much he was bald at the crown, which seemed strange to me because when we were younger, he'd always been in need of a haircut. Usually the most even tempered of men, today I sensed anger in him. He scoffed at the idea that Detective Whitbread had been demoted and encouraged me to try to contact my former mentor in the morning.

"You don't really think the waiter killed Hazel, do you?" he asked me.

"Why would he? The police assume he just saw her there and killed her as revenge on the hotel for firing him. But what if it's someone else? What if there's some other reason she was killed?" My mind had been racing with conjectures during the ride home, but I hadn't wanted to speak them out loud in front of Lizzie. "I don't see why the waiter would kill a woman outside the ballroom. On the other hand, do you remember the incident last year where an anarchist chef poisoned a room full of guests in another hotel? Could it be something as crazy as that?" In that instance, the man had put so much arsenic in the soup that it caused immediate sickness, which saved the victims. No one had died and he'd been arrested.

"Are you thinking it could have been anarchists attacking a young woman at the Blackstone just because they thought she was wealthy?" Stephen asked.

We both knew Hazel wasn't wealthy, no more than Lizzie. It didn't really seem like the act of an anarchist to me.

"Anarchists are mostly known for bombings, though, not something as personal as attacking a single woman. They aim at bankers and rich men usually," Stephen pointed out.

He was right. The picture in my mind of Hazel lying there made me think it must be personal. "It was awful, Stephen. It was as if someone argued with her or was angry with her. Someone who knew her. But who could do that to Hazel? She was such a kind and gentle young woman. And why? What was she going to tell Lizzie? That worries me. I wish I could stop Lizzie from attending all these social engagements until we know the truth."

"You don't think this has something to do with the Spoffords, do you?" Stephen asked. "You've never liked George Spofford and his family, but it's farfetched to think Hazel's connection to them somehow caused the attack on her." He could always read my mind.

"It's not George," I said. I needed to defend myself because Stephen was right. I'd never wholeheartedly approved of the engagement. "He's a fine young man, and Lizzie is very fond of him."

"And he adores her. You can't think there's something wrong in the Spoffords' social circle, Emily. I know you wanted something else for Lizzie, but she's a grown woman now. It's her choice."

I looked at the framed pencil sketch that hung above Stephen's desk. It was a study that Mary Cassatt had drawn for a painting. In it, I sat, bent over some sewing while a four-year-old Lizzie stood leaning against my knee, chin in hand, looking directly at the viewer with a skeptical gaze. She'd been such a bright, intelligent little girl.

Lizzie did well in her studies in high school and, on graduation, she was accepted as an undergraduate at the University of Chicago. She loved to draw and paint, so she studied art history and shared that enthusiasm with George Spofford, a fellow student. He soon courted her with trips to the Art Institute and galleries. Later, there were balls and social evenings with the Spoffords' circle. Lizzie loved it all. I was deeply disappointed when she decided to drop her studies, and I insisted she keep a job as a typist. We weren't wealthy like the Spoffords. I worried that she might need to support herself, to have the ability to be independent.

"The Spofford boy is madly in love with her. You can see that," Stephen said. "And Lizzie will have a wedding and life that will be more lavish than anything we could give her. She *wants* a big wedding with all of Chicago society in attendance. It isn't what you've ever wanted, but it's right for Lizzie, and she deserves every bit of it."

I knew Stephen regretted that he couldn't provide the life of wealth he thought I should have had. Our own wedding had been a small ceremony that took place after my parents were both gone. We even had to keep the marriage secret to protect my position at the university. When I became a married woman the Dean of Women was forced to peck away at objections from male faculty members before she could give me my lectureship. More battles followed with the birth of each of my three children and, even now, it was a trial for every married woman we wanted to appoint. The Spoffords and their friends wouldn't understand that.

It seemed strange to me that my daughter's aspirations were so different from my own. When I was her age, I'd fought hard to pursue my studies. Yet it was her friend Hazel who was completing her degree at the university while Lizzie abandoned all of that. I didn't understand, but I wanted my daughter to be happy in her choice even if I would have chosen differently.

"I think Lizzie is even more excited about the wedding trip than the wedding," I said to change the subject. We'd been over all this before and I would never change my mind about it. Lizzie and George planned a trip to Europe. They wanted to tour museums and galleries, but they also planned to start a collection of their own. Lizzie's eyes lit up when she talked about it.

"And why not?" Stephen asked.

"Because of the *war*." It annoyed me that so many people, like the Spoffords, were able to ignore the bloodshed going on in Europe and assumed it would stop without inconveniencing them one bit.

He sighed. "Like many people, they're hoping it'll be over soon. In any case, there's no reason to believe Hazel's engagement to George's brother has anything to do with the attack, is there?"

"No, not that I know of. I wonder about Hazel's own activities, though. She was active in the Woman's Peace Party."

"You think someone was angry enough about the pacifist movement to kill the girl? Some people say all pacifists are traitors,

I know, but you can't think that has anything to do with the attack. If it did, you're the one who'd be in danger, not Lizzie."

Lizzie refused to be involved in the pacifist cause I'd supported, even though her best friend had embraced it since the outbreak of the war. Stephen also had his doubts about the movement. It was a sore subject between us. Sometimes I felt like everyone around me was blindfolded and only I could see the obstacles they were about to walk into. It was frustrating.

Stephen shook his head. "I can't see any reason for the attack on Hazel, but Whitbread will track it down. He's like a bulldog when he's on a case. You just have to get him to help. In the meantime, we'll keep close watch on Lizzie to be sure she's careful."

"All right. I'll find Whitbread tomorrow." I let out a breath, feeling heavy and tired. Deflated, I gathered my things to head upstairs.

Stephen coughed. "There's something else I need to tell you. The science faculties have sent President Judson a request urging the trustees to offer the laboratories and equipment of the university to the federal government in case of war."

"Oh, Stephen, no. You didn't sign it."

I saw his face redden up to the tips of his ears. "I did, Emily. You know how I feel. There *will* be war and we'll need to support it. We can't sit back and allow the Central Powers to destroy Europe. It's only a matter of time before we're part of it and, at that point, we must do everything in our power to bring the horrendous suffering to an end once and for all. We've been standing by, and we can't go on that way. We have to defend ourselves if nothing else."

I sighed in exasperation. More and more I found myself swimming against the current. When the conflict began in 1914, the public condemned both sides equally, and everyone around us was determined that America should stay out of it. But, as the number of stories about German atrocities mounted, along with

21

news of U-boats sinking neutral ships, people began to waver. And efforts to get neutral countries to force the combatants to discuss peace broke down, despite all the work we put into it. In 1915, Jane Addams had convened a conference of women against the war which even drew women from the warring nations. Nothing came of it. The Woman's Peace Party just wanted to find a way to get Germany, France, and Britain to stop shooting and gassing each other and to negotiate a peace. The thickheaded combatants wouldn't listen.

On the other hand, there were those who believed pacifists were in league with anarchists who wanted to overthrow the government, or with Germany and Prussia, who wanted to conquer all of Europe. Socialists and labor organizers who objected to warmongering by munitions manufacturers were condemned as traitors when they called for improvements in wages and working conditions. The war itself was in a horrible stalemate described by the newspapers as a muddy, bloody mess, and waiting for America to declare war was like waiting for the guillotine to drop. I, as a mother, had a very basic concern.

"'I didn't raise my son to be a soldier,'" I said, quoting the song that had been so very popular all over the country only a year before.

"Emily, it doesn't matter. You saw the Zimmerman letter. The Germans offered Texas, Arizona, and New Mexico to the Mexicans if they'd attack us. The Germans threw down the gauntlet. There's no way for Wilson to avoid war now." A secret communique of the German foreign minister had recently been discovered and quoted in the press.

"But think of the carnage," I protested. I dreaded the prospect.

"Yes, there will be carnage. All the more reason to put every resource into the effort to get it over with as quickly as possible." Stephen was not a bellicose man by nature. He was a medical doctor who always tried to relieve pain and sickness. His research was concentrated on that effort. But he was sickened by the way the war was dragging on, killing so many, and destroying so much. Perhaps he was right, but I was a mother with two sons. The fact that they would inevitably be drawn into the carnage was all I could see.

That, and the need to guard my only daughter from this new, unknown threat.

FIVE

The next morning, I woke with an idea of how to find Whitbread and I wanted to be on my way early since I had a meeting to attend before I could search for the detective. Stopping in the kitchen, I found Stephen. I sensed anger in the way he hunched over a bowl of oatmeal. "What happened?" I asked. "Is it Lizzie?"

"Tommy never came home last night."

"You know Tommy, he probably stayed at a friend's house."

"Emily, this has gone on for too long. I won't put up with it anymore. You have to stop defending him."

"I wish you wouldn't let it upset you so much." Our youngest son was our troublemaker, but I had no time for this.

"Not let it upset me! Emily, I keep telling you he's in with a bad crowd. It's not right. We told him to be home by midnight. If he won't do that, then it's time for him to find another place to live." He was angrier than I expected.

"Stephen, please, don't throw him out. He's barely twenty. He doesn't know what he's doing. If you push him too far, he'll only do something foolish."

"At that age, plenty of young men are supporting families or dying on the battlefields of Europe. Stop babying him, Emily. He's a man and he needs to behave like one."

"He's always felt he's not as good as Jack and Lizzie."

"Nonsense. He's received the same benefits that they have

and what has he done with it? Nothing. He's just a gadfly, racing motorcars, going to bars and brothels. Yes, Emily, brothels. You think Fitzgibbons and his ilk don't go to those places? You'd be wrong. Is he gambling, Emily? Do you even know? I don't."

It wasn't the first time Stephen had threatened to throw Tommy out and make him fend for himself. He thought if we shoved this chick out of the nest, he'd finally fly but, as Tommy's mother, I wasn't at all sure he wouldn't just lose control and plummet. With Tommy I always had a sense that he was plummeting. Sometimes I feared he enjoyed the sensation.

"Let me talk to him first," I begged. "I'm going into the city anyway for a meeting and to try to get Whitbread's help. Take care of Lizzie."

He grunted.

As I walked to the train station I thought more about our youngest son. I knew Stephen's anger came from a deep worry about him. Unlike his older siblings, Tommy hadn't completed his schooling at the University of Chicago Laboratory School. It was a special opportunity for the children of faculty to be able to attend the well-respected private school that was attached to the university. We never could have afforded such an education otherwise. Tommy was so unruly, and skipped class so often, they finally expelled him. Stephen was disappointed, but I knew it was hard for Tommy to see how well Jack and Lizzie did. Jack followed his father into medicine and was studying to be a doctor. Lizzie was another good student, although she disappointed me when she gave up her university studies to marry.

Stephen had been furious when Tommy failed and then resisted all efforts to enroll him in another school. Finally, without Stephen's knowledge, because I knew he wouldn't approve, I consulted our old friend Peter Francis Fitzgibbons who found a job for Tommy in City Hall. Stephen bitterly resented the fact that Fitzgibbons could help his son when he couldn't. Stephen was always suspicious of Fitz's motives. But I could see Tommy was happier. He did whatever it was they paid him to do, and he spent his money on entertainments. His passion was racing motorcars. Unable to afford one, he drove for his wealthier friends.

Distracted by these thoughts, I was walking along Fifty-Ninth Street when I heard a crack, and something fell in front of me. I jumped back from the corner of a large sign that had fallen from above. "Schmidt's Bakery" was painted in swirling white letters.

"Oh, no. Not Schmidt's," I said to myself. I could smell the baking bread and a hint of burnt sugar from the doorway as a rotund little man in an apron came out.

"You are all right?" he asked. He waved angrily at a workman coming down a ladder.

"Sorry, lady," the workman said.

But I was reassured by seeing Mr. Schmidt. The bakery had been a favorite place for our family to go for sweets while the children grew up. I hated the idea that it might close. "I'm fine. Just startled. Why is the sign coming down?"

The little baker wiped his hands on his apron and pointed to another sign leaning against the wall. "Smith and Sons" it read. I was confused.

"Some of the customers, they don't like to come to a German bakery. You see?" Mr. Schmidt asked. "Not you, of course. And plenty others. But some, they don't feel so good going into a bakery with a German name." He looked at the ground, obviously uncomfortable with the situation.

I shook my head. "I understand. I'm so sorry you feel you have to do this, but I understand." People were getting war crazy and some were beginning to boycott anything that was German.

"I was born in Germany, many years ago. But my sons, they never even been there. They are Americans, born here...Chicago. So, we change the name."

"'A rose by any other name,'" I quoted but he didn't understand. "So long as you keep making us your wonderful cakes," I told him. "Excuse me, I must run for my train. Good luck with the new name, Mr. Schmidt."

When I sank into the seat on the train, I thought of the waiter who'd been fired because of his German name. Would that really make him desperate enough to attack Hazel?

The pretty girl with blond curls had been Lizzie's best friend since they were in nursery school. Hazel had no siblings and she had been like a sister to Lizzie, balancing out against Lizzie's two brothers so it was even—girls against boys. Hazel would have been lonely without Lizzie's family, but my children would have been wilder without her. She was always a steadying force in the group. I was thankful that she put up with my little hooligans. Stephen and I got used to Hazel coming to us with tears in her blue eyes to plead for one of our naughty children. It was a joke with us that we knew they'd done something especially bad if they sent Hazel to tell us about it.

Later, she and Lizzie had been inseparable as the boys grew away from them, following their manly pursuits. The girls had graduated together and begun study at the university together, and Hazel had been the one to become engaged to one of the Spofford brothers first. She'd introduced Lizzie to George Spofford when she found out he was interested in art. I knew the two girls had looked forward to sharing the adventure of their marriages and lives as young wives and mothers. Lizzie would miss Hazel so much. And I would miss the check that Hazel always kept on my rambunctious daughter. Many a time Hazel had pulled Lizzie back from some impulsive leap into trouble. Who would do that now?

I had to convince Whitbread to help me find out the truth of what happened. But first I needed to break the news of Hazel's death to the Woman's Peace Party.

SIX

The WPP had offices at 112 Michigan Avenue on the fifth floor. I trudged upstairs to the modest office, which held two old wooden desks, a flank of wooden file cabinets, and a large oval table for the inevitable meetings. Eight women were gathered there when I entered and they immediately muttered condolences. I realized three of them had been present at the luncheon.

"It was a terrible shock," I admitted. "Hazel was my daughter's dearest friend and Lizzie's devastated. And I'm worried because I can't understand why someone would attack Hazel like that."

"Do they really believe the waiter is to blame?" asked one of the women who'd been at the luncheon.

"They arrested him."

"Did anyone see him attack Hazel?" Miss Breckinridge asked.

"No, they found him hiding in a lavatory downstairs," I said. Those who had been present explained how the maître d' had accused the ex-waiter.

"They fired men because their names were German?" Miss Breckinridge was surprised. "Then, when there was an attack, they assumed the man with the German surname must have done it? There are too many prejudices in the assumptions of the police. Didn't anyone question them?"

Those of us who were there sank in our chairs, feeling guilty about not speaking out.

"It was impossible to challenge the authorities just then," I said. "Hazel's body was being carried out and her future father-in-law was wild with anger. I confess I have doubts about the man's guilt. I plan to ask for help from an old friend who I trust could find the truth. If I can get him to investigate, I'm sure he would be fair."

"Hazel would hate to have the wrong man accused, especially if he's been accused because of this war." Miss Breckinridge rose and took down a photograph from a shelf. She held it in front of her so we all could see. It showed a group of women on the deck of a ship. They held a white banner with a single word—Peace.

"The *Noordam*," one of the women said.

"Miss Addams was on the ship," I said. "Hazel went along as her secretary." In April 1915, an international group of pacifists, including members of the WPP, had braved travel in war-torn Europe to attend a conference on peace, sailing on the SS *Noordam*. Hazel traveled with a group from Hull House.

"She convinced her parents to support her on the trip," Miss Breckinridge added. "Here she is at the end." She pointed to the photo, then handed the frame to the woman beside her to be passed around.

"I didn't go myself," she said, and I thought she must have regretted it. I remembered how Lizzie and I had waited for news of Hazel's trip. There was always danger from the U-boats and then the *Noordam* was held up by the English, who had denied passports to their own citizens preventing them from attending. In the end, the Americans reached the Hague.

"She told me about it once," one of the women said as she passed the photograph to the next person. "She said no one came from France but there were Germans and Austrians, despite the war."

"That trip impressed her so deeply she was completely committed to the peace movement when she returned," Miss Breckinridge said. "After the conference, she travelled to Berlin and Vienna with Miss Addams. She said people would bring fragments of bomb shells to them and ask how America could be neutral if American shells were killing their countrymen."

"No wonder she threw herself into the work when she returned," I said.

"She was especially good at digging out the statistics on how much money we were making on armaments and projecting how much more effective it would be to use an economic boycott to pressure the warring parties to the peace table. She hated that it was our bombs that were being exploded."

One of the other women was smoothing her hand over the framed photograph. "Hazel was so patient, too. She was much more patient than I was about our sisters in New England. I've had a hard time keeping my temper dealing with them over this suffrage issue. But Hazel was always so patient and nice." She shook her head sorrowfully.

One of the problems for the WPP was that its constitution called for women's suffrage as well as peace. There were some groups in New England who wouldn't support that. Of course, the pacifist movement had been begun by women in Britain who had used public demonstrations and protest to support women's suffrage before the war, so it was unthinkable to them that the issue would not be in the platform. Most of the Chicago women agreed, but Hazel had been able to communicate with the dissenting New Englanders without the rancor the rest of us felt on the topic.

Disheartened by the memories of Hazel, we decided to adjourn early and postpone our planning for the peace rally until the next meeting.

While the others were gathering their things and heading down the stairs, Miss Breckinridge kept her seat at the table, running her index finger around the edge of her tea mug.

Lizzie blamed *me* for Hazel's recruitment to the pacifist movement, but Sophonisba Breckinridge had been Hazel's professor and mentor at the university, and she was the one who'd encouraged

Hazel to join the WPP. Miss Breckinridge was treasurer, and Hazel had worked closely with her to print the pamphlets and pay for the telegrams to Washington, D.C. that were all part of the effort to convince politicians to try to make peace not war.

"You were Hazel's favorite teacher," I told her.

Her expression was bleak. "I got her involved in the peace party. She was so young, yet she was able to see beyond the foolishness to the rightness of the cause of peace. She deplored the preparedness movement."

"Can you think of any reason someone would want to harm her?" I asked.

"Certainly not. She was serious in her commitment to the cause but, more than the rest of us, she was careful to listen to the other side. I will tell you one thing, though. I think she was having a difficult time with her fiancé's family."

"The Spoffords?"

"Yes. She told me Mr. Spofford was a very big supporter of the preparedness movement, and she dreaded having to listen to him go on and on about it. Apparently, he demands his sons support his enthusiasms and Hazel had to bite her tongue not to protest."

I thought if it had been Lizzie who disagreed with their future father-in-law, she would never have kept quiet. Hazel was more diplomatic than my daughter.

"Is that why she didn't attend the luncheon?"

Miss Breckinridge looked surprised. "The luncheon for the Belgian relief services? Why, no. She told me she felt good about that effort and she was glad she could support Mrs. Spofford in that while she couldn't agree to some of the other things Mr. Spofford was doing."

Hazel had planned to attend? Why didn't she, then? "What was Mr. Spofford doing that she objected to?" I asked.

"I don't know. She didn't say specifically but she seemed troubled." Miss Breckinridge looked up at me. "I didn't want to mention it to the others, but Hazel was leaving us in any case."

"What do you mean?"

"She stopped in yesterday morning. She wasn't scheduled to work, but she came with a notebook full of research she'd been doing for me. You know she sometimes translated French and German documents for us?"

"I knew she was good at languages."

"She gave me that work, along with some statistics she'd been researching, and told me she was very sorry but she wouldn't be able to work for us anymore."

"But why ever not?"

"She didn't say, and I didn't like to press her. Because of what she'd told me before, I assumed it was her coming marriage and the fact that her in-laws didn't approve of her work with us that made her resign. Perhaps your daughter knew about this?"

"If she did, she hasn't told me." It did seem possible that the Spoffords might have demanded that Hazel resign. It disappointed me a bit to think that she'd given in to their pressure. But she was a young girl with her married life ahead of her and Hazel prized peace over conflict in personal as well as public matters. But, if she was giving in to the Spoffords' demands, why hadn't she attended the luncheon that was so important to Mrs. Spofford? Was it a final act of rebellion?

SEVEN

Miss Breckinridge's observations made me even more worried about how I could find out the truth about what had happened to Hazel. I needed Whitbread's help. Fitz would know how to reach him and, as my son Tommy was working for the Irish politician at city hall, I would be able to talk to him as well.

I found Fitz in his corner office. Over the years, he'd moved in and out of similar offices, even being exiled to the wards for a while, but he always returned to some official position in municipal government. He was a big shouldered man whose muttonchop whiskers and thick wavy hair had recently turned white. The veins stood out on his nose, and his eyes were deep set under wiry brows. I had no idea what his exact title was, but he was in the entourage of Big Bill Thompson, the current mayor. Although he was born in Chicago, Fitz affected a slight Irish brogue to appeal to the voters he represented. I found his pretenses exasperating sometimes, yet I knew he was sincerely devoted to making the lives of his constituents better. No subterfuge was too much if it helped him to his goals. His goals were worthy, but his methods were sometimes questionable. Nonetheless, I'd seen enough men motivated only by greed to be able to forgive Fitz his faults in view of his efforts to help folks who needed helping.

Before I could enter the wide-open door of the office, I realized Fitz was having an argument with a group of three men who loomed before him. They leaned toward him aggressively with frowns on their faces. Fitz stood up behind his big wooden desk to defend himself.

They were arguing about the coming visit of a Frenchman who led Allied troops. America was supposed to be neutral, but the government was sponsoring the trip of the French hero.

A well-dressed man spoke up. "It's a disgrace. Marshal Joffre is a hero of the Marne battlefield. Every other American city is welcoming him. Thompson needs to issue an invitation and give him a parade."

I recognized the speaker. It was Richard Spofford, who'd claimed to be a friend of the mayor the day before. I knew he ran an advertising agency and was well connected in the city. He wore a black armband which I assumed must be for Hazel, but his presence had nothing to do with her death. I was a little shocked and I didn't know what to say to him as I'd only met him a few times. I stepped back, hoping to be ignored.

The other two men were egging him on while Fitz folded his arms and waited for a break to respond. "Now, wait a minute, if you please. The mayor has only said it's not clear what the purpose of this visit is. You know he's against sending our boys over there, so he wants to know if these French visitors want to encourage us to enter the war, or do they have some other purpose?"

"The mayor's trying to make this city into a German stronghold in America!" Mr. Spofford turned an unhealthy shade of red.

"Not at all. What he's said is that there are more foreign-born parents of school children in Chicago than American born. That's a fact. It's also a fact that Chicago is the sixth largest German city in the world, the second largest Bohemian, the second largest Norwegian, and the second largest Polish. He said if an invitation is sent to some nation in the name of all the people, then all the people ought to be in favor of the invitation."

There were protests from the men, and Mr. Spofford spoke again. "We're going to go to the district attorney and demand he investigate Thompson's loyalty! You'll see what happens then."

"I expect the district attorney has read the Constitution and there's something about free speech in it," Fitz retorted.

"It says the penalty for treason is hanging," Spofford returned.

"I'm sorry you don't agree with the mayor," Fitz said. "You're welcome to investigate anything you want. But we have business to get to here, boys, so if you've nothing else to discuss I'll be wishing you good day."

The other two men hustled Mr. Spofford out the door. He was still red faced with anger. I was glad he was too distracted to see me. I didn't know what to say to him about the terrible death of his future daughter-in-law. Perhaps that tragedy contributed to his anger and frustration.

After the others left, Fitz greeted me. "Mrs. Chapman, it's always lovely to see you. I'm sorry you had to hear that fracas. There's many who claim the only patriotic stance is war while others think it's Wall Street profiteering that will get our own boys killed in a battle that's not ours. Did you know they tried to shut down a film the other night because it was about the American Revolution and they said it was too anti-British when we ought to be allies with them against the Germans? It's madness." He guided me to a chair. "But did I hear that you and Miss Chapman were at the Blackstone for the terrible event there yesterday?" As usual, Fitz was on top of what was happening in the city. I told him what I knew and what I feared.

"What an awful thing. And you say Spofford, who was just in here, was going to be her father-in-law? You'd think he'd be more concerned about her death than an invite for some French marshal." He gazed at the ceiling, shaking his head at the mysteries of human nature. Then he looked back at me with pity in his eyes. "They say Miss Littleton was a pacifist?"

"She was a member of the Woman's Peace Party, as am I. We organized the rally last New Year's Eve."

"Oh, yes. It's Miss Addams's group, of course. Poor girl. Killed by a waiter who'd been fired, they're saying." Fitz grimaced as if he were itchy and couldn't reach the place that itched. "It's a sad thing that the management of the Blackstone fired a man who'd been working there just because he has a German name. We'd really like people to not turn against our friends and neighbors just because they're of German heritage. They're still good Americans. The mayor has been steady in supporting our German American brethren."

Because they voted him in, I thought. "I think Chief Kelly was a bit hasty in assuming that ex-waiter did the deed just because someone saw him inside the hotel. Why is Kelly in charge, anyhow? I looked for Detective Whitbread, but he wasn't there. What happened to him?" If anyone would know the full story it was Fitz.

"Ah, there's a tale. It seems Superintendent of Police Schuettler is taking advantage of some civil service rules to get rid of a lot of the detectives. There's nearly a hundred of them that were promoted before the civil service exams were in place, so he's saying they're not first-class detectives in the eyes of the law. And the old detectives are stuck because—even if they took the test now—they'd be on the bottom of the heap with all the detective badges already allotted."

"But Whitbread's been solving cases for more than twenty years," I protested. "He was a seasoned detective when I first met him during the Exposition in '93. I can't believe they demoted him and put someone with little experience in his place just because they'd passed a test. That doesn't make any sense."

"True." Fitz shook his leonine head. "But, of course, it's partly political. You know Whitey was never one to bend at all, even for the most influential."

Integrity was a byword for Whitbread, and he hated graft. He refused to be influenced by politicians or wealthy citizens.

Fitz himself had often butted heads with the stubborn detective. Still, Fitz seemed sorry to see him demoted. "He was put over in the Maxwell Street station where there's been a great number of burglaries. There's some gang's been blowing safes right and left, and getting away with it, for several months now. I heard Whitbread's charged with cracking the case or, if he can't do it, he'll be put out to pasture. I don't envy him that task, as it's been tried by others before him and nothing's turned up the villains."

"I need to talk to him," I said. "I'm worried about my daughter. If something this awful could happen to her friend, how can I know if she's safe? We need Whitbread's help. How do I find him?"

Fitz gave me directions to the Maxwell Street station. "You can tell them I sent you over, that'll get you through the door, though what you'll get from Whitey I've no idea." He cocked his head. Fitz knew there'd been a break between me and Whitbread, and he was fishing for details, but I didn't feel obliged to explain.

"Is my son here, by any chance?" I asked. "He didn't come home last night, and we're concerned."

"Well, I'm sure he'll be in shortly," he said. "Don't you worry, now. I would bet he spent the night at Mr. Frommer's flat. They're great friends these days." Leonard Frommer was a new friend of Tommy's. Stephen disliked him, although I thought he was fine. "You've met Lenny, haven't you?" Fitz asked. "He's a little monkey of a fella, but him and Tommy get on well. They're wild for the motorcars." He bent forward and lowered his voice. "I don't know if you're aware of it, but the poor lad's father shot himself when his firm lost all their money last year. It was a terrible sad thing. His da was a great supporter of the mayor, though, so when Lenny couldn't afford to stay at the university we found him a place here."

I wondered if his mother had prevailed on Fitz to get her son a job at city hall, which was no more than what I'd done. It must have been hard for the young man to fall from a place of wealth and privilege to the working class. Fitz moved between both those worlds and could make the boy's landing a little softer. He had a good heart, my old friend Fitzgibbons.

The large door to the corridor was open behind me, and I saw Fitz start to rise. "There they are now, the young scoundrels. You sit back down, and I'll get your Tommy to come to you. I've a meeting to attend, anyhow." He came around the desk. "It's always a pleasure to see you, Mrs. Chapman. You know that."

"Fitz, thank you again for helping Tommy."

"Ah, it's nothing. He's a good lad. If he and Lenny are a bit late sometimes, they're willing to do my bidding into the evenings. You know how it is."

I didn't really, but I could imagine. Fitz spent a lot of time at constituent meetings, parties, even funerals. The mayor's voters were working people, so socializing with them happened after the working day. I wasn't sure what Tommy's duties were, but I was glad to have him occupied.

"Here you are, Mr. Chapman. Come see your mother now," Fitz said as he exited.

EIGHT

My son came through the door, head down, like he knew he was in trouble. It was always like that with my third child. At the age of six, wide eyed and completely fearless, he jumped from shed roof to tree limb, missed and broke his arm. Later, he and a comrade terrorized the neighborhood by throwing apples through windows and, when we finally discovered the culprits, he grinned. After a wallop by his father, he grimaced, then grinned again. He'd steal his brother's ties and his sister's ribbons just to annoy them. He claimed to spurn their academic accomplishments, but I knew he was jealous. He tried so hard one year to get his sums right in arithmetic that, when he failed a test, I found the papers shredded in the fireplace, along with one of Lizzie's essays labelled "Excellent!" I tried to tell him he had other qualities that Jack and Lizzie lacked, but he would run away whistling down the alley behind the house before I could finish. He infuriated his father by his lack of attention when Stephen lectured him. Tommy was never one for lectures. So, how to talk to him now? I feared he was finally at a breaking point with his father.

"Tommy, where have you been? You haven't been home for two nights. I was very worried."

His eyes were red rimmed. He must have been out drinking all night. I remembered Stephen's accusation about brothels and hoped he was wrong. Tommy was short where his father and brother were tall. At the age of nineteen, his face was still rounded with the smooth cheeks of childhood, despite a small brush mustache that he cultivated. Holding a soft flat cap in one hand, he knocked it against his thigh as he stood before me, looking abashed. But I knew he could feign embarrassment when it suited him.

"Sorry. I was out with Lenny and we were really late, so I stayed at his place." He looked much paler than I'd ever seen him. My heart leapt at the fear he might be ill, but I suppressed it. Stephen told me I was too weak when it came to Tommy, that he played me. I knew he was right.

"Your father is very upset with you. I need you to come home and apologize to him, then sit down and talk to him. You must do this for me, Tommy. You've pushed him to the limit this time and he sees your actions as completely disrespectful." I didn't want to tell him outright that Stephen wanted to throw him out. I was trying to navigate between the two of them like rocks in a quick running stream.

"He's right about me," Tommy said, surprising me. "Anyhow, I'm not coming home. I'll stay with Lenny. We've worked it all out." He held out a hand, his palm facing me, against my objections. "Yes, Mother, it's the right thing to do. Lenny and I have some big races coming up and we'll be busy with them, even out of town some of the time. So, it'll be better this way with me staying downtown with Len." He stared past me through the big window to the city streets.

"No, Tommy, you must come home and make it right with your father."

His face settled into a pout that made him look like a little boy again. "Father won't approve. But I'm my own man now and I have things to do." He looked directly into my eyes. "We're getting ready for the Vanderbilt Cup Race. We've got a chance to win it, wait and see."

Stephen and Tommy argued constantly about the motorcar racing. Even if I got Tommy back into the house, there would be no peace. I used to think it was my fault, that Tommy had some of my stubbornness, until I realized he took after his father. Stephen was even more persistent than I was. He was the one who could wear down a stone when he knew he was right. He'd worn me down when I rejected his first proposal, and of course he was right about that. It was when I'd realized the two of them were too much alike that I decided to help Tommy get out from beneath his father's wing by getting him a job with Fitz. Now I needed to support him in his efforts to pull away even further.

"If you think it'll benefit your work, then I suppose sharing a flat with your friend is a good idea. Are you sure you have enough money to pay your share of the rent?"

"Don't worry about that. We've got that covered."

I felt guilty to be relieved that I could return to Hyde Park without anticipating a roof-raising blowup between Tommy and Stephen that evening. I hadn't mentioned Hazel's death yet. I dreaded giving him the news. She'd been his playmate as well as Lizzie's when they were children. "Tommy, something terrible has happened. It's Hazel Littleton. She was killed yesterday."

He turned so pale, I feared he would faint. "I saw it in the paper," he said. "Is Lizzie all right?"

"She's shocked, of course. She found poor Hazel." He looked so sad, I had to restrain myself from rushing over to him, but he took a deep breath and slapped his soft cap onto his head.

"Lenny and I have to go," he said. "Duty calls. Fitz'll be back in an hour or so."

I felt a lump in my throat as he disappeared from the doorway. I wished I could be confident that independence was the best way for Tommy to learn about the world and himself. At least he was safe, working for Fitz.

NINE

As I walked to Whitbread's office in the Maxwell Street station, I prepared myself to face him. I would apologize, then I hoped we could talk to the man they'd arrested, Johann Hoffman. Whitbread should be able to arrange that. He would have when I'd worked with him in the past. Surely the senselessness of the crime would allow him to put aside other work to help me. I needed his connections and authority to find out what was going on in the investigation. Then, *I* could help *him*. I'd even brought a notebook and pencil, remembering how he always preferred my notetaking to that of his men. It was one reason he'd let me come to interviews, but not the only one. He'd never hesitated to use the fact that I was a woman, or my social standing, to get him through doors and into parlors where policemen were not welcome. I needed that kind of single-minded pursuit to find out who killed Hazel Littleton and why. Even if he was assigned to burglaries now, I trusted he would be able to get himself moved to the murder investigation. He was a man who never let the graft around him prevent him from doing the right thing.

The Maxwell Street police station was a rectangular brick building not too far from Hull House. At the desk, I asked for Detective Whitbread and was scrutinized closely by the burly sergeant before he led me to the burglary division on the second floor. Stepping into the room, I was engulfed by the pungent smells of cigar smoke and damp wool. Six scarred wooden desks were ranged in two rows on a wood floor that echoed with the sound of boots. I heard a harsh male laugh from one side and saw another man on a telephone raise an eyebrow as we passed. Tall windows on my right provided most of the illumination.

Whitbread's desk was in the far corner. He looked smaller than I remembered, perhaps because in the past I'd always met him in his narrow office crowded with books and papers. Tall and sinewy, at sixty-two his hair had thinned and turned gray. His eyes still raked me with the sharp gaze I remembered, and his large mustache still flourished under a pointed nose. I felt a pang when I saw him again and I realized how much I missed him.

"Hey, Whitbread, who's the skirt? Got an informer?" I heard a voice behind me, but I knew not to turn and look.

Frowning, Whitbread stood. "Mrs. Chapman is a lecturer at the university, Yardley, so keep a civil tongue in your head." He moved a stack of papers from a chair beside the desk and motioned me to sit, as he looked around the room.

"Ooo, from the university. Has she come to teach us?" someone teased.

Whitbread turned with his hands on his hips. "I'll teach you something, Sullivan, if you don't get out there and find those men we were talking about. Get on with it." He glared, and I heard the scrape of a chair and an incomprehensible mumbling as the man followed Whitbread's directive. When he was gone, the detective sat down again.

"What brings you to the burglary division?" There was a rough map drawn on paper tacked to the wall behind him. It showed the downtown area with multiple stars marking what must have been burglaries. Below it, a narrow bookshelf held works by criminologists like the great Italian researcher Lombroso. I remembered that when I first met Whitbread I was amazed by his interest in the academic study of crime and his willingness to work with a young woman from the university.

"Mrs. Chapman," he said, calling me back to the present, "are you here to report a burglary?"

"Detective Whitbread, I'm here about the death of Hazel Littleton. My daughter Lizzie found her. You remember Lizzie? She's twenty-one now, and Miss Littleton was her best friend. She's terribly upset. We have no idea why someone would attack her like that. And Stephen and I are afraid for Lizzie. That's why I've come...to ask for your help."

Whitbread stretched back in his chair, with a grim expression on his face. "I heard about the murder of Miss Littleton, and I am sorry your daughter was the one to find her. However, as you can see, I am no longer in the detective bureau." He gestured with a long-fingered hand at the room behind me. "We pursue burglaries here, and there are quite a lot of them, as it happens."

I couldn't believe he'd refuse me. "Detective, I'm so sorry for what I did when Alden was suspected of murder." Eight years before, I'd allowed the detective to assume my brother was home at the time of a murder when I knew he was not. "You were right to be angry with me. I should have trusted you to find the real villain. I was wrong. Please don't let your anger at me keep you from helping us find out who did this to Miss Littleton."

A young man came up behind me. "Whitbread, it's Bowman Dairy on South State. They were robbed...the thieves got five thousand. They're saying it's our gang and they want us over there now." He turned and sprinted away.

There was movement in the room behind me. Whitbread stood and said, "I must go. Chief Kelly is the one you should be talking to."

I stood, hesitating. I remembered what Fitz had said about Whitbread's job hanging in the balance. I knew he needed to solve a string of burglaries, but I had been so sure I could convince him to help. His blank refusal stumped me. Was he finally defeated by the system he'd fought for so long? Tentacles of corruption often whipped at the detective, but he always managed to beat them off. This time, they'd tied him down. It was foolish of me to assume he could still help us when he'd already been demoted. How could the police department do this to such a talented detective? I shouldn't be surprised. I knew how the city worked.

Stopping to look down at his desk, Whitbread asked, "How is your youngest son doing these days?"

"Tommy? He's working in the mayor's office, for Fitz." I was surprised that he would question me about Tommy when I'd come to him about the horrible murder.

Whitbread shook his head. "You might want to keep an eye on him," he said. "Fitzgibbons isn't necessarily the best influence on a youngster. He'd do better down in Hyde Park, don't you think?"

I was dumbfounded. It took me a moment to respond. He was preparing to leave. "But that's not what I came for. What about Hazel Littleton?"

He took a deep breath. "I assure you, my reluctance to be involved has nothing to do with our past differences. I cannot help in the matter of Miss Littleton. If I could, I would do so, but there is no way around it. Chief Kelly is in charge and he would brook no interference from me." From what I'd seen of Kelly, I knew he was right. A cloud of despair descended on me. He slid his chair in behind the desk. "Now, I must go. Just ask anyone if you need assistance finding your way out."

He brushed past me, then turned and said softly, "You have good reason to fear for your family, Emily. You should keep them close about you. These are dangerous times."

While he followed the men hurrying out the door, I stood there helplessly. What did he mean about fearing for my family? It wasn't the kind of warning he would give lightly, but I couldn't see where the danger was coming from. I was at a complete loss when I realized I couldn't count on his help.

TEN

Lizzie was disappointed, and Stephen was disgusted by Whitbread's refusal to help us, even when I explained his position was changed and his job was in jeopardy. In other matters, Lizzie denied that the Spoffords had forbidden Hazel from working with the WPP and said if Hazel had decided to cut her ties with the group it was entirely her own decision. Stephen maintained a stony silence when I told them Tommy would room with his co-worker in the city, but Lizzie broke down and wept. Considering their frequent loud quarrels, I was surprised she was so upset. The yawning loss of Hazel made her fragile. My oldest son, Jack, just raised an eyebrow at the news. Broad shouldered and solid, he was immersed in his medical studies and had little patience for the foibles of his younger brother. After Whitbread's warning, I was uneasy about Tommy, but I couldn't do anything about it now, so I let it be.

The next trial was the funeral for Hazel Littleton in the university chapel. I insisted that all our children attend. Tommy and his friend Lenny Frommer showed up dressed in black suits. Tommy looked quite sad. I was glad he was sensitive enough to mourn his old playmate. Lenny hovered around him, as if he were ill. Lenny was short, like Tommy, and the type of young man who was in motion all the time. Just looking at him made me tired, as he jiggled coins in his pocket and shot his gaze around the church. I took one look and gave Jack the task of making sure Tommy and Stephen had no opportunity to lock horns. My oldest son shrugged good-naturedly and stepped over to talk to the young men.

Lizzie was inconsolable. She came with us but, when her fiancé, George, arrived with his family, she clearly wanted to desert us to join them. George was tall and thin with a thatch of blond hair that sprang up from his forehead and fell in a wave to his temple. His blue eyes sought out Lizzie and I saw him relax when he found her. He reached out a hand. Biting my lip, I let Lizzie go with a pat on the arm.

It was a painful service. The pastor and everyone present had known Hazel all her short life. I felt empty and impatient at the mumbled words of prayer. Rituals helped to mark the importance of the day, but no scriptures could explain God's will satisfactorily. How had He let this happen?

The sorry procession out of the chapel was followed by an even drearier trip to the graveyard. At the end of the day we were back in Hyde Park at the Littletons' row house for the after-funeral visitation. Hazel's father taught philosophy at the university. He and his wife, Henrietta, were our neighbors and friends. I found it searing to see them go through these ceremonies knowing they would never have Hazel in their home again. I insisted that our family support them through to the bitter end. Finally, I convinced Henrietta to abandon her guests, some of them my fellow academics who were too thick skinned to respond to suggestions they leave. After helping her upstairs, I tucked her into bed, covering her with an afghan. As I pulled it up, I remembered Hazel crocheting the pale green and blue squares.

"Thank you, Emily," Henrietta told me. She was a small woman who was known for the needlepoint pieces she did on medieval themes. She'd been disconcerted when her daughter became involved in politics. Perhaps she resented the fact that it was through me that Hazel met Jane Addams and later joined her campaign for peace. But we were just two mothers now. "It must have been terrible for

Lizzie to find her, but I'm glad she wasn't alone when she…"
Lizzie had told her in detail about her discovery of Hazel's death.
I wasn't sure Henrietta realized Hazel was gone before Lizzie
found her. Reliving the experience was hard for my daughter,
but it was a gift to the grieving mother. If she couldn't be there
herself, thinking Lizzie had been with Hazel at the end gave
her comfort.

I knew I shouldn't tax the grieving mother's energies, but
I had questions. "Henrietta, we don't know why anyone would
do this to Hazel. Do you have any idea?"

Tears flooded her eyes as she sat up stiffly, and I regretted
my question. "No. She hated the very idea of violence. Hazel
was a pacifist. She didn't even go to that luncheon they said.
I think she'd had a falling out with Mrs. Spofford about it. I don't
think she cared about raising money for the Belgians but there
was something else the Spoffords were doing that bothered
her deeply. I don't know what it was. She didn't tell me." Her
back stiffened and her head was raised. "How horrible this war
is. So many young men dying, but never, never did we think it
would come to this." She gulped down a grim laugh. "James
and I congratulated ourselves that, even if it came to the worst,
Hazel would be spared because she's a girl. Oh, how could this
happen?"

Tears rolled down her cheeks. "Hazel felt she had to do
something to stop it." Henrietta stared into the shadows. "Ever
since the peace march in New York. We were visiting my sister,
Hazel and me. We saw them—women in black like a flock of
crows marching down Fifth Avenue. There were drums, but
nothing else, not a word. They swept down the street like a
plague, stopping everyone, bringing silence. There was just a
banner with a dove. There was nothing to say, just sorrow."

The Women's Peace Parade had been held in August 1914,
just after war was declared in Europe. I knew Hazel had been
there, but I didn't know how deeply it had affected her.

Henrietta squeezed her eyes shut. "After that, Hazel was determined to oppose the war."

I realized that my own involvement with Hull House had little impact on Hazel's commitment to the peace movement. She'd attached herself to pacifism before I had. Her parents had supported her trip to the peace conference with Jane Addams because she was obsessed with acting to stop the madness. Even the opposition of her future in-laws had failed to shake her faith. She'd believed that war was wrong with a rock-solid determination that I could only admire.

Henrietta collapsed in on herself, bowing her head and covering her face with her hands. She moaned. I reached out to soothe her but, when she looked up, the despair on her face stopped me. I sensed she was holding something back. "Henrietta, what is it? You can tell me."

"I don't know what was wrong. She wouldn't tell me. She was so late getting home that night...the night before she died. I didn't tell Arthur. He disapproved of her going to Hull House, especially when she stayed so late, but she begged me to support her. She wanted to help with the settlement work even if it meant staying for the night classes." Henrietta shook her head. "When she finally got back, she was upset. She looked disheveled, like she'd taken a fall, but she insisted she was all right. I should have made her tell me. Why didn't I?"

I reached out to pat her arm. Like Lizzie, she was tortured by regrets that had been bottled up inside her. It seemed to be helping her to confess to me.

"In the morning, she waited till her father left then hurried off to find Lizzie. I tried to stop her, but she promised she'd tell me everything when she returned. She wasn't upset anymore, just calm and serious. She must have thought it through overnight. She's so like her father. When she makes up her mind there's no moving her. She just said she must find Lizzie to explain to her." Her shoulders fell in. "If only I'd stopped her. I never stand up to her or her father. I wish I was like you, Emily. You would have made her tell you." She keened.

"No, Henrietta, you did all you could. You mustn't think otherwise." Why did Hazel need to see Lizzie even before she told her mother about what bothered her? I needed to know, but I feared pressing the woman. "You couldn't have stopped whoever did this."

She grabbed my arm. "She was going to run away. After she left, I went to her room. She'd packed a carpetbag. She was leaving. I don't know where she was going." Henrietta wiped her eyes. "I wanted to stop her. I would have stood up to her this time. But she never came back." Her head dropped. "I unpacked it, so no one would know…"

Hazel planned to run away, and Henrietta had concealed that fact. That must be why Hazel had told Miss Breckinridge she could no longer work for the peace party. It wasn't because of the Spoffords, it was because she was leaving town. "Why didn't you tell anyone? Shouldn't the police know? What was she running away from?" If Hazel was afraid of someone, the police should know. *I* wanted to know. Was that what she was going to tell Lizzie?

"No, no, no. I couldn't tell them." She grabbed my hand. "You mustn't tell anyone, Emily. Promise me. Don't you see, she must have been in trouble? If she'd told me of course I would have helped her. I could have taken her away. But now…" She wept.

"In trouble? Henrietta, what kind of trouble?"

"Oh," she moaned. "The kind any young girl fears. Oh, Hazel, why didn't you tell me?"

I realized Henrietta believed Hazel was with child and planned to escape the disgrace. For many that would be the first thought when a young woman of her background disappeared. That was what Henrietta was hiding. "Of course I won't tell anyone. But what if that wasn't it? What if she was leaving for some other reason?"

"What reason? No, it's the sad truth, but please don't let anyone know. It would ruin her reputation." Her face scrunched up as if she would cry again.

"Was Fred Spofford the father?" I asked softly.

She burst into tears. It would be even more painful for her to think that Hazel could have been seeing any man other than her fiancé. I could see Henrietta wanted to believe it was Fred, but her deep grief showed me she feared it was another man.

I didn't believe it. Not Hazel. She was never so headstrong as my Lizzie. She would never have betrayed Fred Spofford with another man. But I could see Henrietta had brooded over this for days. She fell back, burying her face in the pillow, mourning her daughter but also the thought of a grandchild. Surely not. I wondered if the coroner would find out about Hazel's condition. I hoped not for her parents' sake. I wasn't sure what to believe.

"Why did Hazel have to find Lizzie?" I asked. But it was useless. Henrietta didn't know. It didn't make sense, and not being able to ask Hazel to explain left a gaping hole in my memory of the girl I'd known since her childhood. Could I be wrong about Hazel? And, if so, could I misunderstand my own child?

The grieving mother on the bed rolled her face to the wall. Settling the afghan around her shoulders, I left her alone. I knew I would keep her secret. It would be an awful blot on her daughter's memory if it came out. If it were even true...

Descending the stairs, I overheard a conversation. Mr. Spofford, Lizzie's soon to be father-in-law, and Mr. Samuel Insull, a man who was active in the electricity companies in Illinois, were gathered with several other men.

"Ryerson has the right idea," Spofford said. "There's a vital need to get public support for the universal military training bill. It was left hanging when Congress adjourned in March."

I stopped in the shadows. Of course, life went on without Hazel. Spofford was burying his anger first in the argument about the French marshal's visit, and now in this movement. All these men had probably accepted that Hazel was attacked by a crazed waiter and moved on to topics of public discussion. If I broke in, as I wanted to, and demanded an explanation for the girl's death, they would think me mad. "Leave it to the police," they'd say. I knew I could never betray Henrietta by telling the police her suspicions and that bothered me. How could the police find out what happened if they didn't know the full truth?

"You think it'll pass Congress this time?" Insull asked. The coming war was all that these men cared about. There was no outrage over Hazel's murder.

"It has to. It's only a question of time till we're in this war, and we're totally unprepared," Spofford said. There was a murmur of assent. "Ryerson has this idea to go out and rouse the public sentiment in support, see. And he's being really clever. He wants to do it at cinemas. You know how people won't sit still for a long speech; you've got to plug it out as quick as possible. He found out it takes four minutes for the operator to change the reel for a two-reel feature. So, the idea is to have someone get up and give a pithy four-minute speech, just enough to hold the people's attention and get them behind the training bill." Spofford ran an advertising agency and was in the business of persuading people to buy things, so he admired an approach that would grab people's attention. It seemed cynical to me.

"Brilliant," Insull said.

"Yes, and he's got a name, too. The 'Four Minute Men' like the Minute Men in the Revolution, you see? Now is that clever, or what?"

That was the first I ever heard of the Four Minute Men. I wondered if this was the plan that Hazel had argued about with her future mother-in-law. It sounded devious but, in the end, it just wasn't serious enough to cause her to break the engagement or to cause someone to kill her.

Continuing down the stairs, I tried to think of a way to encourage the remaining people to go home. I was tired. And

I needed to think about what Henrietta had told me. At the foot of the stairs, Tommy and Lenny stood, staring at the group discussing the Four Minute Men plan. My son looked grim. I followed his gaze to Fred Spofford who joined George on the edge of the group. The young men looked bored, but maybe I was too quick to assume they'd forgotten Hazel. It might be the stunned blankness that came with grief. Young Fred must be devastated by Hazel's death. If Hazel had been with child, as her mother thought, did he know? Was he the father?

Why was Tommy so interested in the Spofford brothers? It bothered me that my son and his friend seemed to be glaring at them. I was afraid they'd provoke a scene.

"Tommy, why are you staring at the Spoffords?" I asked quietly.

Lenny perked up and stepped close to me. "Ah, it's just that Fred, there, he's a bit of a blowhard." At my look, he explained. "We know him from the races, the motorcar races. Him and Tommy're rivals. He won that last rally, but we think he cheated. That's what it's all about."

We were at the funeral of Lizzie's best friend and Tommy was worried about motorcar races? Sorrow welled up through my chest and pounded in my temples. I tried to restrain myself. "I think it's time for you to leave," I told my son. "This is about Hazel, not your motorcar races. Go home now, please."

Tommy looked at me with shock but, when I frowned at him, he plucked Lenny's sleeve and led him away. Lizzie sat like a rag doll on the sofa, and I wanted to get her home. Brushing past George and Fred, I hurried to Lizzie. By the time we got our coats and said farewell, Tommy and Lenny were gone.

I was sad to think of Mr. Spofford and his friends plotting to support the war effort at poor Hazel's funeral. She would have hated that. They clearly still assumed the arrested waiter killed her. I wished I could just accept that explanation, but I had too many unanswered questions. If Hazel *was* preparing to run away—

whether for the reason her mother assumed or another—why did she need to see Lizzie before anyone else? Was she going to warn her against the Spoffords? Or was it something else? I didn't see how to get answers without a working relationship with the police. Despite my doubts, I decided to take Kelly up on his offer to work with the university. At least it would get me a contact at the police, something I sorely missed.

ELEVEN

At the Harrison Street station, it seemed strange to find Kelly in Detective Whitbread's old office. In the past, when I worked there, the room was stuffed with filing cabinets, bookcases, and boxes of identity cards. Now it was bare. Kelly sat behind an imposing wooden desk under the window, and there was a small sofa in a corner where there used to be a worktable. Photographs of Kelly with various politicians hung on the wall beside him. I sat in a wing chair opposite the chief who leaned back comfortably, his dark hair shiny.

He smiled. "Superintendent Schuettler was glad to hear of your interest in working with us again. He'd like to do a press release about how the university and the police force are cooperating. What do you say we put something out this week?"

"That would be premature," I told him. "Perhaps we could discuss a collaboration to begin next fall. I'll need to write up the proposal and have it vetted by several faculty committees. I want to propose a project, such as the one we had with Detective Whitbread, where we update some of our statistical analyses to chart any changes since that program was discontinued in 1912."

He flinched at Whitbread's name. I wasn't sure if he realized it was the police department, not the university, that had stopped the work when the numbers could no longer be used to tout police victories over crime. Those victories weren't the object of the studies, but only Whitbread seemed to understand that.

Kelly's reply indicated that the current administration would be as shortsighted as the last.

"Well, of course, you can do that, but we were thinking of something more active, more impressive, like having your students write up how much improved the situation is from when you were last involved. I know how fond you academics are of your numbers, but wouldn't an overview of our progress be a better use of everybody's time?" He smiled like he was patronizing a sweet little old lady. I froze my face to disguise my disgust.

They wanted an academic imprimatur for the current administration. When I was younger, I would have protested violently at such a notion—using what should be an unbiased academic study to forward the ambitions of the current superintendent. I was older and wiser now. This was a game I could play as well as the next man, or woman. "You are so correct about academics loving our numbers, Chief. So, here's what I suggest…to get this through my committees, you understand. How about we have the first set of students update the numbers for us, then we look at the results and see how much progress there is and go from there? I'm sure, with all the work you've been doing, the results will be just what you're looking for." Perhaps not, but we'd deal with that later. My students wouldn't have the advantage of working with Whitbread, who was such a sterling example of a good public servant, but there was value in adding to our data. We did a little polite jockeying back and forth before Kelly agreed to review a proposal from me before I submitted it to the university.

When we finished that topic, I tried to ask for a favor. "I found that Detective Whitbread was very helpful in consulting with my students when we worked with the department in the past," I hinted.

Kelly frowned and hunched over the appointment book he'd pulled out. "He won't be available for this, I'm afraid. Whitbread's in charge of the investigation of a string of burglaries in the financial district." He leaned forward to look me in the eye. "He's one of the old guard who never passed the civil service exam, you know. We've been cleaning house. We've got a lot of new men here now. In fact, this is important enough, I'm going to supervise it myself. So, don't worry about that. We'll find you a nice big room to work in and I'll personally make sure you have everything you need."

And personally make sure we don't find anything that shines an unfavorable light on the police department, I thought. It was going to be a struggle, so I would write safeguards into the proposal to prevent Kelly from sabotaging the project. If he didn't accept them, we wouldn't work with him. There was only a fifty-fifty chance the proposal would be approved by fall.

I started to rise, then sat again, so that I could bring up the real reason for our meeting. "Chief Kelly, before I go, I was wondering if you could tell me about the investigation into the death of Hazel Littleton. She was my daughter's closest friend. I'm very worried about my daughter's safety...after such violence."

He clucked sympathetically. "We all have to be careful in these times. I can tell you that we've apprehended a man who was unlawfully on the premises during the crime, and we're confident of making a case against him."

"That's the waiter who was fired? Johann Hoffman?"

He seemed annoyed that I had that information at the tip of my tongue. Perhaps he'd forgotten I was there when the man was arrested. "He's someone we're looking at. But not because he has a German name. You can't believe everything you read in the papers." The arrest had been portrayed as an anti-German act by local journalists. Kelly moved uncomfortably in his big chair. "I don't want you and Miss Chapman to worry. We have the investigation well in hand. We'll make sure that man is locked up and can't hurt you."

He made me feel like a cowering matron who would have the vapors at the thought of a criminal, rather than a woman who'd participated in numerous murder investigations, as I had done before my break with Whitbread. "Is Mr. Hoffman the only suspect? Surely it seems unlikely that he would strike out at Miss Littleton for no reason."

Unhappy with my temerity in questioning him, he got quite huffy. "This may come as a shock to you, but it would appear that Miss Littleton may have known Hoffman. In fact, there's some reason to believe she became estranged from her fiancé over another young man, and we think it was Hoffman. He and some of his comrades spent time at the settlement house on the West Side."

"Hull House?"

"That's right. Taking classes or some such. We think she met him there. It seems her fiancé, the Spofford boy, didn't approve of her pacifist activities and it was becoming a point of contention between them. Relations were strained. I can only warn you, Mrs. Chapman, to guard your own daughter against such activities. These innocent young women don't know the rough crowd that hangs around those places."

I stared at him. He had no idea who he was talking to. I was the one who hung around with the "rough crowd" at Hull House, not my daughter Lizzie. She avoided the place. Unlike Lizzie, Hazel had worked with Jane Addams on the peace movement, and she'd often been to Hull House. But I had no reason to believe she'd met Hoffman or anyone else at classes there. In fact, I'd heard no hint that Hazel met with any young man other than Fred Spofford. If she had, surely Lizzie would've known and told me. Yet Henrietta Littleton believed it was possible that her daughter had relations with some man. She assumed it was Fred. But had it been someone else? Kelly gave no hint that they'd discovered the girl was pregnant when she died. Would he tell me that, even if he knew? I doubted he would. He'd consider it too delicate a subject for my feminine ears.

With his elbows on the desk, he bent forward. "Now, you mustn't worry if you hear that radical Darrow is going to defend Hoffman."

"Clarence Darrow?"

"That's what we've heard. His office sent over an attorney. Darrow may have been a big name in the city in the past, but he's shot himself in the foot with that trial in Los Angeles, and he'll get no special treatment. He's just taking the case for the publicity."

Clarence Darrow. The famous defense lawyer was active in many labor related cases. But recently he'd gotten into trouble defending two men who blew up a newspaper in Los Angeles. Darrow had attracted all kinds of support by claiming their innocence, then he'd turned around and advised them to plead guilty to avoid the death penalty. Afterwards, Darrow himself was brought up on charges of trying to bribe the jury. The trial of a German American waiter sounded like the type of case he might take, but I had my doubts about the flamboyant attorney. I wondered if he would try to arouse suspicions against someone other than his client. I wished again that Whitbread could take a hand. He was the only one I trusted to find the truth.

I didn't want to overstay my welcome, so I stood up to leave. Kelly looked at me with a gleam in his eye. Had he planted that information about another man in Hazel's life to stir up trouble? No doubt he was caught between the mayor's desire to placate his German American voters, and the outrage from members of the moneyed class that such a horrid crime could happen to a young girl at a society women's function. I feared Kelly would spend more time walking that fine line than looking for the real perpetrator of the crime. I wished I knew what Hazel had been so intent on telling Lizzie. There was so much political posturing in Kelly's attitude. Without Whitbread, would the police find the real killer?

TWELVE

F red didn't approve of Hazel helping Miss Addams with the peace movement," Lizzie said when I ambushed her as she came home from work that afternoon.

"Was she seeing another man? Chief Kelly seems to think she knew this Johann Hoffman."

Lizzie stopped to remove her hat and coat before replying. "No. There was no one else. Besides, how would she know a waiter?"

It appalled me that my daughter should mouth such a snobbish sentiment. No wonder I had reservations about the amount of time she spent in the Spofford circle. As she started toward her room, I stood in her way and nodded sharply to direct her into the parlor. We were going to talk about this before she disappeared. Herding her in, I placed myself opposite her on the sofa. "Lizzie, Hazel's mother believes she was going to run away but she wanted to 'explain' something to you before she left. Do you have any idea what that was about?"

Lizzie's face slackened. "Run away? But why?"

"That's what I'm asking."

Lizzie's brow furrowed, and she bit her lip. Her eyes roamed the room then came to rest on the pattern in the Oriental rug, following its whorls. "Hazel wouldn't run away from *anything*. Are you sure her mother isn't mistaken?" She looked directly at me.

I didn't want to tell her Henrietta's suspicions. It would be a terrible slur on the dead girl's reputation and a betrayal of her mother's confidence. But I needed to know. "Lizzie, if Hazel were in trouble, if she found herself...with child, where would she go?"

Lizzie's mouth dropped open. "Mother, how could you? Is that what her mother thinks? No, no, never. Not Hazel. I promise you, she would never do that."

I believed her. But we all have secrets and it was possible she didn't know her best friend's deepest ones. I took a breath. I was relieved to hear her deny the possibility so vehemently. "If that wasn't why she was leaving, what would Hazel have to explain to you, Lizzie? Did she break off her engagement to Fred Spofford? Was that what she was running away from? Could she have met someone else? Hoffman attended classes at Hull House. Was Hazel teaching there? I thought I heard she might be helping out. Could Hazel have known Hoffman? That's what the police think." She glanced away. I must have come close to the mark. What was she keeping from me?

"Hazel wasn't involved with the classes, Mother. You don't know her like I do. She went to Hull House to help with the peace movement. That's all." Lizzie looked at her lap where she was fingering her gloves. My daughter was what Whitbread used to call a "letter of the law" liar. She would avoid telling you a truth by saying something that was literally true but hid the answer she didn't want to admit to. I knew her methods. I often regretted she hadn't continued her studies to take a law degree. She was a very clever young lady.

"Lizzie, answer the question. Was Hazel seeing another young man? Because, if she was, her fiancé would be a suspect. Don't you see? If he found out about it, he could have been jealous enough to attack her."

"Oh, Mother, how can you say that? Fred would never hurt Hazel. I can't believe you'd accuse him."

"I'm not. But the police might. Jealousy is a strong emotion, Lizzie." Remembering the scene, how could the police avoid thinking some passionate motive was involved? A random attack in a stairwell made no sense. Kelly might be satisfied with Hoffman as the murderer, but anyone else would think Fred should at least be considered as a suspect. Surely Hazel's fiancé would be angry if he found out she was seeing another man, especially someone as disreputable as a mere waiter. And, if one brother could turn violent, I had to worry about Lizzie's future husband. I knew little enough about the family life of the wealthy Spoffords.

"They wouldn't dare accuse Fred. The Spoffords are a very important family. What a horrid thing to say."

"Lizzie, what are you thinking? It doesn't matter how important the family is. Someone did this awful thing. If Whitbread were running the investigation, he certainly would suspect the Spofford boy."

"But Fred would never *ever* hurt Hazel." She had tears in her eyes. "He's heartbroken. George says he's not eating, and he can't sleep at night." She sobbed, and, with a sigh, I moved to console her.

"All right, all right." I patted her back. "I was just telling you what the police could be thinking and what Hazel's mother told me. I saw Chief Kelly today."

She sat up and looked at me, wiping the tears away. "Are you going to help him find out who did this?" It touched me that she had so much confidence in my ability to find the truth. I hated to disappoint her.

"Lizzie, it's not like that. Chief Kelly may want my students to come back in the fall, but he won't involve me in an investigation like Whitbread used to do. It's not the same." Lizzie didn't understand that we could never go back to the days when I worked closely with Whitbread on murder investigations.

"But you *must*, Mother. Hazel didn't know that waiter, so someone else did this. Or he randomly chose her. Or he held a grudge against the Spoffords." She grabbed my hand. "You have to find out."

"Lizzie, what is it? Do you have reason to think you're in danger, too?" She was squeezing my hand, as if she were afraid.

"No, no. It's not that." She let go and looked away. What wasn't she telling me? It must be something Hazel was ashamed of. My daughter could be terribly stubborn, though, and she wasn't ready to tell me. If I pushed her now, she would just shut down and not respond.

Lizzie sat up straighter. "You and Father are coming tomorrow night, aren't you? To the film? Mr. Spofford will be speaking, and I promised you all would come. Jack, too."

I sighed. A film about the war in France was playing at the Strand Theater, and a group of men who supported "preparedness" had a plan to advocate for their views during the intermission. I realized this was the Four Minute Men plan I'd overheard a discussion of at the funeral. The Spoffords were involved and they'd invited us to a dinner party followed by the film. While I was not enthusiastic, Stephen overruled me. He felt compelled to go in order to support the president of the university who was a big promoter of preparedness.

"Mother, I know you don't agree with Mr. Spofford, but this is very important to him. Please come. Do it for George, for me. Please."

George was always trying to please his father. I suspected he'd ignored his father's advice when he proposed to Lizzie. Surely George's parents would have preferred a girl from a different background and with more money. My involvement in the peace movement was frowned on in the Spofford home, but Lizzie never complained. Neither did George for that matter. He was a sweet-tempered young man who was happily in love with my daughter.

"Yes, we'll attend," I told her. It was a large affair that had been scheduled long before the tragedy of Hazel's death. Neither the Spoffords nor my family could avoid the commitment. Hazel would have hated it, though, all those scenes of war. But I was uneasy about Lizzie's welfare and preferred not to let her out of my sight, even if it meant spending an evening with warmongers. The Spoffords' friends were all upstanding citizens of Chicago society, yet it was at one of their affairs that Hazel was attacked. How could I be sure that the true cause of Hazel's death wasn't something rotten in their social circle?

I wasn't looking forward to watching a war film. My brother, Alden, had moved to California to work in the film industry and had written a film that was playing at another theater. I would have preferred to see that one because I knew it would have a happy ending. I wished I could have escaped into the convoluted imaginary catastrophes of that film. But such were the times that I was obliged to see the bleaker story about a bloody conflict that was destined to have a sad ending.

I could only hope the evening would provide some clue about the attack on Hazel. Her mother said the girl complained about some of the Spoffords' activities. I could see how Hazel, being a pacifist, would have objected to the Four Minute Men plan, but I wanted to know more. And I also wanted to see Fred Spofford to judge for myself whether his grief was genuine. I told Lizzie I wasn't in a position to find out the truth of Hazel's death, but I couldn't keep myself from trying to find out as much as I could.

THIRTEEN

In the end, I didn't have much opportunity to observe Fred. When his father had invited us to dine that evening, I was afraid he'd choose the Blackstone Hotel, just opposite the theater. I was relieved we were to go to the Palmer House instead. I couldn't have entered the Blackstone so soon after Hazel's death. And I was sure Lizzie and Regina Spofford felt the same.

Spofford was the type of man who liked to display his generosity. He greeted us in an immaculate evening suit and showed us to a private room with velvet-covered chairs and a huge chandelier. Young George looked a little stiff sitting beside his mother, and he was on alert to fill in the names of prominent clients as his father talked about the advertising agency. There were several other couples at the table.

During the meal, which was served by white-gloved waiters, Mr. Spofford explained how the current plan for the Four Minute Men was hatched at a dinner of the Saddle & Cycle Club. After a heated discussion about the prospect for war and the universal military training bill, prominent citizens including Mr. Donald Ryerson, Senator McCormick, and others agreed something had to be done to develop public sentiment in favor of the bill. Spofford emphasized his own involvement, as an advertising man, in the plan to make brief speeches before moving picture audiences. My participation in the peace movement was politely ignored.

The plan was the same one I'd overheard at the funeral. Ryerson convinced the Strand Theater to allow them to test the program that evening, after which they'd organize an army of prominent men who could go out and deliver this type of speech all over the city. "And to the rest of the country, too, if we can convince Washington." Clearly, George's father was anxious for the evening to be a success.

Dressed all in black, as a reminder of his loss, Fred joined us for dinner but didn't attend the film. When he said his goodbyes in the lobby of the Palmer House, young George confided that his brother was going to a nearby garage to work on his racing car. "It helps to occupy him," George said as he took Lizzie's arm. "He needs to forget his sorrows some of the time. We encourage it."

His parents both looked away, not so much embarrassed by the reference to the recent tragedy as at a loss about what to say. Spofford soon hurried us to the street. Life had to go on, despite the tragic loss of Hazel. No one could really blame the Spoffords for that. But it didn't make me like them any better.

The Strand Theater was at Seventh and Wabash, catty-corner from the Blackstone. It was squatter and more garishly decorated than the elegant hotel. On the façade was a tall arch of light bulbs for evening performances. It had originally been built, back in the 1880s, to hold a panorama of the Battle of Gettysburg. It was almost round, a sixteen-sided polygon built specifically to display the massive painting. Over time, the appeal of the historic battle diminished, and it became first a theater and then, finally, a fancy cinema with an orchestra pit for impressive musical accompaniment.

I was aware of the shadow of the Blackstone as we entered under the marquee announcing *Merl Lavoy's Wonder Battle Pictures Presents Heroic France: The Allies in Action*. On large posters, men in helmets rushed through bomb blasts. It made me dread the future—both the coming hour, and the coming year. A well-dressed crowd poured through the lobby to red velvet seats inside.

After the first episode, which depicted French soldiers on the lines and French peasants in the countryside valiantly defending their country, Mr. Ryerson came out and made a short speech. "Tonight, practically the entire civilized world is at war," he began. He continued with statistics on how woefully reduced the numbers of *our* country's military forces had become, and, finally, he provided frightening statistics on the high numbers of troops deployed in the warring European countries. He used all this to demand support for training our young men. Concluding with predictions of disaster, he warned, "Now is the time for us to act."

It was an argument that we of the Woman's Peace Party profoundly disagreed with. It was obvious that investing time and money in "preparedness" only made it more likely that someone's finger would slip on the trigger and we would be launched into the war without consideration for the costs in lives. Men who were itching to go to war needed too little excuse to plunge the whole country into the mess in Europe. I was unconvinced by Ryerson's speech.

But others were. After rousing applause, Mr. Spofford announced a lunch meeting at the University Club the following week to begin to organize speakers, then the lights were dimmed, and the rest of the film was shown.

If this was the activity of the Spoffords that worried Hazel, I could understand it. As a pacifist, she would have been repulsed. I was repulsed. My heart sank at the thought of all those young men being handed guns. The way the speaker had blatantly manipulated the audience was also troubling. But it was hardly nefarious. Hazel's possible objections to the Four Minute Men movement didn't explain her death, but could explain her estrangement from Fred, if they had indeed been estranged. Was it enough to push her into the arms of a working man like Hoffman? Lizzie rejected the idea but, after the rampant militarism of the evening, I could almost picture that possibility.

In the lobby after the show, there was much back slapping. While Stephen and I greeted the University of Chicago president, Harry Pratt Judson, several people congratulated Mr. Spofford on helping to write the speech. After a while, I found myself at the edge of a group of young men surrounding Samuel Insull, the electricity and railroad magnate. They appeared to be complaining. Young George Spofford was among them. My son Jack moved to my side, his face blank so I wasn't sure what he thought of the discussion. I kept an eye on Lizzie. Hanging on to George's elbow, she looked drawn and exhausted by the evening.

"The government should get away from this red tape," young George said. "A yacht owner who's patriotic enough to turn his craft over to the government can't answer questions as to how many guns he can mount, or how strong his wireless is, or storage space for ammunition, etc. We wanted to get them a thousand or more small craft for scout patrol. But they send all these ridiculous forms to be filled out. Instead, they should send an expert to look at the boats and then have a contract the owner can sign in three minutes."

Insull was a smart looking man of about sixty with trim white hair and a pince-nez on a chain that led to his ear. Although he was a very successful businessman, and despite his British accent, he wasn't always accepted by Chicago society. Perhaps that was why he was so patient with these young men. "The navy is used to dealing with ship builders," he told them. "Keep after them, and if you have any friends or relations in Washington, get them to help. If that won't work and you're still anxious to get in the fight, there are other ways to join." He raised his eyebrows quizzically, as if waiting for another question.

I wondered what other ways to fight the war he wanted to offer them, but the young men were only interested in the plan hatched at the Chicago Yacht Club to offer private yachts to the government. They wanted to chase U-boats.

While George described his plans to arm his yacht with four cannons, and impressed the crowd with his assertion that it could make a speed of twenty-one knots, Jack told me quietly that Insull had encouraged young American men to join French and British fighting forces by going through Canada. "I've heard he's even helped some men avoid arrest by taking that route."

A lot of young people saw the war as a great adventure, despite gritty films like the one we'd just seen. Men like Lizzie's George wanted to sign up for what they saw as "outings" on their yachts. They dreamt romantic dreams about fighting. From the newsreels, they should have known it was no glorious fight but, at that age, young men don't recognize the truth. It was as if there were a huge pool of energy building up behind a dam, just waiting to burst forth in a raging flood of war madness. At least my son Jack seemed skeptical. That gave me some hope.

Lizzie looked wilted in the midst of all that enthusiasm. I tapped her shoulder and told her we were leaving. We found Stephen in a knot of men complaining about something entirely different.

"It's a bad idea but, anyhow, Congress will never agree," George's father was saying. They were talking about a proposal to conscript incomes over one hundred thousand dollars in order to support the troops and their families left behind.

"You're wrong about that," another man said. "There are a lot in Congress who support it. Not only that, there are plenty of radicals who support extending the drastic income tax even *after* the war is over. You watch, they're chomping at the bit to get that money."

"It would be a mistake," a bank president in the group said. "That money needs to stay in the hands of business to reinvest in needed industries. When we enter the war, the government itself will need loans from those businessmen. I know a man who's held a very large loan for the French government. He could have made a better profit by putting it in stocks, but he wanted to help them. Our government is in much better financial shape than the Europeans were when they got into the war. They don't need to confiscate money. And, at some point, the U.S. government may need to borrow it. It's a foolish idea."

I beckoned Stephen away from the conversation. I hated all this war talk. It might be inevitable but, until it happened, I prayed we would remain neutral. With all this emphasis on war, Hazel's death was old news, lost in the tide of public affairs that was rising like a huge wave.

Three days later, President Wilson asked Congress to declare war.

FOURTEEN

W e got the news in special editions of the papers. They printed the speech in full. I will always remember the kernel in the middle:

The world must be made safe for democracy. Its peace must be planted upon the tested foundations of political liberty. We have no selfish ends to serve. We desire no conquest, no dominion. We seek no indemnities for ourselves, no material compensation for the sacrifices we shall freely make...

Even while waiting for Congress to give President Wilson the declaration he requested, war fever spread. Patriotism became the latest fashion, and anything German was disdained. The sentiments grew and grew. By the following year, sauerkraut became "liberty cabbage," dachshunds "liberty pups," and even German measles became "liberty measles." Frankfurters and German shepherds were forbidden. As if such renaming would in any way affect the bitter struggles going on in Europe. By the spring of 1918 the madness came to a head with the lynching of a German American man in a town outside Chicago.

But, in the spring of 1917, the wave of hatred was just forming. Where the most popular song the year before had been "I Didn't Raise My Boy to Be a Soldier" now it was "Over There." Everyone geared up to send our boys, the "Yanks," over there. It made me heartsick.

With all the turmoil going on in the world, my investigation into the death of Hazel Littleton might have ended if I hadn't met Mr. Alexander Mirkin.

We went back to our normal schedule after Hazel's funeral. Stephen and I both had classes to teach and meetings to attend. Jack was deep in his medical studies, spending much of his time on anatomical dissections. Lizzie was pale and inconsolable, but she attended to her duties as a typist and disappeared to her room after supper each night. I couldn't bring myself to interrogate her about her dead friend anymore. If Henrietta Littleton's suspicions were correct, the news Hazel planned to tell Lizzie was purely personal, and I couldn't see how my daughter's safety was at risk. But Lizzie had adamantly denied that Hazel could have gotten into such trouble, and I still had my own doubts. What if there was something else, something more dangerous Hazel had been involved in? And why did she need to tell Lizzie about whatever it was before she told her own mother? After much soul searching, I couldn't bear to damage Hazel's memory by sharing Henrietta's suspicions with the police.

Stephen and Jack took notice of the glum atmosphere and decided they needed to cheer me up. So, when they cajoled me into accompanying them to the Friday evening meeting of the Biology Club at Clarence Darrow's apartment on the Midway, I agreed. The club invited scholars to talk on subjects like Darwin's theories and Spencer's writings, but it was really an excuse to drink sour Italian wine and join in the wide-ranging discussions peculiar to academics. Jack reassured me that even Jane Addams was known to consult the famous lawyer, as if I were unaware of that fact. I knew of the salon Clarence and his wife, Ruby, held in Hyde Park and that it attracted famous visitors, but I really agreed to attend that Friday evening in the secret hope that I could learn more about the case against Hoffman. If Darrow was providing the defense, his office must be actively investigating the murder.

Bundled up against the cold, the three of us set out. Our path took us by Stagg Field, where canvas tents flapped in the wind and formations of khaki-clad young men in pointed brown hats marched over well-trodden icy ground. Dirty piles of frozen snow left from the winter bordered the walk. As we passed the soldiers, their leather boots and belts creaked in the cold.

"It's the Reserve Officers' Training Corps," Jack told me. He held fast to my elbow to keep me from slipping, making me feel older than my forty-seven years.

"Military science." I spat out the words. "What's the university coming to that we have *military science* as a field of study?" I'd come to the university when it first opened because it offered the chance to do research in important areas like science and sociology. From its beginning, the new university even allowed women to do advanced research. I was certain that military science was never on the original prospectus.

Stephen spoke over the muffler wrapped around his chin. "It's Judson. That was his idea. He's gung-ho on it. Some people think he's trying to make his mark. When he was appointed president after Harper, he had big shoes to fill and a lot of the faculty held him in contempt. It's unkind but true."

Judson was the second president of the University of Chicago. He followed William Rainey Harper, the vigorous young scholar who founded the school. By comparison, Judson was more of an administrator, and some even thought of him as a mere accountant. That was probably because he got the school out of debt and made enemies along the way. An even financial keel didn't count much with the pre-eminent scholars on the faculty. Judson was the one who'd established the R.O.T.C on the campus. Personally, I thought he'd done well by the university, but I hated the militaristic tendencies he encouraged. What was it about men who had never been soldiers themselves that made them so enthusiastic about supporting military training?

The marching men were such an anomaly on campus that I ground my teeth in exasperation. How could they calmly tramp around the half-frozen field like that, with the devastation that was happening on the battlefields of Europe? It was appalling.

Sensing my indignation, Jack patted my arm. "With Wilson's declaration of war some sort of militarism is inevitable, Mother. But tell me, why haven't you come to one of Darrow's gatherings before now? You knew him when he was younger, didn't you?"

Stephen cleared his throat. "Your mother didn't always approve of Darrow's conduct when he was younger."

I kept my gaze on the ground, looking to avoid patches of ice. "He was a disgrace."

Stephen defended Darrow, explaining to Jack, "It was a long time ago. Ruby's not his first wife. He was married before. We knew him when your mother and I were both residents at Hull House, before we married. Darrow helped with the legal actions after the Pullman Strike." Jack smiled at the thought of his parents being young, or perhaps at my apparent dislike of Darrow.

"We were grateful to him for defending the strikers," I said. "But those were the years when he and another bachelor rented an apartment at the Langdon. They preached 'free love' and other radical ideas."

"Some of the young women from Hull House were especially fond of Darrow," Stephen said, smirking.

"Hah! They fawned on him. I'll never forget the ruckus he caused when they heard about his marriage to Ruby. He'd been leading them on, claiming that he believed in free love and vowing never to marry again."

"Several of the women were quite upset," Stephen said and chuckled.

It was no laughing matter. "Two of the women behaved very badly. They were bitter. It was a huge embarrassment at the time and one for which I had very little patience," I told Jack.

Recalling how I'd personally chased one of the girls away from Darrow's flat, I cringed at the memories.

"But, after that, he was active in supporting labor, wasn't he?" Jack asked. I was active in labor causes, so I'm sure he assumed I'd sympathize with Darrow.

"Yes, but we cannot forgive him for what he did in Los Angeles. He swore those men didn't set those bombs, then he turned around and had them plead guilty to save them from the death penalty. He lied to all of us in the labor movement."

"He managed to save them from death," Stephen pointed out.

"And then he was tried himself for bribing jurors," I said.

"He beat that."

"A hung jury got him out of that pickle and now he's back in Chicago, broke and looking for cases," I said. The men were silent, letting my wrath cool. Darrow had done a lot of good in his time, but he was no saint and there was a lot to forgive. I was old enough not to be shocked to find out a widely admired man had feet of clay, but it rankled, nonetheless. I knew too many people who *had* remained true to their ideals to waste my sympathies on the charismatic lawyer.

FIFTEEN

After crossing the Midway, we arrived. The Darrows rented a large apartment on the fifth floor of a building called The Hunter, which overlooked the university. Ruby welcomed us, taking our coats as we entered the big L-shaped room that was lined with books. They had knocked down walls, put up shelving, and laid a huge, red Oriental carpet. Soft leather chairs and sofas were placed around the room. Two wicker rockers stood by the hearth. A fire burnt brightly at one end, while big windows displayed a view of the lake, trees, and the Japanese garden left from the Columbian Exposition. Already a dozen people were scattered around, and a table with wine and fruit stood near the entrance so guests could help themselves.

Clarence Darrow sat in one of the rockers, joking with a young physicist who was scheduled to give the talk that evening. Stephen warned me that although it was called the Biology Club, it was open to all topics.

Darrow showed the wear and tear of recent years. He was a tall man with a shambling aspect. That night he slouched in his chair, his straight hair falling over his fine blue eyes when he argued. Considered handsome with his cleft chin, he had a lot of charm, although I'd never warmed to it, myself. I recognized a number of faculty in the room along with some graduate and undergraduate students. I wasn't surprised at the young women clustered at the foot of Darrow's chair, hanging on every word.

When I sat down with my glass in hand, I nudged Stephen beside me on the couch. He knew my opinion of Darrow's flirtations. Stephen grinned, and I noticed Ruby across the room glaring at the gaggle of girls. There was no time for me to approach the man before the speech began.

I confess my mind wandered as the young physicist attempted to explain a new theory of relativity that was beyond my ken. The discovery he described was considered earth shattering by the academic theorists and I sensed that they could see far into a future I couldn't grasp. When the session broke up into separate conversations, I took the opportunity to get up and walk around in hopes of talking to Darrow. I was refilling my glass when I heard someone ask him what he thought of Mayor Thompson's continued support for American neutrality.

Darrow condemned the mayor. "He's like a biting adder, lurking in the grass. He and the others are being used by German agents in a conspiracy of treason. There can be no peace while Prussian militarism lives. I want to see it destroyed."

I couldn't help thinking of the boys marching on Stagg Field. Wasn't it a sign of American militarism winning to see them on a university campus like that? I was surprised by the vehemence of Darrow's comments. If he was so firmly against the Germans, why would he take Hoffman's case? Perhaps Kelly had gotten it wrong. Uncertain of my facts, I sought time to think by drifting to the far end of the room, avoiding the discussion. Everything these days was about war. I was trying to distract myself by reading the spines of books, when I heard my name called.

"Mrs. Chapman, may I introduce myself?"

I turned to find a tall, slim young man with a clean-shaven face approaching me. He had brown hair that fell to the right side of his head in long flat strands that reminded me of Darrow. He pushed a strand away from his round spectacles with one hand as he held out his other hand to me.

"My name is Alexander Mirkin. I work for Mr. Darrow and I'm representing Mr. Johann Hoffman, the waiter who is accused of murdering Miss Littleton."

"And you are telling me this because you think I can help you?" I was glad to make the contact, but I didn't want to appear too eager. I wanted to find out what this young man knew first.

"Mrs. Chapman, I've been told that your daughter was present when the crime was committed. I wonder if I might come to see her, so she can tell me in her own words what happened that afternoon." He stared at me earnestly, then, when I didn't respond immediately, he rushed on. "When Mrs. Darrow told me who you were, I couldn't help taking the chance to approach you. A very great injustice will be done to Mr. Hoffman if he's condemned for this crime merely because of his German surname."

I had my own doubts about the fairness of the investigation, especially since Whitbread wasn't in charge. But the request to question my daughter was not what I was looking for. I hesitated to involve Lizzie in a criminal trial. "My daughter is very upset. Hazel was her closest friend. They even planned to marry two brothers on the same day." I wondered what Regina Spofford would do about that now. She'd planned it as a highlight of the social season. I didn't see how the plans for George and Lizzie's wedding could proceed without reminding everyone of the horror of Hazel's murder. Perhaps Lizzie would have to settle for a small, intimate wedding after all.

"I'm sure it must be very distressing for her, but I'd be grateful if she'd talk to me. I'm sure she wouldn't want to see a man railroaded."

"I'm surprised Mr. Darrow would take such a case…he's so pro-war and anti-German."

"It's my case, but Darrow supports it. He's more committed to our involvement in the war than I am, but it does seem inevitable now. I don't think there's much hope left, do you? Anyhow, Darrow wouldn't condemn a man only because he has a German surname. He's not that far gone."

Having heard Darrow accuse the mayor of Chicago of being a traitor, I couldn't help wondering about the young man's motives, but I could see his interest was in their client. I was uneasy about the German waiter. Kelly's suggestion that he was romantically involved with Hazel didn't ring true, yet he might have killed her for other reasons. How could I know? And, of course, the possibility that there was some involvement with Hull House disturbed me, given my own longstanding relationship with the settlement house. At least Mirkin would investigate the murder. At this point, no one else was willing to do so. And perhaps I could be in a position to monitor the young attorney's progress.

I told him he could call the following afternoon.

SIXTEEN

I'd prepared the front parlor, putting out my mother's tea set on a little round table. When Lizzie came in wearing a black mourning band around the arm of her white shirtwaist, she was in a dark mood. I told her about the imminent arrival of our guest, and she frowned at me angrily. It was Saturday, so she was home from work early. Because she'd been out to dinner with the Spoffords the night before and had left early in the morning before I saw her, I hadn't had a chance to warn her about the young lawyer's visit.

"Lizzie, I thought you'd welcome Mr. Mirkin's investigation. You're not satisfied by the police arrest of Mr. Hoffman and neither am I."

"Oh, Mother, having you and Detective Whitbread investigate isn't the same as having this lawyer try to put the blame on someone other than his client."

"But you don't think Mr. Hoffman killed Hazel?"

"I *know* Hazel didn't have any romantic entanglement with a waiter, which is what you say the police think. But George's father believes Hoffman killed Hazel. He thinks Hull House is hiding a nest of saboteurs and spies for Germany, and that Hazel somehow knew something about it and Hoffman killed her to keep her quiet."

"Lizzie, you don't believe that, do you?"

"I don't know what to believe. I just don't think talking to the lawyer who's representing the man the police arrested for

Hazel's murder will help. I wish you and Detective Whitbread would investigate. The police claim Hoffman was Hazel's lover, and the Spoffords believe he's a German spy. I want you and Whitbread to find the truth."

"I'm sorry, Lizzie. I've told you, Whitbread just can't help this time. And I haven't been involved with that kind of investigation for a number of years. Talking to Mr. Mirkin might at least be a way to find out what's happening with the case." As defense lawyer, Mirkin had every right to look into the facts of the case and I was longing to know details, for my own satisfaction.

"Well, it's too late now. I think that's him at the door," Lizzie said when the doorbell rang.

I went and ushered the young man in. He was thin and moved with a nervous energy that seemed barely restrained. While Delia brought the tray from the kitchen, I made the introductions.

"Thank you for seeing me," Mirkin said. Lizzie stared out the window, her arms crossed on her chest. "I would be grateful if you could tell me what you saw the day Miss Littleton was attacked. I know the memory must be very distressful to you, but it could help me to clear an innocent man." He held a handkerchief at the ready in his hand. If he expected my daughter to be a tender plant, he was mistaken.

Lizzie turned to face him. Her jaw was set, and her eyes narrowed. "Mr. Mirkin, why would I think that your client is an innocent man? He's been arrested by the police. If he murdered Hazel, I have no reason to want to help him, or you. She was my oldest and dearest friend, and she didn't deserve to be attacked like that."

I saw the young man's eyes widen behind his wire spectacles. His head snapped up and he looked Lizzie directly in the eye. "I'm sorry," he said. "Of course, it was a terrible thing. But, Miss Chapman, I want to find out the truth of what happened to your friend. The police claim Mr. Hoffman was acquainted with Miss Littleton, but Mr. Hoffman assures me that is not the case. What if the police are wrong? Do you believe that Miss Littleton was involved with my client?"

"No, Hazel was engaged to Fred Spofford. My mother has told me the police claim she had a romantic relationship with your client. She wouldn't betray Fred Spofford like that. But that doesn't prove your client innocent. There could be other reasons for him to attack her. He was fired from his job."

"Merely because his name is German. Surely you don't think that's fair!"

"But he *is* German, and the reason he was at Hull House was for socialist meetings. They oppose supporting the Allies."

"They believe that men are getting rich by selling arms to the Allies," Mirkin countered.

"And Hazel was attacked outside a meeting of women from wealthy homes, who were raising money to support the Belgians against the Germans. How do you know he didn't strike her down to demonstrate against those so-called warmongers? For that matter, how do you know he didn't do it on instructions from the German embassy as a way to promote terror and confusion? My fiancé and his father believe there are German spies planted here. They've already been exposed in New York and other places. Mr. Spofford believes Hazel could have heard something damning and been killed to keep her from speaking about it."

I remembered the bruises on the dead girl's face, as if someone had wanted to keep her from crying out. I couldn't help thinking the motive for Hazel's death was to keep her from talking. There was something she'd been intent on telling Lizzie.

Mirkin's mouth hung open slightly as he listened, and I saw a light of admiration in his eyes. Lizzie had that effect on young men, but it was something she mostly ignored. I felt a little sorry for him. He was staring as if he'd just noticed her blooming complexion, and her figure brimming with life and energy. *Oh, Lizzie, you've struck again.*

But he rallied. "Yes, certainly a spy network was uncovered in New York, but we can't condemn every German American for the actions of some, can we? Mr. Hoffman does attend political rallies, but they're for workers' rights, not in support of the Kaiser. There's no suggestion he's a spy. I confess, having met the man, he's a pretty worn-down kind of person, disappointed at losing his job and desperate to find a way to scratch out a living." He looked up. "And besides, aren't you worried that if Hoffman *isn't* the man and someone else did this, you might be in danger yourself?"

"Oh, nonsense," Lizzie said. "I'm not in danger. I would feel it if I were."

"Did Miss Littleton 'feel' it?" he asked.

She hesitated, looking at me. Neither of us wanted to share the information from Hazel's mother that she believed the girl had packed up to run away. Henrietta had told that to me in confidence and I shook my head slightly to indicate Lizzie shouldn't repeat it, even though it might indicate that Hazel *had* felt threatened. Lizzie shrugged. "I don't know. Why do you believe Mr. Hoffman's denial? Do you know him so well you can vouch for him?"

Mirkin hesitated.

"He's just your client so you take his side, isn't that so?" Lizzie asked, giving me a significant look as if to say, "I told you so."

Mirkin appeared to withdraw within himself before he replied. "I didn't know Mr. Hoffman before I was hired. But I believe it's unfair that he was dismissed from his job simply because he has a German name, and I think it doubly unfair that he was arrested on the spot for the same reason. This business of him knowing Miss Littleton at Hull House was only brought up after they seized him merely for being of German heritage." He held up a hand to stop Lizzie from talking. "I have no love of Germany and the Kaiser, but my family came from Russia to escape the pogroms during which people were driven from their homes merely for being what they were born to be. I won't stand by and see that sort of unthinking prejudice get ahold of people here. We're better than that."

Lizzie cocked her head to one side as if reconsidering her opinion of the young man.

"Exactly what do you want from us?" I asked.

He turned to Lizzie. "Did you see Mr. Hoffman that day? You found Miss Littleton, didn't you?"

Lizzie closed her eyes with a flash of pain. I reached for her hand, but she pulled away. Shaking herself, she answered. "No. I didn't see anyone. After the speeches, I went to the doorway where Hazel's note said she'd be waiting. I pushed through the curtains and opened the door. She was lying on the stairs, bleeding from her forehead. I went to her, I shook her, but she didn't answer. Then I screamed for help, but it was too late. She didn't speak. She just looked at me with those big blank eyes, all the life gone from her." Lizzie shivered. "She was lying on the stairs. Whoever killed her must have run down the stairs."

"I'm sure that was very horrible for you," Mirkin said. He paused in respect for the painful memory, then he continued. "I visited the hotel yesterday. At the bottom of the stairs, there's a door to an alley in the back. Mr. Hoffman was found *inside* the hotel. If he'd done the killing, why would he come back inside when he could have escaped through the alley?"

"Surely the police must know this," I said.

Mirkin turned dark eyes on me. "They have Mr. Hoffman. If they can prove he murdered Miss Littleton, the murder is solved. But the mayor doesn't like the idea of pitting German Americans against the rest of the population, so they've come up with this idea of a romantic relationship with the lady as a motive."

"What a terrible thing to do to Miss Littleton's reputation! Her poor parents have enough grief without enduring the slander of their dead daughter," I protested.

"That's why I need your help. The police aren't looking any further than Hoffman. Do you know of anyone else who had a reason to hurt Miss Littleton? Or someone who had a grudge against the women's group who ran the luncheon? Was there anyone else in Miss Littleton's life who would attack her?"

"Of course not," Lizzie snapped. "Hazel was loved. She was completing her degree at the university and planning her marriage to a man who loved her. She was committed to the pacifist cause, but we all knew that war was inevitable. Isn't it much more likely that Mr. Spofford is right, and your client was involved in dangerous activities that led to Hazel's death? The police just don't want to rile the mayor so they're not looking into that possibility."

I was glad to see my daughter roused from the lethargy of grief, but I wondered if she and the young lawyer knew what they were getting into. I'd been involved in murder investigations, and I knew from experience they could expose more rifts and dark secrets than were ever anticipated. I doubted whether either of these young people had any idea of how deeply you needed to dig into relations, motives, and sometimes irrelevant sins of others, including the dead person, to get at the truth. Whitbread understood, and he taught me to bear the consequences of such investigations, but these young people had no idea. However, I could see they were both determined to pursue the truth.

"Why do the police believe Miss Littleton had a romantic attachment to Mr. Hoffman?" I asked. "What's their evidence?"

"It's not true," Lizzie insisted.

"I'm not sure," Mirkin said. "They seem to think they may have met at Hull House. Mr. Hoffman attended meetings and classes there."

"But Hazel didn't teach at Hull House. She would only have gone there for pacifist meetings," Lizzie said.

"I think she did teach," I said. "I recall someone mentioning she was involved in other activities at the settlement."

"I didn't know," Lizzie said. "But that's all the more reason to think Hazel might have stumbled on a conspiracy, isn't it?" I could see it hadn't occurred to Lizzie that Hazel had a life beyond the one that overlapped with her own. If she didn't know about the classes her friend taught, what else didn't she know? I wondered if the rumor of a romantic attachment had some truth and Lizzie just didn't know about it.

"There's no more evidence of any conspiracy than there is of a romantic relationship," Mirkin said. "My client says he never met Miss Littleton." He looked down at some notes in his hands, as if hesitant to ask the next question. "Why didn't Miss Littleton attend the luncheon? Wasn't it Mrs. Spofford's event, and wasn't she Miss Littleton's future mother-in-law?"

I remembered the empty chair at our table. Regina Spofford had planned to have Hazel on her left and Lizzie on her right, showing off her soon to be daughters-in-law. It had been awkward when Hazel never appeared.

"They didn't always agree about politics," Lizzie said. "But that was just because Mr. Spofford believes in preparedness and Hazel was a pacifist."

"What did her fiancé think?" Mirkin asked.

"He sides with his father, of course. But he doesn't care so much about that. Fred Spofford is always busy with his race cars. That's what he really cares about...besides Hazel, of course."

Mirkin raised an eyebrow and glanced at me. If a young man was so consumed by his interest in race cars, perhaps a young woman might look elsewhere. I could see Mirkin was perplexed about how to pursue this line of reasoning without alienating my daughter.

"Lizzie, was there any tension between Hazel and Fred Spofford? Did she disapprove of the motorcar racing?" I asked.

"No. Hazel came to the races, the same as I did."

Mirkin cleared his throat. "Miss Chapman, if the police could get the idea that Miss Littleton might have a romantic entanglement, could her fiancé have a suspicion of something like that, even if he was totally wrong?"

"That's ridiculous." Lizzie went quite pale and I felt hollow myself. Poor Hazel. How people could speculate about her when she wasn't here to defend herself. It seemed very unfair.

"Mr. Mirkin, I'm afraid there's no more Lizzie can tell you."

He sipped his cup of tea, which must have been quite cold at that point. His hair fell into his eye as he put the cup down. "I do thank you for your time. I hope you can see that it's by no means certain my client is responsible for Miss Littleton's death." He looked up at Lizzie and then me. "The police have little incentive for further investigation. They won't mind if they sully your friend's reputation if it means they can convict Mr. Hoffman without inflaming anti-German sentiments." I knew that was true.

He folded his napkin and placed it on the table. "I'll be trying to disprove the accusations against Mr. Hoffman. I want to go to Hull House to find out if anyone has proof of the relationship or of any other circumstance that might have led to the attack." He nodded at Lizzie as if to acknowledge Mr. Spofford's conspiracy theory. "I would also very much like to interview the Spoffords, although I have little hope they'll cooperate with me. I wonder if you might help me to find the truth."

"Why should we believe you want to find the truth?" Lizzie asked. "You just want to find evidence to clear your client and who's to say you won't damage the reputation of Hazel or others in that quest?"

It wasn't a polite exchange, but I was glad to hear Lizzie speak up. It reminded me again of my ambitions for my daughter. She would have made a great lawyer.

Mirkin suppressed a smile as he looked at the ceiling. "Look at it this way, you could correct me if I get off course. I don't think there's anything to this conspiracy theory, but we could follow up on that." He turned to me. "I'd really like your help when I go to Hull House, Mrs. Chapman." He obviously knew of my involvement there. "And, if you would agree, Miss Chapman, I would very much like to meet the Spofford family. If only to eliminate Miss Littleton's fiancé as a possibility."

"I'm willing to introduce you to Hull House staff," I said. "But I'll expect you to be fair and evenhanded with any information you uncover." I looked at Lizzie. "I admit I'm disappointed with how the police are proceeding. I'm not satisfied that Mr. Hoffman is responsible...at least not yet."

"I assure you that if I find Mr. Hoffman *is* responsible, I will advise him very differently than if I continue to believe his assertions that he's innocent," Mirkin said. I hoped he was being truthful. I wasn't confident that a protégé of Mr. Darrow's would live up to that statement after Darrow's defense of the bombers in the Los Angeles trial, but I reserved judgment.

"Miss Chapman?" Mirkin turned toward Lizzie. "Will you introduce me to the Spoffords?"

"I'll consider it."

It was more than I expected after the verbal fencing. He and I arranged to meet at Hull House the following Monday.

After letting Mirkin out the door, I thought how different this would be from the times when I'd assisted Detective Whitbread. It wasn't the first time I'd been enlisted to save someone from the hangman after the police had made an arrest, but it was the first time I had so many doubts about the accused. What did I know about Hoffman? It was a long time since I assumed workingmen were all innocents. Many people who suffered from unreasonable practices—like the firing of men for having German ancestry—collapsed in despair, but not all. Some fought back as viciously as they were oppressed. I didn't necessarily believe in Hoffman's innocence.

SEVENTEEN

We arranged to meet Mirkin at Hull House on Monday afternoon. Lizzie insisted on coming. I had a meeting to attend at city hall in the morning and my daughter came along. But at the door to the city council area, she shied like a horse, saying she had an errand and would meet me later. I mentioned that I wanted to try to see Tommy, so we should meet at Fitz's office on the fifth floor.

I found my way to the meeting of the judiciary committee. I'd come to support a socialist alderman who was friendly to Hull House and who was being accused of speaking in a treasonous manner at a recent West Side meeting. I'd attended that meeting, during which he merely stipulated the reasons for America *not* to get into the war, along with the common accusations against the forces of Wall Street. Many people believed the bankers supported the war for their own financial profit. The alderman staunchly defended himself to the committee and I was among those who applauded him. The meeting adjourned after a few windy patriotic declarations by the committee members. As I rose to leave, I noticed movement at the back of the room.

A man stood near the door, waving a handful of circulars with the bold headline "Do You Want to Die?" I assumed he supported the socialist alderman who was against getting into the war. Too late, of course, since Congress had just declared war, but he was entitled to his opinion. I saw him knocked to the floor by a man who didn't want the circular and who yelled, "Get out of here, you should be ashamed of yourself!"

"I'm not. I'm proud of myself," the man with the circulars said, standing back up.

They might have come to blows, but the sergeant at arms intervened, keeping them apart.

I stiffened, alarmed at the threat of violence, but the crowd elbowed the combatants out of the way to get on to their next meetings, and the fear in the room dissipated. I waited until most had gone before proceeding to the elevators. There was so much pent-up anger in the air in those early days of the war.

On the fifth floor, I headed for Fitz's corner office. I was surprised to see Lizzie already waiting on a bench as my meeting had been shorter than I'd expected. She looked up and was surprised to see me, too. "Mother."

At that moment Lenny rushed up. "No luck, miss. He's just gone off on a job for Fitz. Oh, Mrs. Chapman, how do you do? Miss Elizabeth here was looking for Tommy but he's gone out, I'm afraid. Are you here to see him? Or is it Mr. Fitzgibbons? He's out, too."

"Thank you, Lenny. I was hoping to see my son, but we have an appointment this afternoon, so we won't wait. Just tell him I was looking for him, will you? Lizzie, shall we get something to eat before we go to Hull House?"

In the elevator Lizzie told me she'd decided to look for Tommy instead of doing her errand.

"Why? Do you think he knows something about Hazel's death?"

"No, no, of course not. I just wanted to see how he was. I didn't get to talk to him at her funeral. We were all so close when we were younger. I'm sure he's feeling sad about Hazel."

Of course, I knew they were close. Lizzie seemed to be anxious to excuse her actions. It seemed odd. But I was glad that she'd thought of her younger brother. I still hoped I could reconcile him to our family.

EIGHTEEN

I t had surprised me when Lizzie insisted on going with me
to Hull House. In the past few years, whenever I'd tried to
interest her in the activities of the settlement house, she'd
always declined. It was as if that were my world and she planned
to inhabit a different one, the world of wealth and beauty that
the Spoffords enjoyed.

Once, when I reminded her how much she'd appreciated the
Hull House art gallery when she was younger, she said, "Mother,
look at the Art Institute. I know Miss Addams and Miss Starr
wanted to expose people in the tenements to beautiful things
but look at how feeble that collection is compared to what Mrs.
Palmer and others have established at the Art Institute. And
those collections are available to *everyone*. Can't you see how much
more they've been able to do? Of course, Miss Starr had the best
intentions, but you have to see that she never had the resources
to do what Mrs. Palmer did for the Art Institute."

Her insistence on accompanying me this time made me uneasy.
What if something about Hazel's work at Hull House led to her
death? Surely, Lizzie was not involved. But, if she showed up now,
would someone assume she knew more than she did? Would that
put her in danger? I didn't see any evidence for Mr. Spofford's
conspiracy theory, but I couldn't dismiss it either. He'd told Lizzie
there was a nest of spies at the settlement house. I was confident
that wasn't true. But I still had no idea why Hazel was attacked.

On the way, we witnessed another scene that did nothing to reassure me. We took the train and changed to a trolley car to get to Hull House. As the trolley made its way along Twelfth Street, a fight erupted between a drunken man in a stained white apron and several other men in working clothes. The drunk stood up and began yelling, slurring his words.

"Dis is a rich man's war," he said, then he pulled a knife from his pocket and raised it in the air. "I'm sick and tired of dem all blaming de Kaiser. He's a good man." I could smell a cloud of whiskey.

Someone screamed. The trolley jolted to a stop.

The man stumbled and grabbed a pole. "Dat *Lusitania* had no business on de water."

A uniformed policeman stepped onto the trolley and put his hands on his hips as he looked the man up and down.

The drunk ogled him. "I tell you, Americans have done things just as bad as the Germans did to the Belgians."

"Right. Had a bit of a nip, have you?" the officer said. He reached out to grab the knife, but the man swung away from him, stumbled, and landed in Lizzie's lap.

"No, get away!" I yelled, using both hands to push his shoulders. Lizzie also pushed and he landed on his backside on the floor. He looked startled, his mouth open. I pulled Lizzie to me.

"It's all right, Mother."

The large policeman lunged across and straddled the drunken man. Reaching down, he plucked the knife from his hand and pulled him up, wrenching the man's arm behind him. "Are you all right, miss?" he asked. Lizzie assured him she was fine. He pushed the drunk out the door. "Come along now. We've got a place for you to sleep it off."

My heart was still beating fast and my breath was short. Lizzie soothed me. But the picture of Hazel lying on that staircase was in my head. I bit my lip to bring myself back to the present.

The man's struggle was pretty pathetic. As he was pushed off the car into the arms of another officer, he yelled back at us, "De Kaiser is good man!" Passengers shook their heads and we lurched forward. Not everyone supported our entry into the war, it seemed. That man was no pacifist, however. Two stops later we reached our destination. My heartrate had come down to normal, but the incident confirmed my fear about letting my daughter roam the streets of the city alone.

As we descended the trolley car to meet Mirkin on the doorstep, I looked up at the red brick and dull yellow trim of the old Hull mansion with affection. More than twenty-five years had passed since Jane Addams had abandoned her wealthy background to live among the immigrants of the West Side. A few years later, I came to the city from Boston, thrilled to be one of the first women graduate students at the newly opened University of Chicago. I felt I had grown up with the settlement house. Now, there were more than a dozen buildings, filled with classrooms and workshops, an art gallery, theater, communal bathhouse, and playground. When I first arrived in Chicago, I never would have imagined Hull House could grow to be such a force. Nor had I imagined I would be the mother of three grown children by this time. We had survived a lot and thrived during turbulent times in Chicago.

For years I worked at Hull House, trying to accomplish something, even if only in fits and starts. Not all our reform efforts were successful. Over the years there were some failed strikes and lost elections, but there were also new laws and regulations we could be proud of. Recently, some people withdrew support or ridiculed Miss Addams for her efforts in the international peace movement, but I was still proud of what we'd accomplished.

Beside me, Lizzie looked up at the house. She'd been there plenty of times while growing up but now she came looking for conspiracies and spies. I hoped she wouldn't find them. It hurt me to realize that Lizzie considered the successes I valued as puny. She saw the wealth and power of the Spoffords as much more effective than the efforts of the Hull House reformers. With that in mind, the settlement house looked older and smaller to me that day.

Inside, Miss Addams met with us and suggested we use the octagon room for interviews. In her fifties, she was a solid figure. Her hair was graying, pulled back tight against her head, and her eyes were deep set and shadowed. As always, she was dressed in a stylish suit with a small watch pinned to her lapel. She was intimate and welcoming as she ushered us in. Gracious to everyone who crossed her threshold, she was sincerely interested in every problem brought to her door.

She was very sad about Hazel and apologized for not attending the funeral. "I've been sick on and off since my trip last year. And I'm sure Miss Littleton's parents would not appreciate the notoriety my attendance might bring. The press are relentless in their criticism of the pacifist cause these days." She sighed. "It was so different last year. But it would have been a shame to distract from the services by my presence."

"Miss Littleton believed in the cause of the Woman's Peace Party," I said.

Miss Addams shook her head. "She did, and she was a great help. But now that we have war, we should, perhaps, not talk against it but work for the proper conduct of it." She told me she was organizing a meeting of the Woman's Peace Party to mobilize for war by doing social service or helping the Red Cross. I wondered what Hazel would have thought about that.

"Hazel helped out with some classes," she said, when I asked about the dead girl's work at Hull House. "I'm afraid Miss Holden, who's been so helpful with organizing the day-to-day schedule, isn't here today. I believe she recruited Miss Littleton to teach some of the English language classes. I'll ask some of the others to talk to you, but I suspect Miss Holden would be the best source of information. She'll be back tomorrow."

When Mirkin asked about the Young Socialists Club, Miss Addams said, "They've met here for many years. I think a Mr. Kurtz is the speaker these days. They sometimes organize demonstrations but most of the time they have lively debates. I think there may have been some disturbance lately, but that's not unusual. They have a lot of strong opinions. If something happened, I suspect Miss Holden has kept it from me because she thinks I'm ill. They meet on Thursday evenings, you see, and the meetings are open to anyone, so you're welcome to come back and join in. I'm not acquainted with Mr. Hoffman myself but I'm sure Mr. Kurtz could tell you about his involvement."

Lizzie brought up Mr. Spofford's theory that Hazel might have learned of a German conspiracy. Miss Addams was not offended but she thought it was unlikely. "Certainly we have many German Americans in our clubs and classes, but we also have French, Italians, Bohemians, and others. As you can see, very little is secret here. People are walking in and out of the meetings and anyone may attend. We certainly don't mean to host any spies, and we have no reason to believe anything so nefarious is going on. You must understand, many in the labor unions and socialist party oppose the war because they believe that wealthy men are profiting from it. They think the East Coast bankers have loaned a lot of money to Britain and France, and they want us in the war to protect their investments. It's not that they think well of the Kaiser or support Prussian militarism. They just don't trust Wall Street. Let me send up some people who may be able to help you."

When she left to find some staff members for us to talk to, Lizzie said, "Still, there could be things going on here that Miss Addams isn't aware of. Since anyone can attend, they have no idea if there *are* German spies."

"In my experience, there is much more to do with learning English and job skills, or art and drama going on here," I said. "They have political discussions but they're about labor laws more than anything else. There are other private German clubs where very pro-German people go."

Mirkin, Lizzie, and I talked to several staff members, but no one knew of any connection between the German waiter and Hazel. Hoffman attended meetings of the socialist group, but that was only to be expected of a working man at that time. He'd been active in a movement to unionize the waiters but played only a small part. They also recommended we talk to Miss Holden and Mr. Kurtz.

"I haven't heard anything to suggest a pro-German conspiracy, have you?" Mirkin asked when the last staff member left.

"No," I agreed.

"The police were right that both Miss Littleton and Mr. Hoffman were involved in Hull House activities. It's possible they could have met. We can't disprove that," he said.

"But Hazel would never become romantically involved with a socialist waiter," Lizzie insisted. "She never mentioned the man to me, and she would have. It's much more likely she saw or heard something without knowing it was important."

Mirkin shuffled some papers. We'd arranged ourselves around a simple table to do the interviews. I was glad a desk that once stood in the corner had been removed. Every time I entered that room, I remembered a Christmas day many years ago when I found a dead man sitting there.

"No doubt Mr. Hoffman was beneath Miss Littleton's notice," Mirkin said. "But what if her fiancé suspected her affections were engaged elsewhere, as the police do?" He turned to Lizzie. "If it wasn't Hoffman, could she have met someone else here who would interest her in that way?"

"No." Lizzie looked at me. She and I knew that Hazel's mother suspected there was another man. "Hazel just disagreed with Fred about politics. I'm sure that's all it was."

The literal liar, again. Hazel had disagreed with her fiancé about war and peace, but I suspected there was more. "Lizzie, are you absolutely sure Hazel wasn't seeing another man?"

"Hazel was very busy with the peace work and the wedding plans. She didn't have time to meet anyone new. She never told me about meeting someone new. Never."

"She was still committed to Fred Spofford and planned to marry him in June?" I asked. Lizzie didn't answer immediately. She looked down and shuffled some papers. Why did she hesitate? Perhaps she remembered that Hazel's mother believed she was planning to run away. Or did she know something else about Hazel's relationship with her fiancé?

Finally, Lizzie spoke. "She may have had doubts."

Mirkin pounced on that. "Doubts about marrying Mr. Spofford? Did they argue?"

"No," Lizzie said. "Fred thought she was nervous about getting married, but he didn't take her seriously. He didn't believe she'd withdraw from the wedding, not after all the planning his mother and her mother and all of us have done. He hushed her and told her not to worry, it was just jittery nerves. He even kidded her about it. She couldn't get him to take her seriously."

"But she was serious, wasn't she?" Mirkin said. He was quick to understand.

"No."

"Lizzie, did you get the sense Hazel was seriously thinking of breaking off her engagement?" I asked. "Is that why you didn't want to talk to her that day? Were you afraid she was going to call off the wedding?"

Lizzie took a big breath. "I was afraid of it. But not because of Hoffman. At first, Hazel liked all the social events. It was so much more exciting than the university lectures we were used to. We both liked it. But, after a while, Hazel wasn't as interested. She didn't like the balls and parties as much as I did. She worried that her parents weren't happy with her choice, you know. Fred was so involved with the motorcar races, and he took it for granted that Hazel would do whatever his mother asked. She got involved in the Woman's Peace Party and I think she used that to avoid social engagements. Mrs. Spofford spoke to her about it. She spoke to both of us about obligations, things we needed to do.

"I was angry with Hazel for not coming to the luncheon. I had tried to make her understand how much more good we could both do when we were married. I thought she could at least support the Belgian refugees. I couldn't believe she would insult Mrs. Spofford by not showing up and I think the money raised at that event is a lot more useful than all the telegrams the WPP sent about staying out of the war. So, when I found out Hazel was outside, I made her wait." She moaned, clearly regretting her delay in going to her friend. "But why didn't she come in? She could have. She was supposed to attend. Mrs. Spofford was keeping a seat for her. Why did she have to talk to me *outside* the ballroom? Now I'll never know." Lizzie looked devastated and my heart went out to her. She squeezed her eyes shut as if trying not to cry.

It occurred to me that Hazel might have feared Lizzie's angry reaction to the news if she was breaking the engagement. She might not have wanted to confront her friend publicly, or she might have wanted to allow Fred to tell his mother himself. That could be a reason to not come in and face her. I suggested that to Lizzie.

"You think she didn't come to the luncheon because she went to see Fred that day and broke off the engagement?" Lizzie asked. I knew we both wondered why she'd packed a bag and planned to run away.

"Perhaps we could ask Mr. Spofford," Mirkin said.

"Oh, I don't think the Spoffords are going to talk to the lawyer for Mr. Hoffman," Lizzie said, rummaging in her pocket for a handkerchief. She blew her nose. "Fred's not going to talk to *you*."

"But he'd talk to you," Mirkin said.

"Fred is mourning Hazel's death," I said. "Lizzie can't just confront him about whether she was going to break off the engagement."

NINETEEN

George drove us to the motorcar derby in his new Jeffery Touring Car. The early April day was unusually mild, but I was instructed by Lizzie to dress warmly since the car was mostly open, despite the raised top. She had anchored my straw hat with three pins, and I soon saw why she'd purchased a long driving coat with wide lapels and a broad hat with netting that was tied firmly beneath her chin.

George himself wore a long coat and flat tweed cap. He was hugely proud of the big machine. When he helped me to climb into the back with Mirkin, I saw it was unexpectedly spacious inside. I had insisted on bringing Mirkin, who I introduced as a friend of the family with an interest in motorcars. I didn't tell George that Mirkin was Hoffman's lawyer. Lizzie rolled her eyes but didn't reveal Mirkin's connection to the murder case. The truth was I didn't want Lizzie to go on the expedition at all. Until we knew who killed Hazel, I was afraid for my daughter. But when Lizzie insisted on going, I insisted on coming along and bringing Mirkin. She scoffed at the idea that Fred Spofford had anything to do with Hazel's death, but I wanted to talk to the young man myself with the skeptical lawyer at my side.

George hid his dismay at the presence of another male by babbling on about the vehicle's features. It had leather seats and a cloth tonneau cover that could be raised or lowered to protect the passengers depending on the weather. With George and Lizzie

Mirkin sat back in his chair. Reaching into his briefcase, he took out a newspaper, folded to a middle page. "Mr. Spofford may be mourning his fiancée's death, but apparently that doesn't stop him from participating in motorcar races."

He pointed to a paragraph that announced a road race on Wednesday. Frederick Spofford was listed as one of the drivers. And so was Thomas Chapman.

in the front seats, and Mirkin and me in the back, we headed for the race at Speedway Park in Maywood.

Once we were underway, the two men began a shouted conversation during which Mirkin demonstrated his bona fides by mentioning auto manufacturers like Stutz, Mercer, and Duesenberg.

"Will Oldfield be there?" Mirkin asked, continuing to impress with his knowledge of the racing world.

For Lizzie's sake, I regretted that Mirkin seemed more congenial to me than my future son-in-law was. I was rooting for the young lawyer in this contest of male wills. But then I saw George's adoring glance at my daughter, and I knew how much he cared for her.

"Not likely," George answered. "This is just a warmup to test the track for the June race. That's Barney Oldfield," George explained for my benefit and Lizzie's. "He's one of the top racers. He's got a custom Delage these days." He said that to Mirkin, as if a man could appreciate the importance of the name, while we ladies would not.

Lizzie straightened and turned toward us in the back. "George's father says motorcars are the future. A lot of his firm's advertising is for the auto manufacturers. That's why it's good to have a car in the races, it helps to show how much they know about the industry. It's really important for the company." She knew I thought it was callous of Fred to be racing so soon after Hazel's death. She smiled at me pointedly to show me she was gritting her teeth at having to keep Mirkin's occupation a secret from George. She knew I wanted the young lawyer along, and that I wanted to avoid a fuss. When Mirkin smiled mischievously, Lizzie turned back to the front.

George was oblivious. "You wait and see. In a few years everyone will own a motorcar. Just look at how convenient it is today. We don't have to wait on a train schedule, we can just come and go as we choose. It's a new world out there." George made me a bit nervous when he turned to address us in the back. I wished he would pay more attention to the road ahead. Seeing Lizzie's shoulders tighten, I knew she was concerned, too.

George noticed her tense. He laughed. "No reason to fear," he told her. "Let me show them what this girl can really do." With that, he shifted the gears and we roared forward with the scenery flashing past us in a blur. I grabbed the side of the seat with both hands.

"I thought your brother was the race driver!" Mirkin yelled. That only made George drive faster.

Lizzie frowned. "Stop it, George. It's too fast."

He laughed and increased the speed. Lizzie shook her head as she gripped her door. George swerved to the left to pass a horse-drawn cart. The poor horse reared up in fright.

"Lunatic," Mirkin said under his breath. He sat up and yelled to George. "Plenty of power in this, but how does it do in the city? Do you have to downshift a lot? I hear that's a problem with some of these touring cars."

Instantly, George dropped his speed to a crawl to demonstrate gear shifting despite the sparse traffic on the road.

"George, you nearly scared Lizzie and me out of our wits. Kindly refrain from speeding like that," I cried out. I could see Lizzie shivering and I was angry.

The touring car made an alarming noise as he seemed to race the engine while keeping it in a low gear. It was like reining in a horse that was ready to gallop, only much noisier. I was afraid we would leap ahead in a burst of speed but, when George replied, he spoke in an even tone. "Sorry to alarm you, Mrs. Chapman. But Lizzie's used to it. She's been out with me lots of times and she loves the speed as much as I do, don't you, Lizzie?"

I waited for my normally outspoken daughter to rebuke him. I was shocked when she merely shrugged and didn't even turn around to face me. George, on the other hand, took his eyes from the road to grin at me. I wondered why Lizzie didn't complain, but then I realized his response to her silence was to slow down. Perhaps she had her own ways of reining him in. Mirkin patted my gloved hand on the cushions. With my other hand, I clutched the side of the seat.

"So, George, I hear your brother Fred is racing today. Aren't you surprised that he'd do that so soon after Miss Littleton's passing away?" Mirkin asked. It was a bold question and Lizzie turned toward him with narrowed eyes, but George didn't seem to mind.

Clearing his throat, George replied, "Fred is broken up about losing Hazel. We all are. But it does seem better for him to continue on. Hazel would have wanted him to. She used to come to the races to cheer him on. She knew how much it meant to him." He glanced over at Lizzie. "It's a way to forget...when things are too horrible. Between Hazel, and the coming war, and the uncertainty of tomorrow, it gives you something to think about that isn't so grim. You know what I mean, don't you, Lizzie?" He might have reached out to her, but at that moment we neared an intersection. After the turn he said, "Besides, we were already signed up for this race and we have sponsors we need to keep happy. It's business."

"I didn't know Miss Littleton," Mirkin said. "I've heard she worked at Hull House, isn't that right?"

George navigated a street with a mixture of motorcars and horse-drawn vehicles. Lizzie looked away at the passing scenery. As we got nearer to Speedway Park, there were more motorcars. In the distance, I saw the stands and outbuildings of the oval track. "Society women are involved in all sorts of charities," George said with a quick glance at Lizzie. "Hazel didn't have to go over to the West Side to do good. My mother was always telling her that and, after the wedding, she could have worked on other charities, closer to home. Like Lizzie does. I wouldn't say anything bad about someone who's gone, but Hazel was a bit headstrong. She didn't have the background to work in my mother's clubs. They depend on large donations. Her parents didn't have that kind of money, but my mother was showing her how much good she could do with the Spofford money once she married into the family. Hazel just wasn't used to it yet."

If this was how the Spoffords viewed Hazel, it must be how they saw Lizzie. They thought her lack of wealth was what drew Hazel to the settlement house. As a Spofford wife she wouldn't have to deal with the messy conditions of Hull House, instead she could attend functions at the Blackstone and other elegant venues. And she could contribute more than those who went to live and work among the people in the settlement house. But they were wrong. In my time at Hull House, many society women had contributed funds, time, and influence to help further the progressive agenda. *They* never would have agreed with George's view that their contributions were worth more than those of the residents who worked in the community. Yet I suspected their husbands might. I'd made friends with women very like Mrs. Spofford but, unlike her, they never spurned the work of the settlements. It irked me that Lizzie had become so involved with people who looked down on the work of Hull House. She was clearly beginning to believe that the money and power wielded by people like the Spoffords were more important and more effective.

"So, you don't think Miss Littleton could have gotten herself involved with a young man she met at Hull House?" Mirkin asked. His blunt questioning made me feel guilty that I'd introduced him as a family friend.

"Of course not. Who suggested such a thing? Hazel wasn't used to the level of society my family inhabits, but she'd never do anything so crude. It's an insult to suggest it."

"It's the police who suggested it. They arrested a man named Hoffman and are saying he knew Miss Littleton from Hull House. Who do *you* think murdered her?" Mirkin asked.

"That waiter, of course. He's a Hun. They're all barbarians. Haven't they proved that? We know what they did in Belgium and the ones here are loyal to the Kaiser. What are you getting at, Mirkin? How can you bring up such a thing in front of Mrs. Chapman and Lizzie? What do you think you're doing?" He downshifted and pulled into a large open lot opposite a row of low stone buildings. We were behind the viewers' stands for the racetrack.

"I'm so sorry," Mirkin said. "I didn't mean to upset the ladies. It hadn't occurred to me that a German surname was enough to incite a man to bloody acts." His sarcasm was lost on our driver.

"Of course it is," George said, as he hopped out and hurried to the other side to help Lizzie and me out of the car. "What do you think's been going on over in France, for heaven's sake? What's wrong with you, man?"

George stood with Lizzie and me, one on each arm, glaring at Mirkin as he extricated himself from the motorcar. Then he turned us toward a tent that had been erected with strings of flags flying in the wind and people milling about. "This, ladies, is the auto derby."

TWENTY

We were outside Speedway Park itself, a huge oval with a grandstand on one side and an open viewing area on the other. There was a large space for spectators to park their motorcars and a branch of the railroad ran along one end of the racetrack.

With Lizzie on his arm, George led us into a tent pavilion in the corner of the parking area where tea, sherry, beer, and whiskey were being served. Tired from the ride, I leaned a little on Mirkin as we followed. Inside, I saw a few women, but the atmosphere was oppressively male. Deep belly laughs and guffaws filled the tent and one corner was a fog of cigar smoke. I could smell it from the opposite end where George and Mirkin found us white folding chairs beside a long cloth-covered table. They brought cups of lukewarm tea to us, then returned with mugs of beer for themselves.

While they stood and talked to other men, I nursed my tea. As I craned my neck looking for Fred Spofford, I avoided a conversation with Lizzie for fear I would offend her with negative comments about George. I didn't want to provoke an argument with her, but I was hard pressed not to speak my mind about his dangerous driving. How was I going to tolerate my daughter's soon to be in-laws? But I had to, or I'd risk estrangement from her. I hated to think Lizzie could go months without seeing us, but I knew her stubborn determination, second only to her father's. If she took offense at my attitude toward her husband or his family, she might shut me out. When she was a child, I could have the final say. Now, she was growing beyond me, and I feared our connection could become so attenuated as to break altogether.

"I don't think it was a good idea to bring Mr. Mirkin," she said. She watched him as he circulated among the men near our table.

"I don't know why you say that. Mr. Mirkin appears to fit right in with this crowd."

"You haven't told George he's Hoffman's lawyer."

I looked around. "You're right. But it seems too late now. Where is George?"

"He went to see Fred down at the garages, to tell him their father couldn't come today. Usually he's here to cheer Fred on, but he had another function to attend."

"You said Hazel came to the races?" I asked. I wanted to know more about the dead girl's relationship to her fiancé.

"Of course. They're Fred's passion. George's too, although he'd rather back his brother than race himself. I think he's a little jealous of how proud their father is of Fred's racing. It's quite dangerous, though. They're trying to break records for speed when they run on this track so—if they miscalculate a turn, or if a tire bursts, or something breaks—it can be fatal. A friend of Fred's died one time but, fortunately, I wasn't here to see it." She shivered.

What were they thinking? I hated the idea that we might see someone die during the spectacle. It wasn't what I'd come for. Could someone here have killed Hazel? Men who would risk their own lives with so little reason might think taking the life of a young innocent like Hazel Littleton was easy. But why? I couldn't even think of a frivolous reason. Looking at Lizzie I felt panic. What about Lizzie? What did she see in people who gathered to watch dangerous races?

Lizzie turned to face me. "Mother, I know what you're thinking. You think they're just spoiled, rich boys. But you're wrong. George and Fred are keen on the future. Motorcars are the future. And they care about this country and making sure we protect ourselves. You think people like the do-gooders at Hull House and liberals like Mr. Mirkin are somehow better than George and his family. You're wrong about that, too. Do you know how much good George and I can do with his family's connections and influence? They work at knowing the right people, so they can get things done. Not everyone can be content with the committee meetings you have in academia. It takes so long to get anything done there it's ridiculous." Having had her say, she turned away to scan the crowds in the tent.

So, Lizzie saw Stephen and me as helpless, powerless academics in a world of stronger forces. Our way of life wasn't enough for her. She wanted more. I wanted to tell her she was wrong, but she'd have to learn that from experience. I just hoped her illusions didn't draw her too far away from us.

Mirkin appeared. "Fred Spofford is working on his motor. They say he won't appear before the race. I found out which garage he's in, if you want to come with me to talk to him."

Lizzie looked at me with doubt in her eyes. I whispered, "I want to find out if Fred thought Hazel was seeing someone else."

At that moment George claimed Lizzie's attention like an anxious beagle. He insisted she accompany him to some event in the private drivers' tent. When she protested, he explained there were business clients he needed to see in his father's absence. I nodded to Lizzie to go. She followed her future husband to mix with the powerful people he courted. Lizzie rolled her eyes and gave me a shake of her head as she walked away. She knew the world she chose to enter with her future husband was foreign to me, but she believed in the promise of a future that it represented.

I stood up. "Let's go and talk to Mr. Fred Spofford."

TWENTY-ONE

We found Fred in one of the many garages that backed up to the grandstands. Each was like a cave with an electric lightbulb hanging from the ceiling and oil lamps placed around the work area. Like many of the men, Fred wore a one-piece overall, heavy boots, and a tight-fitting leather cap with the ear flaps folded up and the ties hanging free. Big round goggles, like a pair of insect eyes, perched on the top of his head. He hovered over a motorcar that was stripped down to the minimum.

He was happy to show off his darling to visitors, so he never questioned our arrival. He knew me from family occasions, although I think he mistook Mirkin for one of my sons. Despite what I said to Lizzie about how I was wrong to mislead George about Mirkin, I didn't enlighten Fred. It was more important to find out if Fred was connected to Hazel's death, no matter what Lizzie thought. Pointing out the features of his race car with great pride, he told us it was a Mercer.

The covering of the long motor was folded back to reveal the inner workings. Two seats were in the middle, with long leather straps to belt in the driver and his racing mechanic. The body was a bright yellow, and the steering wheel was on a long thin column that looked as if it could snap like a matchstick. Fred moved around nervously, wrench in hand, stopping to tighten or loosen various fittings.

I expressed our sympathy for the loss of his fiancée and explained that I wanted to find out why Hazel was killed. "You knew Hazel better than anyone else. Do you have any idea who could have done this to her?" I couldn't bear to describe her death in any more detail.

He turned away and I found myself peering over his shoulder at the engine mechanisms. His hands moved nervously over the metal. "Poor Hazel," he said. "She was my mother's pick from all the girls, but then she got into pacifism with Miss Addams and Mother was unhappy. I didn't care." He wiped his hands with a rag, stepping back from the car. "I mean, I sort of agreed with Hazel. Why should we have to spill blood for France and England? But it's a lost cause. I told Hazel as much. We'll be in the war pretty soon now, I told her, and I was right. If you're careful, there are ways to stay safe, but if you're not, you're going to be cannon fodder. Hazel didn't want to see that, and I appreciated that she worried for me. George thinks he can use his yacht to hunt U-boats and that'll keep him here in the States. But if I have to go, I think it should be aviation. I want to fly." He pulled down the engine cover, clicked the latches, and patted the boxy structure.

"I've heard the French have some American fliers already," Mirkin said.

"That's right. There's a guy that Insull helped to get out of town when he was in trouble over gambling debts. He's over in France now in a group of American aviators. That's where I'd want to be, I think. Anyhow, a lot of people in our set don't appreciate the pacifists, but we're going to war, so that's no reason to do what was done to poor Hazel."

"Did you think someone killed her because of her pacifism?" I asked.

"No, I'm just saying some people feel pretty strongly that if you're against our getting into the war then you're a traitor."

"Did anyone think Hazel was a traitor for her pacifism?" I asked. There had been acrimonious debates but to kill a girl over such disagreements seemed farfetched.

"No." He rubbed at a spot on the chrome bumper of his race car. "I'm just saying some people really have it in for pacifists."

"Who do *you* think killed Hazel?" I asked. He seemed drained of emotion to me. Perhaps he was still in shock at the violent death of his betrothed.

"All I know is they arrested some Hun. You know how bloodthirsty they are, so I assume the police are right and he did it." He looked up from the rag in his hands. "People don't realize how dangerous all these Kaiser lovers are. You've no idea how many have been planted here as spies and saboteurs."

Mirkin watched intently. I almost told Fred that Mirkin was Hoffman's representative, but the young lawyer hurried to pose a question before I could speak. "Did Miss Littleton know the man they've arrested? I've heard she worked at Hull House and he took classes there. Do you have any reason to believe they met? The police have even suggested the man might have romanced her."

Fred frowned, then shrugged his shoulders. "Hazel? That's ridiculous. Hazel was going to marry me in June. A double wedding with my brother and Miss Chapman." He rubbed the side of the race car with a soft cloth.

"You had no reason to doubt she'd go through with the wedding?" Mirkin asked.

"Of course not." His pale face turning red, he faced Mirkin. "Listen, Hazel was involved in Miss Addams's peace party and pacifist marches but all that would've changed once we were married. There are lots of committees and ladies' clubs my mother's involved in. She'd have those activities and, I suppose, children eventually. She'd give up that other stuff. My mother said marriage would settle her down, and my father says that, even if we go to war, married men will get exemptions. Hazel would have liked being married. She and Lizzie would have had a great time." He bit his lip and turned back to the car. "Poor Lizzie, I'm sure she's missing Hazel. We all are."

How cold he sounded and how disconnected from the flesh and blood girl who'd been murdered. Of course, for a young man of his class, marriage was less a romantic commitment than a coming-of-age family ritual. Faced with a field full of pretty daisies that were the eligible young women, a young man like Fred would pick one that fit in the bouquet on the table at home. The young couple would be expected to develop deep feelings of devotion, if not romantic love, over time. It was a tradition that I had seen work for better or worse for many society women. I hoped that Lizzie's affection for George was something more than this kind of bland, if comfortable, arrangement. Hazel had been a sweet girl. No doubt Fred's mother had felt she would be able to mold her into the perfect wife for her son. I remembered that Miss Breckinridge had believed Hazel was withdrawing from the WPP to please her future in-laws. Perhaps she was right. Regina Spofford was due for a big surprise if she tried to mold Lizzie like that, but Hazel had been a kinder, milder girl. It seemed to me that while Fred had been sincere in what he thought was his love for Hazel, now, with her death, he was at a loss as to what he should feel. No doubt his mother would find him another candidate when mourning was over. He wasn't really a cold-hearted fellow, he was just young.

Fred had said his piece and was not interested in further discussion. He looked stubborn, like one of my sons when they wanted to block out the world by concentrating on some small task that let them ignore me. I sighed. Another man entered, and Fred introduced him as his mechanic. Leaving them to prepare for the race, I took Mirkin's arm and encouraged him to steer me back to the viewing stands. Before we could reach them, I saw Tommy and Lenny pushing a green racing car out of another garage. Tommy straightened and greeted us with surprise.

"Mother, you're here. That's great." He patted the engine proudly. Like Fred Spofford, Tommy wore a one-piece overall, boots, and a leather skullcap with big goggles stuck on the top.

He had thick gloves on his hands. I looked at the open seating area with the straps. How difficult was it to stay on those seats while speeding along? I was physically queasy at the thought of my son in that seat in his car.

"Tommy, this is Mr. Mirkin. We came with Lizzie and George."

Lenny came up behind us. "I hope you're rooting for us and not Fred Spofford," he said, grinning.

"I'll just be glad if you make it to the finish line in one piece," I said, eyeing the machine. In the tea tent I'd been wondering why my husband was so opposed to the motorcar racing. It seemed like a sort of picnic with a sporting event. Now that I saw my son beside one of the race cars, the whole endeavor looked a lot more dangerous.

"We were asking Mr. Spofford about Hazel Littleton," Mirkin said. "Did you know her? Did she attend these race meets regularly?"

Tommy looked down at his hands, pulling at one of the gloves. Lenny spoke for him. "She was here sometimes. Not sure she totally approved, though. But since Tommy knew her through Lizzie, we'd say hello. I heard her trying to tell Fred he should give it up. Not that it's likely. No telling what she would have done after they were married, though. Maybe she'd make him stop racing."

Tommy frowned. "He didn't care what she said," he growled. "Come on. We've got to get to the race." As Lenny ran back to the front of the car, Tommy turned to me. "I don't suppose Father is here?"

"No, Tommy. You know how he feels about this racing."

He got into the seat while Lenny cranked the noisy motor. "Wish us luck," Lenny yelled as he hopped into the seat beside Tommy, who shifted, and the car started to move. "I suppose you're cheering on Spofford. Just don't put any money on him," Lenny yelled. As if I would gamble!

They chugged away, and we returned to our party who were ready to climb up into the grandstand to view the races. What a lot of fuss over some noisy motorcars. Did no one remember that Hazel had her life cruelly taken from her so recently? Why were we no closer to finding out who killed her? As Lizzie mounted the stairs on George Spofford's arm, a heavy weight of foreboding pressed on my shoulders. Despite the bright green leaves starting to bud on the trees beyond Speedway Park, it was going to be a dismal spring.

TWENTY-TWO

I n the grandstand, George seated us in a special box. Below, we could see the wooden board track of the speedway. George told us it was two miles long. The featured race of the day would be 100 miles but, before that race, they staged war games in the infield of the oval, accompanied by an aerial display of planes over the field. Intended as a raucous celebration of the declaration of war, it discouraged me.

"With the war on, they're not sure how many more races will be held," George told us. He yelled as the noise of the crowd and the airplanes was deafening. "Fred's counting on the Vanderbilt Cup race. That's held out East every year. He's thinking he has a shot at the cup."

I remembered Tommy or Lenny mentioning that race. I was surprised by how all these young men clung to their plans, even when we were teetering on the edge of war. I silently prayed they could accomplish those comparatively harmless dreams to race for the Vanderbilt Cup. At least they weren't killing each other. Perhaps Lizzie was right, and it was a typically male outlet for the sorrow that Fred couldn't express. To escape the bleak reality by plunging into the excitement of racing might be some kind of solace for a young man, so I withheld any criticism of the competitions. Perhaps Stephen was wrong to be so opposed to them.

When a loudspeaker finally announced the race, the air was filled with the roar of motor engines. Cars lined up four at a time and started in a blast of engine exhaust and screeching tires. My stomach rose to my throat when the metal monsters began barreling around the track. Forty of them swished past, climbing the raked edges of the corners and zooming down the backstretch on the other side. People around us hollered and waved flags or hats.

I saw Fred's yellow chassis first, then later the green of Tommy's car. The drivers and mechanics looked like little dolls that could easily fly out of the racing cars, especially when they tilted up on the turns. I held my breath, thinking it would be over when they completed the circuit, but George laughed at me and explained they would go around fifty times before it was over. I sat back down, wincing at the noise.

Mirkin stood with his arms folded at the far side of our box. His gaze traveled often to Lizzie who paid no attention to the race. Perhaps she was remembering how she and Hazel sat in this same box when they were here together. Before I could move to her side, Mirkin stepped up and bent over her. He left and returned with a glass of water. She took it absentmindedly. I frowned at George Spofford who leaned over the front railing, cheering and waving his brother on.

"Look," he said. "There's your son, Mrs. Chapman. He and Fred are dueling."

I stood to follow his pointing hand. At the far end of the oval, the yellow and green cars drove up the banked side of the turn. I gasped, fearing the green one—Tommy—would go over the edge. But they shifted down and rounded the turn into the backstretch. Neck and neck, they were surrounded by other racers. At the next turn, the green chased the yellow up the side, but another car along the edge behind them swerved, spun around, and ran off the track. The crowd screamed. A great ocean wave in the sea of people below us swept to the left with a roar. This was what they were waiting for. The possibility of death heightened the thrill for the people below me. The crowd in the Roman

Coliseum must have sounded like this. Blood pounded in my ears. The yellow and green cars careened down the side of the turn and flew off the track, into the oval of grass in the middle. Tommy!

The green car stayed upright. I held my breath as it bumped along, leaping into the air in a cloud of dust. My heart turned over. Was I witnessing the death of my son? I strained to see the rag doll figures of the boys. *No, no, no. Why didn't I listen to Stephen?* Tommy would be crushed by the heavy metal of the motor, or he would be flung out and dashed against the hard ground. He would be broken to pieces by such a fall. Before I could scream, the car jolted to a stop with Tommy and Lenny still strapped in. I thought my head would burst.

Behind them, the bright yellow motorcar rolled end over end in a heart-stopping leap. The crowd roared at the spectacle. Fred Spofford's race car landed upside down, with a bone jarring stop. A body had flown off from one side, but the driver was twisted around the steering wheel under the car. All the weight of that glossy machine crushed him. People screamed. I strained to see... was he alive? Engines still growled as other race cars continued to round the course. I couldn't believe it. A group of play-acting soldiers from the pre-race demonstration had scattered but, when the dust began to settle, they rushed back to pull a body from the wreck. A wagon with a red cross on it bumped over the grass toward the injured men.

"Fred!" George yelled. "That's Fred." He looked around wildly, then jumped over the railing and dashed down the grandstand toward the track. Some of the other men followed him, ducking under the barrier and dropping into the crowd below.

Lizzie, Mirkin, and I rushed to the railing. I grasped it and bent over, trying to see what had happened to Tommy's race car. Were they hurt, too? My breath caught in my throat as I saw Lenny cranking the green car's engine, then leaping into his seat. Tommy steered the car back onto the track and streaked away, leaving a cloud of smoke behind him. I was lightheaded with relief to see my son was all right, but I hated that he was continuing the race. How could he do that? How could he leave without knowing the fate of the men who had crashed? Yet the crowd around me cheered. I hunched down, covering my ears. Mirkin took my elbow and helped me to a seat. The smell of the exhaust was nauseating.

One of George's friends came panting up the stairs of the grandstand and climbed over the railing. "He's dead. Fred is dead," he told us. Lizzie sank down in a seat, white faced with shock. I put my head in my hands. How had it come to this?

Cheers erupted from the crowd and they continued waving their flags and hats, oblivious to the death that had occurred right in front of them. Slaughter was the outcome of the day. I wanted to get up and demand Tommy stop racing, but I couldn't fight against the roar of the crowd.

TWENTY-THREE

Fred and his racing mechanic both died in the crash. George sent word that he needed to take care of his brother's body and Mirkin volunteered to find us a way home. He left us in the box with a couple of George's friends, as the crowd streamed out of the stadium below us. The race was completed, but the award ceremony was shortened, and the crowd seemed to come to its senses with the news that two men had died. Perhaps it was only my imagination, but they seemed satisfied. They got what they'd come for, danger and death. Shutting my eyes, I tried to rid myself of the sight of the crowd. They disappointed me. They took the loss of the young men so much in stride, I hated it. What chance was there for any of us if we held young lives so cheap?

Hearing footsteps behind me, I opened my eyes and turned to see Tommy. He still wore his oil-streaked overall with his goggles pushed up on his cap. His face was filthy. He held the thick gloves in his hands, kneading them, as he stood in front of me.

"Mother, Lizzie, we heard about Fred," he said. Lenny was hovering behind him.

I was relieved to see my youngest child in one piece. But I couldn't for the life of me understand why he'd acted as he had. "You went back on the track after the crash. Why did you do that?"

"We had to," Lenny said over Tommy's shoulder. "Our backers were watching, and we had to keep racing, or they wouldn't put up the money for the Vanderbilt."

"It's what we've been working for all year," Tommy said, "to get to the Vanderbilt. If we blew it in this race we'd be out." He saw the look on my face. "You don't understand. That's what you do if there's a crash. If you're whole, you keep racing. It's not just us, it's everyone. Everyone does it." He took a breath as if to say more, but Lenny grabbed his arm and he swallowed.

My throat was too choked up for me to speak. I blinked back tears.

Lizzie was slumped in her seat. "First Hazel, now Fred," she moaned.

Lenny stepped up in front of her. "I know. Isn't it awful? Do you think..." He looked at Tommy who was frowning at him. "You don't think Fred did it because of Miss Littleton?"

"What do you mean?" I asked.

Tommy shook his head, but Lenny continued. "It's just that...it shouldn't have happened. When we were on the track... it looked like something was wrong. He should've been able to pull up. It looked like a problem with the drive shaft."

"Stop it, Lenny," Tommy said.

"No, I have to say it. Spofford could have done it himself, you know. He could have done something to make it happen. Maybe he couldn't go on without her...Miss Littleton. Maybe it was just an accident, but we did wonder, Tommy...you know we did."

Tommy looked like he wanted to hit his friend, but he contained himself with an effort. Then he turned to Lizzie and, squatting down, put an arm around her, so she could weep into his shoulder.

"Excuse me." Mirkin joined us. "I've gotten tickets for the next train but there's someone who wants to see you."

He stepped forward and Detective Whitbread appeared behind him, wearing a suit coat with a loud check, wool knickers, and a plaid cap. It reminded me of all the times I'd seen him in disguise when he was hunting criminals. He must have been working. How had the burglaries brought him to Speedway Park? He wouldn't attend an auto derby on his own time, unless he'd become a completely different person since I last worked with him. He was always relentless when he was on the track of a suspect. I was sure that explained his presence.

"Mrs. Chapman, Miss Chapman." He swept off the cap and gave a little bow. "My condolences on the demise of young Spofford. Presumably his participation is what brought you to the races? Or, perhaps, you came to see Mr. Thomas Chapman race?"

I took a deep breath. "We came with my daughter's fiancé. He's gone to see about his brother. It's an awful shock for all of us, especially so soon after Miss Littleton's death. His parents will be devastated." If I told him I was there pursuing an investigation he refused to get involved in, perhaps it would shame him, but I couldn't tell him that with so many people around. It was petty of me to resent his refusal when I knew he had no choice in the matter, but the death of Fred on top of Hazel's horrible murder frightened me.

"Did I hear you say Mr. Spofford's driving seemed reckless?" Whitbread asked. He was looking at Lenny and Tommy, his dark eyes raking them. His tone was sharp and demanded a response.

Tommy frowned and stood up from Lizzie's side, keeping a hand on her shoulder.

Lenny responded, stepping into the breach. "Well, we did wonder. We heard what happened to Miss Littleton—a horrid way to go." He stepped from foot to foot, as if bursting to say something. "The Spoffords think they own the world. Everything comes so easy for them. If she wanted to break off the engagement, Fred wouldn't take it lightly. What if he struck out in anger, then couldn't live with what he did?" His eyes were wide. "You don't know what it's like when you're out there on the track. All the time, one wrong move and you could end it. Maybe he couldn't live with what he did, and he just let go."

"Lenny, how can you say such a thing?" I asked. I wondered if he was speaking for my son as much as for himself. He sounded so envious. I looked at Tommy who hung his head. Was my son blinded by envy of the wealthy young man? Was Tommy afraid to voice it, so his friend was saying it out loud? It never occurred to me that my children would grow up to believe the lack of wealth was such a hindrance. Lizzie wanted to marry into it and Tommy envied it. Stephen and I had failed them if they really saw the world that way.

"Do you have some reason to believe Mr. Fred Spofford was involved in the death of Miss Littleton?" Whitbread asked. He folded his arms and cocked his head, considering the racing mechanic. I could see Mirkin at attention, catching every word.

Tommy's face was scrunched up in a grimace, as if he were holding back tears. He swallowed then groaned. "Lenny heard them arguing."

Whitbread's wiry eyebrows shot up. "Mr. Frommer?"

Lenny looked around for some place to run. "It's true," he said finally. "It was the last time she came to the races. Spofford's father was here. I saw Miss Littleton arguing with Fred in the drivers' tent. But then, after that, she came out to say hello to us, and Fred followed and grabbed her arm to take her back. He made some comment about how she'd gotten into bad company at Hull House and led her away. He looked angry."

Tommy was very white. I could see that my son and his friend believed Fred had killed Hazel in a jealous rage. Could the young man we'd spoken to before the race be so roused that he would hit out at his fiancée? Tommy and Lenny saw him in a different light, as a competitor. Could they be right? If Fred murdered Hazel in a fit of rage, then suffered unbearable regret, the vicious crash was a spectacular way to repent.

Whitbread listened attentively but, when I looked across at him hopefully, he shook his head. "You need to tell Chief Kelly about that. He's investigating Miss Littleton's death. I am not involved."

What was Whitbread investigating that brought him to the auto derby that day? And why did he join us after the crash? Was he investigating the Spofford family for something other than the murder? Realizing there was nothing we could do to help George, we broke up, everyone drifting away in shock at the day's outcome. Lizzie and I each took one of Mirkin's arms to lean on as he hurried us away to the train station.

TWENTY-FOUR

Lizzie, were you there when Hazel argued with Fred? What was it about?" I asked when we were safe at home. There was something going on. If it had led to Hazel's death, then I needed to know. I kept seeing the race car crash in my mind's eye, over and over. The way a young person's life could be snuffed out so unexpectedly was a hard shock.

"I was there that day, but I was on the other side of the tent. Hazel saw Fred at Hull House, I think. He denied it, and she didn't believe him, but I don't know what it was about or why he was there."

"Why would that lead to an argument? Was she getting Fred involved in Hull House activities and his father objected?" Perhaps Fred's father didn't approve of how he was influenced by Hazel. I pictured the young man bent over his beloved motorcar. Had he been sabotaging it himself when I saw him? It didn't seem possible. I didn't believe that Hazel had persuaded the young man to work at the settlement, either.

"I don't think so. Fred claimed he was never there. He spurned the work at Hull House as much as George does. Their father objects to the socialists, he says they're unpatriotic, traitors even." Lizzie sat down on the couch in her father's study.

Stephen, entrenched behind his desk, was as shocked by Fred Spofford's death as we all were. So far, I hadn't told him that Tommy had been in the same race. "Lizzie, do you believe Fred could have hurt Hazel and then allowed himself to crash because he regretted it?" he asked.

Lizzie bit her lip and thought for a moment. "I can't see it. I just can't see it. The police seem to think Hazel met that German waiter at Hull House. Did Fred find out, follow her there and confront her? Then, in a fit of jealousy, did he go to the Blackstone and attack her? I can't imagine either one of them doing those things. Hazel wouldn't have been seeing a waiter and Fred would never have harmed Hazel."

"Passion can make people do unimaginable things," Stephen reminded her.

She looked at him. "That's just it. There wasn't that much passion."

"You can never be certain about other people's passions," I said.

"I can, though. Hazel was my best friend. She loved Fred, but more like a brother. She had no siblings, you know. She would tease him and make fun of him. She wanted to marry him, and I think they would have been happy, like George and I will be. But it wasn't a Romeo and Juliet thing. I think if she took up with a waiter—and I don't for a minute believe she did—but if she had, Fred would have dropped her. He would have been disgusted. He wouldn't have killed her, though. Not like that." She shivered, and I knew she was seeing her dead friend on the staircase.

She was very certain of her opinion, but she was also very young and didn't know what passion could do to people. Love was a passion but so was hate. Who hated Hazel enough to kill her? Lizzie believed Fred didn't love Hazel enough to kill her, but could he have come to hate her enough to do it?

"What was Fred doing at Hull House if he wasn't following her to expose an illicit love affair?" I asked.

Lizzie frowned.

Stephen said, "Lizzie, if you know something, you should tell the police. Even if Whitbread isn't the detective on the case, the police want to find who killed Hazel. If you have information that would help them, you need to tell them."

"It's the Spoffords," she said. "But I don't see how it could matter to the police. They're very keen on the war. Mr. Spofford and his friends have actively promoted the need for us to get into the war."

"That's why they have their Four Minute Men organization," I said, not seeing how that would lead to Fred Spofford going to Hull House.

"Yes, but that's not all. They think the Germans knew we'd get into it eventually and that they've got spies planted over here. They complain that the government isn't doing enough about rooting out spies and saboteurs. Mr. Spofford and some of the other men have lent their motorcars to the Justice Department. He was very keen to get George and Fred involved. But, when I asked George, he said he'd taken an oath of secrecy."

Stephen was contemptuous. "An oath? It sounds like a boy's club. Some of these wealthy men don't have enough to do with themselves."

Lizzie didn't like it when we disparaged her future in-laws, but Stephen was never one to hold his tongue, and she knew he would scoff if she protested. Instead, she turned to me. "Mother, you must be able to find out if Fred was at Hull House. Someone must know what he was doing there. Fred didn't kill Hazel. I know he didn't. But maybe Hoffman killed her because of some connection to Fred. You know Hull House. You can find out, can't you?"

It was a challenge to me. Lizzie thought Stephen and I were biased against the Spoffords, and she was right in a way. If I hesitated to use my connections at Hull House, she would think we were siding against her and protecting the German waiter. She was quick to take offense because she was quick to comprehend. I needed to step carefully. I looked at Stephen, but he just raised an eyebrow.

"Mother?"

"Yes, of course. I can ask if anyone knows if and when Fred was at Hull House and what he was doing there. We still need to talk to the socialist group that meets on Thursday nights. And you should go to the Spoffords and see if you can do anything for them. This must be a terrible blow."

"Mrs. Spofford will let me know what she wants from me," she said. "But we can't let Tommy go around saying Fred killed Hazel. What a horrible thing to do, destroying his reputation when he's died."

"Tommy?" Stephen said. "What does he have to do with this?"

"He was in the same race," I said. I saw Stephen stiffen. "But it wasn't Tommy who said that. His friend Lenny suggested Fred might have spun out purposely because of guilt over Hazel. It was nothing but wild speculation." I hated to think the bitter words sprang from a rivalry between the young men.

"Lenny was just speaking for Tommy," Lizzie said. "But he's wrong. They're both wrong. Fred would never have hurt Hazel." She looked back and forth between me and her father as if challenging us to dispute the fact. Until we could find out who attacked and killed Hazel so viciously, Lizzie would have no peace. She was roused from the apathy that had seemed to overcome her since her friend's death. But I was not at all sure how to unravel the tragedy. At least if Lizzie saw me try, to the best of my ability, she'd know I valued the truth over my allegiance to Hull House and the peace movement. I didn't want her to feel torn between her fiancé's family, who had just suffered such a terrible loss, and her own family. I looked across the desk at Stephen.

He rose and came around to comfort her. "Oh, Lizzie, my little girl."

TWENTY-FIVE

T he young socialists' club that Hoffman belonged to met
early on Thursday evenings. On the drive to Speedway
Park Mirkin and I had made plans to attend that week's
meeting together. I knew Lizzie resented him for his role as
Hoffman's attorney, but I felt obliged. If we were following in
the footsteps of his client, surely he ought to be involved. Lizzie
scorned my scruples, but she was prepared to give up all caution
when she plunged into the search for Hazel's killer, and she insisted
on going with us.

We took the trolley and then a horse-drawn car to Halsted
Street. Dark was beginning to settle around the buildings by the
time we arrived, so we didn't dawdle outside before we entered
through the main door of the old Hull mansion.

I led the way to a room in the basement, where Lizzie, Mirkin,
and I took seats on wooden folding chairs in the back. At the front,
a bearded young man in work pants, suspenders, and a rough shirt
was striding back and forth lecturing to the group. He stopped
a moment when he saw us, and I wondered if he suspected us of
being police spies, but he only shrugged and continued.

"This war is a capitalist plot to profit from the blood of the
workers," he said. He had a slight accent, so it sounded like "dis
var" instead of "this war." "We have no conflict with the working
men of Europe—no matter if they're English, French, German,
or Russian. The workers are our comrades. But they are the ones

sent to the trenches to pay with their blood so the warmongering classes can make money from armaments.

"Don't be deceived. They may say it's a war to make the world safe for democracy, but what they mean is it's a war to make the world pay for plutocracy. The rich will get richer and the poor will die in the trenches."

There were cheers from people in the front rows. A deep resentment filled the room. They knew they were the poor, and every day they saw that their lives were of little value to the people who employed them, wore what they sewed, or ate what they slaughtered. Looking around, I saw many young people and a few middle-aged men. Most wore cloth caps and work boots. The men had lined faces and hard muscles from their work. The young women had braids anchored to their heads with hairpins and wore dresses in coarse fabrics. They looked tired yet still vigorous as if this type of meeting struck a fire in their breasts after long hours of tedious work for low pay.

Of course, I recognized these types of people because of all the work I'd done as a factory inspector. When I first came to Hull House I'd worked for Florence Kelley, visiting the sweatshops of the city to ensure labor regulations were obeyed. As a sociologist who'd interviewed workers and tabulated so many statistics about their lives, I feared the speaker was correct. The people who would pay with blood for our entrance into this war would be the young workers in this room. I glanced at my daughter. She was used to committee meetings of silk-dressed matrons in flower-scented rooms. But she followed the speaker intently, a frown on her face. Tonight, she wore a simple wool dress with an old plaid coat. She knew the settlement house well enough to know her fashionable gowns would not be appropriate here. Mirkin had his chin in his hand, eyes half closed as he listened. I couldn't tell what he thought of the speakers.

When the meeting ended, we followed Mirkin to the front of the room where he introduced himself as Johann Hoffman's lawyer.

In this company, his connection would be a positive thing. The young speaker's name was Wilhelm Kurtz. He looked at us warily but acknowledged Mirkin as worthy of notice. "It is only because he has a German name that they accuse him," he said. "It is unjust. He was a good worker, but they cut him off. Him and nine others."

"Mr. Hoffman was a member of your group?" Mirkin asked.

"Yes. There is nothing illegal about that." Kurtz was red in the face behind his substantial beard and the ringlets of dark hair that fell on his forehead.

Lizzie stepped forward. "Did Mr. Hoffman know Hazel Littleton?" she asked.

The young man looked her up and down in a manner that I resented. "The lady who was killed…how would a poor waiter know such a fine lady?" He was jeering rather than answering the question.

Mirkin jumped in. "Miss Littleton was active in the Woman's Peace Party. Perhaps your group communicated with them? Since you also oppose the war effort?"

Lizzie glared at Kurtz who took out a toothpick and rudely stuck it in his teeth. He waved a hand. "There are many ladies who claim to be pacifists."

"But not all of them have been killed," Lizzie retorted. "You know who Hazel Littleton was. You know Johann Hoffman. Did they know each other?"

He stopped picking his teeth to return her stare. "What if they know each other? This is enough to accuse him?"

Lizzie stamped a foot. "Why won't you tell us? Is it because you know he's guilty? Did her fiancé, Fred Spofford, find out they knew each other? Did he threaten Hoffman?"

I was surprised to hear Lizzie take this approach. In the past, she'd insisted Hazel hadn't known Hoffman. Now she was suggesting she had? Or was it a tactic to irritate the unwilling witness?

At Spofford's name, Kurtz straightened up, alert like an animal that sensed danger.

"What is it?" Mirkin asked, putting a hand on Lizzie's arm to keep her from Kurtz. "Did Mr. Spofford confront Hoffman?"

"Confront Hoffman? About what?" Kurtz asked. "What do you think? No, no, Hoffman the waiter had nothing to do with the lady. It was the lady who had to do with that Spofford. He lies. This Spofford calls himself Langer. He come to the meeting, tries to start trouble." Kurtz was even more red in the face and he waved his toothpick around, lecturing us. "He is big fake. He says he works at stockyards. He tries to get people to say they support the Kaiser...says he wants to help spy for Germany. Hoffman thinks he is madman, wants to tell Miss Addams, but she's not there. The Littleton girl comes to see, she says, 'Fred, what are you doing here?'"

Mirkin understood before Lizzie and I could take it in. "You're saying Fred Spofford came to your meetings and pretended to be someone named Langer?"

"And Hazel recognized him and exposed him," Lizzie said, equally fast to comprehend.

"Police spy. Trying to make trouble." The large young man stomped to the table where he grabbed up a knapsack. Rummaging in it, he pulled something out and threw it on the table. It was a metal badge that said "American Protective League" across the top and "Secret Service" on the bottom.

Fred was a spy? It seemed so wildly different from the image I'd had of the wealthy young man obsessed with racing motorcars. "What did you do when you found out?" I asked.

The bearded Kurtz got even redder. "We took this away, then we told him go, never come back. Ever." He looked at our shocked faces. "That's all. We didn't do anything to him."

"Really?" Mirkin looked grim. Lizzie was rubbing a finger over the metal badge.

Kurtz raised his hands in protest. "What do you think? We rough him up, punch him a few times, throw him down the alley, so he don't come back. Police spy!"

TWENTY-SIX

When we had gotten all we could from the angry socialist, I led the way upstairs and boldly interrupted Jane Addams who was meeting with architects in the library. Seeing my distress, she sent them away and talked to us, quickly sending for her current assistant to explain what had happened with Fred Spofford at the socialist meeting.

Miss Holden was an angular young woman in her thirties wearing a gray smock and skirt. That she'd been pulled away from a painting class was obvious from a smudge of blue paint on her cheek.

"Yes. There was a disturbance the week before last at the socialist club meeting. Of course, there's hardly a meeting of theirs that doesn't disturb *someone*. We put them in the basement after we had complaints from the reading group and the children's choir. They're opposite the English classes now. Miss Littleton, bless her soul, taught one of the English classes for seamstresses. She didn't mind so much but Mr. Lampert, also teaching English, kept complaining about the noise. Very noisy, those socialists. Always debating one thing or another."

At Miss Addams's raised brow, she hurried on. "I was called down that night by Miss Littleton. It seemed they were accusing a young man of being a spy and provocateur. They had him on the floor by the time I arrived. They showed me some badge or something they'd found in his pocket, but he wasn't police…I asked.

And, when he said he belonged to some secret society, I told him that he was not welcome, appearing under false pretenses like that. I insisted they let him up and escort him to the front door, which they did. I followed to be sure there was no more violence. They tossed him a bit rudely out on the sidewalk, but I could see he was quite all right. He wanted to come back in to see Miss Littleton, but I told him no and sent him away. It was unpleasant but, if the young man wants to protest, I have to say he was to blame for misrepresenting himself. It really was his own fault, and I could see he wasn't hurt in any way."

Miss Addams thanked the woman and sent her away. When she was gone, Lizzie handed Miss Addams the badge that Kurtz had taken from Fred Spofford. Jane held it in her hand, rubbing the metal with her thumb. "The American Protective League," she said, almost to herself.

"What are they?" I asked. Lizzie and Mirkin both looked to Miss Addams for information.

"I'm very much afraid they are the future," she said, then she sighed. She looked at home behind the broad table spread with blueprints for another addition to the settlement complex. She was adding a little theater and music rooms. But she looked haggard that night, as if the past months had added years to her age. There were dark shadows around her eyes when she looked up. "After being so firmly neutral in this country, it seems we're becoming wild in our pro-war sentiments. Unfortunately, our young men will soon be the ones to pay for that excess of emotion." She contemplated Mirkin, biting her lip as she looked at him, then turned back to me. "There will be plenty of men too old to be called to the battlefield who are already feeling they have to demonstrate their patriotism. They'll do it by finding someone at home, here behind the lines, to attack. Safe from having to wield a bayonet in France, they're anxious to prove themselves by finding an enemy here." She shook her head with disappointment.

Seeing we still didn't understand, she continued. "The socialist club has been preaching its philosophy for years. It's only now, because the socialists oppose our entry into the war, that they are accused of treachery. Some men are desperate for an enemy they can face here, so they spy on their neighbors, looking for something they can pounce on to accuse them of supporting Germany. They confuse the socialists with anarchists. There are anarchists, and they advocate violence, but they are clearly a minority of working men. They're not socialists as they advocate for no government at all. They aren't supporters of the Kaiser for the same reason. They oppose government of any kind. They certainly have been responsible for acts of violence in recent years, but not in support of Germany or any nation or government.

"And the anarchists don't support socialism, or any 'ism' for that matter. We have never supported anarchist violence here at Hull House. The group that meets here is socialist, with no plans for violent action. The great majority of the socialists just want to improve the lot of the working man. They aren't dangerous. But they do support labor strikes, and they do disagree with our entrance into the war." She addressed me directly. "It has only begun, Emily. Soon, any word spoken against the government will be enough to condemn a person."

"That's the goal of this American Protective League? To suppress any dissent?" I asked.

"Yes. It's the brainchild of one of those advertising men. A man named Briggs. We've heard of it from some of the society wives who are our benefactors. It's organized as a secret society, with an oath not to reveal any of their actions. It's a kind of men's club but with serious consequences for anyone who comes under their scrutiny. They're preparing to chase down any men who try to avoid the draft, when it comes, and they've been known to try to force Lutheran preachers to declare support for the war or face internment. I'm afraid it's only a symptom of the war madness that's descending on all of us."

Lizzie appeared to be thinking very hard. "Hazel was teaching English across from the meeting. She saw Fred pretending to be a working man and unwittingly exposed him. Couldn't Hoffman have attacked her later to get back at Fred for spying? We should let the police know."

"That's a lot to suppose," Mirkin said. "The socialists threw Spofford out of the meeting. There's no reason to assume they extracted any other punishment."

"But what if he heard something more damaging? What if he knew about some plot?"

"Then why not go after Spofford? There's no reason to hurt Miss Littleton," Mirkin retorted.

"How do you know? Maybe they couldn't get to Fred. Maybe Hoffman came upon Hazel by chance and took the opportunity to shut her up. Maybe she heard something incriminating about some anarchist plot. Maybe they both did, and they got to Hazel first, then Fred."

"Who said anything about anarchists? Didn't you hear Miss Addams? It's a young socialists club," Mirkin said. "You're making all that up. There's no proof whatsoever that Hoffman hurt Miss Littleton or Mr. Spofford. Isn't it more likely that she was angry with Spofford for being a spy? Perhaps it was enough to make her break off the engagement. Maybe *he* lost his temper and attacked her and later, regretting it, he killed himself and his mechanic on the racecourse. Isn't that more likely?"

I cringed, remembering that Mirkin had heard this theory from Lenny at Speedway Park. As Lizzie feared, a rumor like this would be terribly damaging to poor dead Fred Spofford's reputation.

"Fred would have known about the Blackstone luncheon, the socialists wouldn't," Mirkin continued.

"Hoffman would have known. He was a waiter there," Lizzie pointed out.

"He'd been fired," Mirkin responded.

"All the more reason for him to attack Hazel," Lizzie countered.

"Lizzie, Mr. Mirkin, please," I said, raising my arms. "Stop this." I could see that Miss Addams was distressed by the conflict. "We haven't found anything yet to prove either one of your theories."

Lizzie wouldn't be stopped. "The police need to know about Fred Spofford and the socialists. If you won't do anything, I'll go to Chief Kelly myself."

"Lizzie," I began, but Mirkin cut in.

"I'll be sure to let them know that Miss Littleton and Mr. Spofford were heard arguing before her death."

"How dare you try to cast aspersions on Fred when he's only just died? Have you no sympathy for what his family is suffering?" Lizzie protested.

This time, Miss Addams rose to her full height, which wasn't very tall, but she got the attention of both young people. I was appalled that I'd brought such discord to her house. Miss Addams put up her hands to make them stop. "Lizzie, dear, go to the police if you must, but be aware that these socialists you're speaking of have met here for many years with no problems and certainly no plots against anyone. And, Mr. Mirkin, you must do what you can for your client, but try to have some sympathy for the family of the young man who has died so suddenly. Tell me what I can do to help you find consolation for these terrible losses."

Lizzie and Mirkin both looked a bit shamefaced at that. I was glad to see they realized that whatever had happened it was not the fault of Miss Addams or the settlement house. Her appeal produced silence from them, if not peace. I announced our departure and herded them to the door, thanking a worried Miss Addams for her assistance.

Outside, Mirkin escorted us to the next trolley car but stepped back from it when we were safely aboard. "Please forgive me, Mrs. Chapman, I have things I must see to. I trust you two can find your way home without my help."

As the trolley trundled along, I pondered everything that we'd learned while at Hull House. The news that Fred Spofford was spying on the socialist group, looking for German saboteurs, was unexpected. But I was concerned that both Lizzie and Mirkin had leapt prematurely to conclusions based on this new information. I'd learned a long time ago that when you uncovered something like this it was only the beginning of a thread that you had to follow to the end. It could take you to unknown places where you might find even more unexpected things.

I felt as if I'd been leaning on a couple of canes that were abruptly pulled away. It wasn't that I couldn't follow the threads myself, although it was a long time since I'd done that type of work, but I needed someone to help me keep my balance as I felt my way in murky waters. I needed my old mentor, Detective Whitbread.

TWENTY-SEVEN

The next day, Lizzie announced that she was going to the Harrison Street station to tell Chief Kelly what we'd discovered about Fred and the American Protective League. When I offered to go with her, she said, "I'm sorry, Mother, but I'd rather do this on my own."

I protested but, in the end, let her go on without me. I had university work I'd been neglecting and spent most of the day dealing with that. Late in the afternoon, I made my way to the lace curtain Irish area where Whitbread had settled with his wife, Gracie, and her siblings. It was several years since I'd visited their four-story town house. Unable to have children of her own, Gracie had raised the brood left behind after the bloody days of the Pullman Strike. When rents went up while wages went down in 1894, the factory town had gone on strike. The labor action quickly spread to a nationwide railway strike until federal troops were called to Chicago. During the riots, Gracie's fiancé was shot dead, and she was saved from a bullet by Henry Whitbread. In the end, to the surprise of all, he took her away and married her. It was an intense, violent time burned in all our memories. Our nursemaid, Delia, was Gracie's younger cousin, which helped to keep the connection with the family after my break with Whitbread. But I seldom visited any more.

The steep stairs were well worn. Delia had told me that after her brothers and sisters married, Gracie opened a sort of boardinghouse, taking in more young people to replace the ones that left. I pulled the iron knob for the bell, and the tall black door was opened by a teenaged girl in an apron. She led me in, with little formality, to a hallway between two drawing rooms where several young men slouched, reading newspapers and playing checkers. I followed her through a long dining room, the table set for about sixteen, and into the large kitchen where Gracie and a younger woman were dishing out platters of boiled beef and cabbage. The air was wet with steam from the cooking and the smells were heady, rich, and earthy.

"Emily, it's been such a long time," Gracie said, wrapping me in a moist embrace. She was a large-boned woman, with hair that was mostly gray now, pulled back into a large bun on the top of her head, with wispy sprays around her face. She wore a flowered dress with a collar of fine lace protected by a massive white apron tied around her substantial waist. Her deep voice carried, echoing through the house, and her face was powdered. When she embraced me, I caught a scent of lilacs that was mostly overwhelmed by the steamy mists from the food. "This is Deirdre now helping me get the food on the table. You've come just in time and you'll have to join us." She held me away from her. "You've come to see himself, I've no doubt. He'll be along any minute now, but you'll not get a word from him till he's had his vittles. Come on."

She handed me a plate and waved toward the dining room, where Deirdre was adding a setting and calling to the young men to bring another chair when they came. Soon we were all gathered around the table. Just as napkins were being shaken from their round wooden holders, Whitbread strode in, wearing shirtsleeves, and took his place at the head. I was near Gracie at the foot of the table. His sharp eyes saw me, but he remained silent as one of the girls said grace. After that, there was pandemonium as they passed around dishes, everyone serving themselves. I was briefly introduced by Gracie but afterwards ignored as the young people traded jibes and news, and Gracie held forth on how her brothers and sisters were faring. Whitbread seemed content at his end, digging into his meat and potatoes, and occasionally shooting a question at one of the young men near him.

It was only after the meal, followed by pie, that Gracie dispatched me to Whitbread's study in the front of the house. She refused my offer of help with the clearing up, saying she had plenty of hands. Several of the men were already busy washing and drying under her supervision. As usual, she had everything organized, and I could hear her teasing the men as I made my way to a wide door on the right of the staircase. I knocked.

"Come in," Whitbread called.

He sat in a leather armchair behind a large desk. It wasn't a big room, but one wall was filled with bookshelves crammed with legal volumes and textbooks. Files lay scattered on the flat desk, beside a bottle of ink, several pens, and a pen knife. The house was electrified, but an oil lamp with a glass shade lit the room, along with a standing lamp beside his chair.

"Mrs. Chapman, come in." He rose to his full height and gestured to a cozy armchair in front of the desk. I could imagine him counseling some of the young people who inhabited his home by sitting them down and listening. At work, he was always on his feet, moving, restless and impatient. I saw that Gracie had found a way to give him a den where he could relax while still roving through the world via the volumes surrounding him. He had one open on the desk. It was a city directory. When he sat back in the chair, waiting for me to begin, I felt like a child brought before the principal to explain a misdeed. It was no more than I deserved.

"Thank you for seeing me. It's been a long time since we've visited like this."

He remained silent. The fault was mine for the break. He didn't have to say it. He gave in enough to ask after my family.

"They're fine, or they were." I looked him in the eye. "It's Lizzie I'm worried about. That's why I've come. I know I broke your trust when I didn't tell you about Alden. I know I was wrong. I regret that." It had taken me a long time to realize how much I regretted it. When it happened, I believed lying to Whitbread to protect my brother was the only course of action open to me. Whitbread found the real killer despite my mistake, but he never forgave me for not trusting him to do the right thing. We were both older now. I wondered if he believed me. He was unrelenting in his opinions of right and wrong. My own father died when I was young and, sitting there, in the presence of the man who'd been my mentor for so much of my adult life, I realized how much I missed him. "If you can't forgive me, please listen to me for the sake of my daughter. Lizzie doesn't understand why we can't turn to you for help."

His dark eyes were adamantine but, as I watched intently, he took a deep breath, shifted in his seat and clasped his hands in front of him. Hearing men's voices and a clicking noise, I realized they must have a billiard table in the next room. He sighed. "Mrs. Chapman...Emily, it's been a long time since those days and the world has become more dangerous than we could ever have imagined." He closed his eyes.

There was a shout and laughter from another room. "You hear that?" He opened his eyes and gestured. "Listen to it now, because in a few months that sound will be gone. In a length of time shorter than any of us can believe, all those young men will be taken away. We'll miss those voices, and those of us left behind—because we are too old or too ill—will not fill that void. We hang on a precipice from which we will jump willingly, and people are looking up instead of down. I was angry with you for doubting that I would clear your brother if he was truly innocent. But that was a long time ago. I only think of it when I see Alden's name on a billboard for a new film."

My brother had taken his wife and children out to California, where he went to work in the moving picture business after the debacle at the Selig Studios in Chicago. "Yes. He's still working out there," I said, letting my breath go with relief. It seemed that, in a world darkening with war, Whitbread was willing to forgive me. It said a lot about how dire he considered the situation that he would let go of our long disagreement. But perhaps it was that we were both growing older every day, and my apology was sincere enough to get me forgiveness. Whatever the reason, it was a great weight lifted from my heart to be able to consult him again.

Whitbread leaned forward. "I was telling you the honest truth when I said the investigation into the death of Miss Littleton is out of my hands. Kelly will brook no interference on my part. He's jealous of his newfound rank." I sat back in disappointment, but Whitbread fingered one of the pens. "Still, he'll be taken by surprise like everyone else when all the young men under his command are led away to battle. There will be a draft. They haven't agreed to it yet, but it's unavoidable. Once committed, they'll need more than a million men. It hasn't occurred to anyone yet that the very streets they walk on will be emptied of all the young and vigorous. Only we old broken-down men they'd already sent out to pasture will be left."

"You'll never be broken down," I protested.

"Thank you. I'm not sure Gracie would agree. But it means Chief Kelly will soon be distracted. He'll want to hang the man in custody and have done with it. Your daughter doubts the man's guilt, is that it?"

I realized, then, that he was willing to help. Swallowing, I took a breath before pouring out all we knew about the case. I reported in a straightforward, organized manner, as he'd taught me to do so many years before, and I watched as he took it all in, occasionally asking a question. He pursed his lips when I talked about the auto derby, where I'd last seen him. I still didn't know why he'd been there.

When I finished, he shook his head. "The American Protective League. I've had my suspicions about that group."

"Vigilantes," I said.

"Vigilantes who have the backing of the Bureau of Investigation. The bureau's federal, part of the Department of Justice. This league was formed when some of the businessmen offered to provide motorcars for the bureau. But they want to do more, play detective, root out German spies, even if it's just the local baker who refuses to curse the Kaiser."

"Do you think Fred Spofford really pretended to be a socialist to infiltrate the meetings at Hull House?"

"Sounds like a boyhood prank, doesn't it? But these Protective League men are much more dangerous than that."

"Lizzie thinks that Hoffman attacked Hazel as revenge for Fred's spying. Could that be true? Is Lizzie in danger? She went to tell Chief Kelly about it, I couldn't stop her. Will they come after her? I'm afraid for her."

"I certainly wouldn't advise her to willy-nilly go after that socialist group without finding out what's behind it. They've found saboteurs and spies on the East Coast, and there are bound to be some here, but whether a socialist group that has been meeting for years has fallen prey to that kind of influence is impossible to say without more evidence. More likely there are some anarchists sprinkled among them. The anarchists are far more secretive and dangerous. In these cases, it is always advisable to proceed with caution."

"Lizzie lacks all caution. That's what I'm afraid of."

"In that, she no doubt takes after her mother," he said. "What does Dr. Chapman think?"

"He's as concerned as I am. You'll help us, won't you?"

"I'll do what I can. I have an ongoing investigation I cannot abandon." He frowned. "You said Lizzie's gone to Chief Kelly, but Mr. Mirkin thought Miss Littleton and Fred Spofford might have broken off their relationship when she found out he was spying, is that right?"

"Yes."

"I can tell you that the motor crash that killed Spofford was not an accident. The front axle of the race car was tampered with. But it *is* true he could have done that himself."

"How awful." I replayed the crash in my mind. If Fred had sabotaged his own machine, he'd killed his mechanic, not just himself. The other man was flung from the race car and plummeted to the ground. I couldn't believe the Spofford boy would do such a thing. But anyone who could kill Hazel must be beyond my understanding. Whitbread was asking something. "I'm sorry, what did you say?"

"You should have your daughter confront her fiancé about his brother's activities. Try to be present. See if you can find out more about the league. Surely George Spofford is also a member. I will look into the activities of the group Hoffman belonged to. There are rumors that the socialists are helping a waiters' union organize a strike for the near future. It's always possible that a rogue group within a union will do something violent. It seems unlikely but, if the Spofford boy found out about something they planned that was illegal, it's possible they killed him to keep it secret. I can't promise results, and we will have to be discreet when it comes to Kelly, but I'll see what I can do. You can contact me at the division." He rose to escort me to the door.

Gracie heard us and rushed out to give me a pie and urged me to return soon. When I was in the doorway, Whitbread coughed.

"You have two sons, Emily."

I knew he was thinking of the coming conscription. "Yes, but Jack's in medical school and Tommy works for the city."

"Take care," he said. "Soon, they'll both be at risk."

"Oh, stop with the doom and gloom," Gracie said, hitting him on the chest. "He's always going on like this and I tell him, what will be will be. We can't change it. We'll weather it. We always have. Our love to your family."

I left them feeling lighter. With Whitbread on our side, I knew sooner or later we would find the truth behind Hazel's terrible death, and Fred's, too. I knew from experience that there could be aching revelations involved, but eventually the truth would burn through, sear out the evil and, like Gracie said, whatever it was, we would weather it.

TWENTY-EIGHT

Lizzie and Stephen were both pleased when I told them Whitbread would help us. Lizzie had told Chief Kelly about the socialist group at Hull House and Fred's attempt to spy on them. She reported that Kelly still preferred his own story of a romance between Hazel and Hoffman, but he was pondering the idea that Hazel's murder could be an action by the socialist group if the girl had learned something they considered dangerous. Kelly walked a fine line between the anti-German patriotism that was so rampant and Mayor Thompson's refusal to condemn the German Americans who'd voted for him. Still, anarchist bombings in the near past offered cover for Kelly. If he could blame Hazel's murder not on all German Americans, but only on German American anarchists, he might have a convenient explanation that would satisfy everyone involved.

But the next morning newspaper headlines announced another set of burglaries in a building downtown. Seven different businesses in the same building were hit, their safes blown open. I knew Whitbread would need to investigate those crimes. It would delay any investigation on his part into the deaths of Hazel and Fred. When I explained that to Lizzie, she was impatient.

I had already committed to attend a meeting at the Palmer House Hotel of the bakers' union, which was on strike. I'd agreed to act as an observer for a group that was coming from the state capitol to try to mediate. Since I was unavailable to do any further investigations, Lizzie announced that she would go in search of George to ask him about the American Protective League.

There were many groups of workers organizing strikes at that time. America benefited financially by selling to the warring European nations, but many workers' wages had not risen enough to meet rising prices. As a result, there was a lot of labor unrest. Confident that Whitbread would return to the investigation of Hazel's death as soon as he could, I made my way to the strike meeting.

The union had rented a large room. Working men in their Sunday best milled around, mostly ignoring the rows of chairs. Many loud conversations drowned out the speakers who stood on a platform at the front of the room. I stood on tiptoe trying to see what was going on. The head of the union rapped a wooden gavel, and the noise dropped to murmurs. Many of them were in a guttural German I didn't understand.

"Gentlemen! We have received a 'no' from the owners. They won't agree to the two-dollar wage increase. And they won't agree to union oversight over the hiring and firing of the foremen." There were some angry shouts and a surge of voices. "We must stand firm. We must stand together."

Suddenly, I heard a bang. The doors at the back were flung open and uniformed policemen marched in followed by three men in expensive suits and two others carrying briefcases. The crowd parted letting the men down the middle aisle. The hair rose on the back of my neck. What was this?

At the open doors I saw Lizzie looking around, and I waved to her. She pardoned her way through the clumps of men who were trying to see what was happening at the front.

"Lizzie, what is it?"

"I found out where George is. Come with me."

"Not now. I must hear this."

There was a shuffle at the front. More policemen entered at the back of the hall and the union leaders looked worried.

The head man spoke reluctantly. He introduced the United States district attorney, a Mr. Clyne. He was a short man with black-rimmed spectacles who pulled a sheaf of papers from his briefcase and established himself at the podium, glaring around the room, waiting for silence.

"What—" Lizzie began to ask, but I hushed her.

Suspense hung in the air like a cloud. Men exchanged glances as if puzzled and a little afraid.

Clearing his throat, Mr. Clyne introduced himself, his colleague from the district attorney's office, and the three men who were the owners of the largest bakeries in the city. There was a rumble as the working men perceived he was on the side of the owners. Clyne glared out at them. "There will be no disturbance here today," he said. "You'll note we have the police on hand to keep order."

The crowd moved like an animal realizing it was surrounded. Men turned around to see a line of policemen filing in the door, marching down the side aisles. Then the workers turned back to the front where the first two policemen stood at attention before the platform.

Satisfied that he'd made his point, Clyne looked down at his pile of papers. "It has come to our attention that the current labor action on the part of your union could impact the war preparations in defiance of the War Act. I am here to tell you we will not allow that to happen. The people of this country will not allow food shortages to sabotage our efforts against the enemy."

Men shouted angrily and, near us, one man made a loud statement in German.

"He said that we're helping to starve people in Berlin by supporting the British," Lizzie whispered. She had studied German before leaving the university.

I put a hand on her arm and pulled her over to the wall. "Hush, Lizzie, I'm only here to observe."

"Is it true?" she asked. The men were shouting and stamping their feet.

It was a complicated question. "Some of the people who oppose the war think it's unfair for the British to blockade the German ports and not allow even food to be imported. It's been going on long enough that there are serious food shortages in Germany that impact civilians as well as the military," I told her. The bakers resented being accused of depriving the American public of bread when many of them had family starving in Germany. I knew what they were talking about because I'd been following the arguments for and against our entrance into the war. Lizzie hadn't been paying enough attention to the world situation, wrapped up as she was in the plans for her wedding and her entrée into the world of Chicago society.

"That's terrible. He says children are starving." Lizzie was shocked.

"Yes, well there are two sides to the argument. It's nearly impossible to tell if a ship is carrying only food and not military weapons. That's the argument the British would make. A German U-boat sank the *Lusitania* because the Germans claimed it carried weapons, not just civilian passengers. The British avoid doing that by not letting *any* ships through their blockade."

Clyne stepped away from the podium and spoke to the union leader, who whacked his gavel for order, then Clyne stepped back. "This is a warning to all of you," he said, looking straight out at them. "We are aware that most of your union members are of German heritage. We're investigating the claims that some of your leaders are reservists in the German army." After he made this accusation, the noise level dropped. The men froze. "This country is at war with Germany and the United States government will not put up with any attempt to sabotage the war effort. You will stop this strike at once. If you refuse the current offer, then I am here to tell you that camps are being established for enemy aliens, which will be available to house any man who sides with Germany against us. This is not a threat; it is a promise."

There was silence as he looked out at them for a full minute. I couldn't believe what he said. It was legal for a group of workers to strike. It was their only weapon against rapacious employers. Sometimes they were successful, and sometimes not, but striking was always an option. Clyne had just removed that right with a few words. Shoving the papers into his briefcase, he nodded to the policemen at the front and marched back down the aisle followed by his colleagues. When the doors slammed behind him, the other policemen stood uneasily around the edges of the room.

Lizzie stared at the closed doors. "I don't believe what I just heard. How can he say that?"

I bit my lip, reminding myself I was there only as an observer, but I couldn't keep from shaking my head. How had it come to this? The right, the need to be able to strike was something we'd fought for over the years. Would that right really be swept away by this war?

At the front of the room, the bakery owners were talking to the union leaders. They appeared to be as shaken by Clyne's performance as the bakers were. There was a swell of noise as the men began to react to the ultimatum. They were angered by the threats.

The union leader pounded his gavel again. He had to strike it a dozen times to get attention. He looked worried, but his message was not as bad as it might have been. "We have achieved the two-dollar increase in salary," he said. There was a moment of confusion followed by a cheer. He pounded again. "We have also achieved the reduction of work hours we proposed." A bigger cheer went up and hats flew into the air. The leader nodded at the bakery owners. "We have not gotten the right to approve the foremen." There was a groan and boos, until the gavel struck again. The leader stared out at them. "The strike is over. You will all report to work tomorrow. *Everyone.*" Another pound of the gavel proclaimed the meeting over.

"That's not fair," Lizzie said. "He's blackmailing them to stop the strike."

"I think the bakery owners are as shocked by Clyne as the workers," I said. "They've agreed to most of the demands. I don't know if they would have done that if Clyne's threats weren't so vicious. They don't want their bakers rounded up into camps any more than the workers do."

There was a strange hush as the men poured out of the room. They blinked as if coming into sunlight, skirting the policemen at the edges of the room as they left. They should have been triumphant at what they'd won, or angry at what they'd lost. Instead, they were afraid.

"Camps?" Lizzie asked. "Would they really send them away to camps?"

It was a new idea, and a shocking one, but I had to believe it was true after hearing it from the district attorney.

TWENTY-NINE

When the room was empty, I asked Lizzie about George Spofford and the American Protective League. "He went to a meeting at the Athletic Club this afternoon. We can find him there," she told me.

When I cautioned her that we wouldn't be allowed into the club building, as it was a males-only institution, she reassured me that they had parlors where women were permitted. Lizzie was sure George's meeting would run late but she was determined to confront him. I was glad she wanted me with her so I could judge the young man's reaction myself. At the club, we were ushered to a side parlor off a corridor leading to the room where the league was meeting. The floors were covered with oriental rugs in black and red, while the walls were paneled with varnished maple, elaborately carved in sham gothic style. If they were trying to imitate a medieval monastery, the god worshiped here was money.

When the usher left us, Lizzie opened the door, so we could see passersby. "I want to watch for George," she explained. She was clearly affected by what she'd seen at the bakers' union meeting. "Will they really lock people away like he threatened?"

I sighed and sat down in a chair with a view of the door. "War changes everything, I'm afraid. There've been bombs set by saboteurs in New York. In response to that, the government will give local authorities power to do a lot of things in the name of protection."

"You mean someone like our baker, Mr. Schmidt, could be taken away?"

I thought of the Smith and Sons sign our baker had put up. "Luckily, Mayor Thompson is grateful to the German Americans who voted for him. But people will need to be careful. There's a lot of fear of spies and saboteurs now that we've declared war," I said.

When the meeting was over, we watched worried-looking men stream by. Stepping to the doorway, I noticed George's father in the corridor. This time he was dressed all in black. He looked drawn but fidgety as if he were walking on burning coals. There was nowhere he could go to escape the fact that his son was dead, and I felt sorry for him. A smaller man stopped in front of him. "We've got to do something about this, Spofford. This is the third time they've hit a whole building."

"You don't have to tell me. They blew six safes on three different floors the night they hit us. I'm not sure what we *can* do, although Makum had a thought." Spofford tapped a passing man on the shoulder and brought him into the discussion.

Lizzie spotted George in the throng. His face lit up at the sight of her, and I couldn't help liking him for that. He was a very handsome young man, in dark clothes suitable to mourning. His pale face and light hair made him seem vulnerable, and the expression in his vivid blue eyes as they rested on my daughter was one of relief. I looked at Lizzie and realized that she'd dressed carefully, in a white linen suit with black satin lapels and blouse, and a black straw hat with black and white satin roses. They made an irresistible couple when he rushed over to her, taking her gloved hand. How had we produced a daughter who was so beautiful? No wonder he'd been attracted to her. But it wasn't only her beauty. Lizzie was warm and caring, and I could see that George craved that. Sometimes her spirited responses must have surprised him, but he clearly admired her all the more for being different from his family.

Lizzie broke the spell. "George, we've come to ask you about Fred. Did you know what he was doing at Hull House? We've found out he was there, and that he argued with Hazel. Did you know about that?"

George's eyes widened, and he grabbed her elbow. Looking back at the passing crowd, he quickly walked her into the small parlor, gesturing for me to follow. He led her almost to the window seat. "Lizzie, be quiet. You can't talk about these things."

She pulled herself away while he looked back at the open door. After digging in her purse, she pulled out the badge that Kurtz had shown us. I hadn't seen her take it away from Hull House, but Lizzie could be crafty when she wanted something. It was in her hand when we talked to Jane Addams and she must have kept it. Now, she thrust it in George's face. "What is this? What is the American Protective League, and what is this Secret Service?"

When George tried to grab the badge from her, she stepped back and held it away from him.

He put his hands in his pockets. "Lizzie, please, put that away. It's secret. I took an oath. I can't tell you about it."

"There's a secret society, and Fred was spying for them at a meeting of socialists, is that it?" Lizzie lowered her hand with the badge. The two young people stared into each other's eyes, barely a foot apart. "Did Hazel find out, George? She was disgusted, wasn't she? Did she want to call the wedding off? Is that what happened? George, did Fred kill Hazel because she found out and she was going to leave him?"

Was Lizzie finally able to picture Fred killing her friend? She must have mulled it over all night and decided it was possible. Or maybe she just wanted to shock George into telling her what was going on. She seemed to know how to motivate her fiancé.

George's mouth hung open. "Of course not. Lizzie, what are you talking about?" He put a hand out to calm her, but she jumped back.

I heard a rustle behind me and saw Richard Spofford standing quietly in the shadow of the doorway. The young people were too involved with each other to notice anyone else.

"You can't believe Fred would have hurt Hazel," George said. He stood up straight. "She found out. It's true. She saw him at the settlement house and then followed him to his garage to have it out with him. They argued, and she ran away." Lizzie's arms dropped to her side and I saw tears in her eyes. George saw them, too, and hurried on. "He came and found me that night. It was very late. He was upset by the argument and by the fact that she left alone, wandering around by herself so late at night. He told me that she'd threatened to break off their engagement. I pointed out to him that, if she couldn't support his work for the league, then maybe it was better to find that out before they married." George had a stubborn look on his face.

Lizzie stared at him. "You said he was angry. I think that when he found her the next day, he—"

"Lizzie, what are you saying? He wouldn't ever have hurt Hazel." George reached out and grasped her arm. "Listen to me. It's not as if there was another man. If she left him for someone else, he could have flown into a rage…any man would." He was colder in his anger now, standing still like a statue as if he were blocked by a stone wall. He seemed to think in absolutes. Sexual infidelity was insufferable while other indiscretions could be forgiven. I hated to think what he would do if Lizzie grew fond of another man. His anger on the point was more than I'd ever seen in him. The thought of a rival for her love cut to his core. I felt an icicle slide down my back.

"Betrayal with another man would have insulted his honor, but this was war work," he said. "Fred was doing his duty and, if Hazel couldn't see that, then I told him that he should break it off with her, and he agreed. He wasn't happy about it, but I made him see that's what he had to do."

"How do you know he didn't lose his temper when he confronted her? How do you know he wasn't the one who killed her?" Lizzie gulped back a sob as she said the words. She was seeing a side of her betrothed that she'd never encountered before. Growing up in our world, Lizzie had seen us battle for ideas and causes, but she had no experience with the depth of passion between men and women that could lead to violence.

"Stop this, right now!" It was Spofford speaking from behind me. He closed the door and strode over to stand between them. "How dare you?" he said to Lizzie. "My son is dead because he was doing his patriotic duty. Hazel Littleton was killed by one of those German traitors. She brought it on herself when she foolishly exposed Fred in front of that group." I realized that the Spofford family had known about the confrontation at Hull House all along. "They killed her in revenge, and then they killed my son. How dare you accuse my dead son of Hazel's death? If you ever speak like this in public, I'll sue you for slander."

He loomed over Lizzie as he said this. All his anger at the death of his son was focused on her. I stepped between them, pushing her behind me. The man was filled with grief, mourning the death of his youngest child. My heart went out to him. What if it had been my Tommy who died in that crash? Of course, Spofford couldn't bear to hear the son so recently lost maligned like this. Lizzie was wrong to accuse Fred in his hearing. Questioning George I could understand, but all of this was too much for a father.

"I'm so sorry about Fred," I told Spofford. "We only just learned that he was attending meetings of the socialist group at Hull House. Lizzie is as shocked as all of you to lose first Hazel and then Fred. It's horrible. She's just asking about this protective league, so we can find out the truth about these deaths. She spoke too rashly, but she wasn't trying to hurt the memory of your son."

Lizzie quivered behind me. I hoped she would hold her tongue.

"Father," George said, reaching out to the older man.

"Enough." Spofford stood up straight and took a step back. "The work of the American Protective League is none of your business. It's a group of patriots determined to save this country from the spies and saboteurs that Germany has planted here for years. It's work by brave men like my Fred that will save us in this time of crisis." He looked at me and his eyes narrowed. A blast of dislike radiated from him. "We know about you, Mrs. Chapman, and the people you associate with." His nostrils flared, and his pale skin reddened at the cheek bones. "It's fortunate for you that your husband signed a petition to support the university war work. That has helped you...so far. And your daughter's association with my family assures some measure of patriotism on the part of your family. But beware, if you or your associates speak or work against the war effort, we will expose you and all the rest of your kind as traitors."

I was shocked. I wanted to allow the man some leeway in his grief, but his comments were insulting...and so arrogant. His disdain for the people his group spied upon was as incredible as the threats made in the bakers' strike meeting. His attitudes belied everything I held to be most American, like freedom and equality. "Mr. Spofford, I'll excuse your saying such things only because I believe you are out of your mind with grief over the deaths of Fred and Hazel."

"Father, please." George put a hand on his father's shoulder to pull him back from where he stood, glaring down at me. But the older man shrugged him off before finally retreating another step.

"You are lucky to have the connection to our family," he said. He looked at Lizzie and then George. "With Fred gone, we won't wait for a June wedding. George's mother is already making the arrangements. There'll be a military draft in May or June, so the ceremony will be before that."

You could have knocked me down and I wouldn't have felt a thing. Here was the man who had just threatened my daughter, now announcing that her wedding would be moved up. He was insane.

"Father." Young George looked embarrassed rather than surprised. I realized the Spoffords had already discussed the need to ensure George's exemption as a married man by moving up the date of the wedding. I was repulsed.

"What is it?" Spofford asked, seeing my expression. "Is there now some question?" He turned to Lizzie. "You were prepared to marry George in June, weren't you? Do you wish to withdraw from your engagement because you cannot support his involvement with a patriotic organization? Or do you *want* him to be sent to the battlefield in the first draft?"

"Father, please," George protested. "I haven't talked to Lizzie about all of this."

"Don't be a fool, George. Miss Chapman knows her position will be much improved by the marriage, even if her mother does not." My mouth dropped open. He turned to me. "As I said, your position is tenuous, Mrs. Chapman. You'd better hope this marriage takes place as soon as possible and that your daughter's influence will help to keep you out of trouble." While I knew Spofford could be demanding, he was an attractive man who practiced charm in most of his dealings. It was only now that I was seeing into his soul, and it was a bleak prospect. "If for any reason this wedding does not happen, I promise you, you will regret it." With that, he marched from the room.

"I'm so sorry," George said. He spread his hands. "This only came up after Fred...Fred's accident. They're saying there'll be a draft in June. My mother is afraid I'll be drafted, and she wants to move up the wedding. She's afraid she'll lose me, too." He looked anxiously at Lizzie. "I tried to tell her it's not necessary, but she's right, isn't she? There's no sense getting drafted as an unmarried man and then getting married and having to go off to Europe, is there?" He appeared to be insensible to the threat his father had made against me.

I stepped away, and Lizzie looked up at him. "What about Hazel and Fred?"

"Why, they're dead, aren't they? I wish it weren't so, but it is. There's nothing we can do, and there's so much before us." He reached out to touch her cheek. "Dear Lizzie, you can't believe Fred would have done anything to hurt Hazel just because she sided with some foolish socialist group. Please say you'll marry me now...right away." He looked on the verge of tears.

Lizzie blinked. She stepped back from him and looked at me, then back at the anxious boy in front of her. "Fred wouldn't have done it for some foolish group, no." She stared into his eyes as if trying to see into his soul. There was no subtlety in George, he'd confessed everything he'd tried to hide from her. Seeing him near tears, she stood on tiptoe and brushed his cheek with a kiss then left the room. She hadn't refused him. My stomach plummeted, but I followed without comment.

THIRTY

There was an old horse cab at the door, so I secured it to take us to the train station. Once we were safely inside, I tried to talk to Lizzie. I was worried that she would feel obliged to marry George even if she had doubts. I certainly did.

"You don't understand," she said, looking out the window but not seeing anything. "You heard George. Fred wouldn't have killed Hazel for some secret league, but he might have if there'd been another man. *Oh my God.*"

"Lizzie, what do you mean?" I'd been surprised by the vehemence George put into his declaration that only jealousy would have caused his brother to attack Hazel. But I still didn't believe that Hazel had an understanding with Hoffman or any other man in that socialist group. For a moment, I feared that Lizzie herself might be harboring affections for someone other than George. Was that why his attitude shocked her so much? Or was she really so young that she didn't understand how much of a blow to a man's self-esteem such a betrayal would be?

Lizzie shook her head. "Don't you see? George means it. He's telling the truth when he says that if Fred found out Hazel was seeing another man, he would have been mad enough to attack her."

"But George only said that Fred would have flown into a rage. He insisted that Fred would never have *hurt* Hazel. And you said he didn't have passionate feelings for her, that he didn't care enough to kill her. You said he could have just broken the engagement," I reminded her.

"I was wrong." She looked into my eyes. "I've never seen George like that, Mother. I never, ever would have believed it. Not of Fred. Not of George."

"But you also said Hazel *wasn't* seeing another man, didn't you?" I wondered if she was telling me the truth about that. It was too late to keep Hazel's secrets.

"I said there was no one new in her life. There wasn't." She bit her lip as she looked at me. "Oh, Mother, it was Tommy."

"Tommy?" It wasn't possible. Tommy, my boy who was always in trouble and demure little Hazel? It made no sense to me. Hazel had chosen Fred and the world of privilege inhabited by the Spoffords. She had also chosen Hull House and the work of the reformers. But Tommy? My spendthrift, motorcar enthusiast son who hadn't even finished high school? It was beyond anything I had ever imagined. It couldn't be true.

"Oh, Mother, how can you be so blind? Tommy has always loved Hazel, from when we were small." I looked at her blankly. "The three of us were always together. We were friends in all our games and mischief." That I could remember, the three of them running around the neighborhood, but Lizzie and Tommy were the leaders. Hazel was a quiet little girl who moderated their rashness—at least that's what I'd always thought.

"Hazel was the only one who could pull Tommy back," Lizzie went on. "We used to climb out on the roof tiles. You never knew."

I certainly didn't. It was a steep-pitched roof that could only be reached from an attic dormer. I shivered at the thought of young children out there.

"Tommy would show off, walking on the drains. Hazel made him stop. She never yelled at him, she'd just look so worried, practically in tears, and he would see it and collapse by her side and promise not to do it again. She was the only one who could make him go back and apologize to Father, too, after Jack and I gave up on him."

"But they were children," I said.

"Yes, and then Tommy got wilder and wilder, so that even Hazel couldn't put up with him. But when they met again at the motor races, I saw it coming. I warned Fred to spend more time with her. And I warned Hazel that Tommy was selfish. She knew I didn't approve, but she didn't care." Lizzie paused, taking a breath. "That's what I was afraid she'd come to tell me at the luncheon. I was sure she was going to break off the engagement because of Tommy. George thinks it was because of Fred's spying. Hazel would have hated that, but she loved Tommy, Mother. I know she did, even though I didn't want to admit it. Don't you see? She must have told Fred. She wouldn't lie to him about that." She bent toward me, her eyes wide. "Fred was mad with anger... he must have been, don't you see? She told him she loved Tommy and he killed her."

She clutched her forehead in her gloved hands, and I sat back, unable to believe what she was telling me. She'd been so sure that Fred lacked the passion to kill Hazel. But George's blunt declaration of how his brother would react to betrayal had clearly shaken her.

How could I not have known about such a thing? It turned everything around. I thought of the time I saw Tommy at city hall the day after Hazel's death and I remembered my words with him after Hazel's funeral. And the auto derby. Fred's crash... could Tommy have engineered that? Did *he* believe that Fred killed Hazel? No, even then, Tommy wouldn't have murdered the man and his mechanic in such an underhanded way...would he?

We climbed out at the station. Lizzie walked on in a fog, thinking hard. At the track for the Hyde Park train, I stopped. "Lizzie, you go. I have to find Tommy. Tell your father I'll take a later train." She looked at me calmly, and I added, "Don't tell your father anything about Tommy and Hazel."

I hesitated, worried about her. She was sad. "Lizzie, no matter what George and his father say, you don't have to marry him if you don't want to. You mustn't feel obliged." I was torn. I knew I should stay with her, to help her face her feelings about the Spoffords, but I blamed myself for not realizing Tommy had loved Hazel. I should have seen it. I'd misunderstood Tommy so badly already, I had to go to him to make it right.

She shook her head looking at me steadily. "You want me to break off the engagement? Abandon George and his family just when they've lost Fred?"

"But, Lizzie, you can't marry him just to console him. You heard them. They want to move up the wedding just so that he can get an exemption from the draft." I hated to have to say it. It sounded so dishonorable. As a pacifist, I ought to approve of their attitude, trying to save their son. But, somehow, I was ashamed for him.

Lizzie let out a short laugh at that, and I took a step back. "Mother, if I refuse to marry him, what then? What if he's drafted and dies in the trenches? How do you think I'd feel then? He's afraid. Why shouldn't he be?" She sighed. "Mr. Spofford is right. I wanted to marry George. I could see us having a wonderful life, having children, accomplishing things you never dreamed of. You and Father would have been proud of me in the end. We could've had a good life together if it weren't for this horrible war. Now we can't escape it. And you can't really believe it would be right for me to break off my engagement and have George forced into the army, can you?"

"But the war will end, Lizzie," I said, my voice unsteady.

"Not for us…there's nothing but the war for us. Go and find Tommy while you can." I wondered if the ultimatum she'd received about her marriage to George Spofford was the cause of her despair. When she turned away to board the train I stood still, uncertain which way to go. Lizzie needed me. But so did Tommy. As always, in the end, I knew that Lizzie was the stronger one. I rushed away.

THIRTY-ONE

Tommy was not at city hall, but I found Fitz there and convinced him to help me. He had a car and driver who took us first to the apartment Tommy shared with Lenny, but they were out. Fitz said they would probably be at the garage where they worked on their race car.

As we drove down to that area, I saw armies of motorcars staring out from behind huge plate glass windows along South Michigan Avenue. Building after building hugged both sides of the wide flat road.

Fitz noticed my gawking. "They're calling it Motor Row," he said. "We've got more automobile dealers than most anywhere else. We've got better paved, flatter streets than New York, you know. And after Ford built a showroom at Fourteenth Street, all the others followed."

I craned my neck to look at the heights. The buildings were mostly two stories, with some on the corners rising to four or five.

"They've got repair shops and parts storage above," Fitz told me. He laughed. "Would you believe they've got elevators to take the motorcars up and down? It's a wonder."

The wonder was the number of buildings and the way they pushed their wares out to the street with the huge windows. I hadn't had any reason to visit this part of town for several years and it felt like an invading force had set up camp in the area south of the Loop. How had I missed that?

We turned right and drove a block to cross Wabash into an alley filled with smaller garage buildings.

"Fred Spofford had that one," Fitz said, pointing to a green painted door with a big padlock. "Poor boy, I heard about the crash." It was getting late and our car shone its headlamps down the narrow way. Further up, light spilled from a wide doorway. "Ah, they're here," Fitz said.

We found Tommy and Lenny in shirtsleeves, tending their green race car as if it were some kind of live animal in its stall. The garage was well lit with oil lamps hung from the rafters and nailed to the walls. They'd taken one wheel off the car.

"Mother." Tommy stood up, wiping a tool with a rag.

Lenny bounced up beside him. "Hi, Fitz, what's the occasion?"

"Mrs. Chapman wants to speak with Tommy," Fitz said. "You go along home now, and I'll wait out in the car."

Lenny looked as if he was going to object, but he thought better of it when he saw my determination. Grabbing his jacket and cap, he said, "We can finish this tomorrow night." Then he brushed past Tommy to follow Fitz out the door.

It was a place of cold concrete, with black streaks of oil on the floor, and reddish rust on the pails and barrels piled in the corner. Tools were neatly hung on a peg board and lined up on a tall table. It was as alien to me as I knew a library would have been to Tommy. He'd always had to be holding something in his hands to be happy. Unlike the rest of the family, he had no affinity for books and learning. He could learn only by doing.

"Tommy, I came to talk to you about Hazel." His face was blank. "You loved her, didn't you?"

Tears welled up in his eyes. "Mother." He dropped the tool and rag, then hung his head.

I went to him and put an arm around his shoulder. "I'm so sorry, Tommy. I'm so sorry about Hazel and I'm sorry that you're suffering. We didn't know how you felt."

He gulped back some tears, unwilling to weep in front of me. How many tears had he already shed in solitude? He hated showing weakness, and tears were a sign of weakness to him. "I loved her," he said, staring into the shadows beyond the doorway. "I loved her more than anything." A rush of relief coursed through my veins. He was finally talking to me, as he hadn't done since he was a child.

There was a bench against the wall. I led him to it, and we sat down.

"Tommy, how long had you been seeing Hazel?" Lizzie had said they met at the motorcar races, but when had they been able to be together?

"I hadn't seen her for a long time. But she came to the Speedway when Spofford was racing." Tommy brushed at the hair on his head. "He's a spoiled brat...I mean he was. I know he's dead, but Lenny and me had to work hard for everything we got. Spofford's daddy gave him anything he wanted."

Having seen Mr. Spofford with George, I thought Tommy had an idealistic impression about their relationship. He'd envied Fred, but he didn't know what it had cost the boy to get approval from his father.

"Hazel was engaged to marry Fred," I said.

Tommy looked into my eyes. "But Hazel and I found each other again. She dropped by the garages at the races and was surprised to see me. She started teasing me, just like when we were kids, and it was as if it was just the two of us in the world. It took my breath away, and she felt it, too.

"Then she got called away. But, after that, she'd look for me, and I looked for her, too. But I didn't belong in the stands with all the highfliers. Hazel didn't care. She'd slip away and come see me." He wiped his hands on his overalls. "Lizzie got her knickers in a twist about it. She told me to leave Hazel alone. She was right. I didn't deserve her..."

"Oh, Tommy."

"Lizzie was right. What did I have to give her?" He tore his hair with both hands. "It's my fault she's dead."

"Tommy, stop it." I grabbed at his hands trying to keep him from harming himself. His eyes were full of tears.

"Don't you see," he groaned. "Spofford found out."

Without warning, a light shone in my eyes. I shut it out, putting an arm around Tommy's shoulders, and blinking a little in my blindness.

"Stay still. Put your hands up," a voice from outside yelled.

Tommy shrugged me off, calling out to me, "Mother, get back." He stood with his hands up as several men rushed into the space.

I was startled to hear a familiar voice. "Thomas Chapman, you are being arrested for the burglary of the Stewart building, the Roanoke Insurance Company, and the First Bank of Illinois." It was Detective Whitbread. I stood up. "Mrs. Chapman, please step away."

Another detective grabbed Tommy by the arm and put large steel cuffs on his hands. Tommy hung his head, and I heard him groan.

"Detective, what's going on?" I exclaimed. Tommy wouldn't look at me, but just stared at the ground.

"Take him to the wagon," Whitbread said, and they led Tommy away. My heart was pounding as I stood there bereft. "I tried to warn you," Whitbread told me. "We've had our eyes on him for a while now. Your son is part of a gang." He pointed to the shiny green race car. "Where do you think he got the money for that? He drives a getaway car for them."

"It's here," one of the uniformed men yelled. He was climbing among the barrels and tipped one sideways to show a pile of bills and a bar of gold.

"No," I protested, although in my heart I knew it was true. I was ashamed of myself for pretending ignorance. Of course. How else could Tommy and Lenny afford a race car? Stephen was right.

But why did this have to happen now, just when I was reaching out to my son? Arrest and disgrace on top of the murder of the woman he loved. Oh, Tommy! Whitbread looked at me glumly.

Fitz returned, pushing his way through the men to my side. He took my elbow. "Whitbread, what's going on?"

Whitbread frowned. "Your city employees have been supplementing their salaries, Fitzgibbons. They've been driving for the gang that's blowing safes all over town. You must have suspected."

"No, of course not," Fitz blustered.

A small man with sharp features came up to Whitbread. "That's all of what's here, but it's only a small part of the take. Must be their share. We found this, though." He held up a pair of overalls, like those I'd seen the racers wearing at the auto derby. They were stiff and stained. In his other hand he held a metal wrench, brown with rust.

Whitbread fingered it. "That's dried blood." He looked across at me. "It could be Miss Littleton's."

I nearly lost my footing, but Fitz held me up. "No," I moaned. "No."

Whitbread's features were stiff. "I'm sorry, Mrs. Chapman. We'll be charging your son for the burglaries. I don't know if the overalls and wrench have anything to do with the attack on Miss Littleton or if there's some other explanation, but we have proof of the burglaries and we're arresting your son. You can see him in the morning, if you want. But, for now, you should let Mr. Fitzgibbons take you home."

I grabbed his arm. "Whitbread, Tommy didn't kill Hazel Littleton. He was in love with her." I touched the stiff overalls in his hands, then shivered. I released him and stepped back.

"That is something Chief Kelly will need to investigate. Your son was seen outside one of the burglaries, and we've found part of the stolen money. I know nothing of the murder investigation. It is possible Miss Littleton found out about the burglaries and was silenced."

"No, please. Yes, it may look like he's involved with the burglaries. Driving a car, yes. He could have done that, but he loved Hazel, Whitbread. He never could have killed her."

"I can't help with that," he said. "But I *am* arresting him for the burglaries."

I wanted to protest, but how could I? Once again, I had to take the part of my family, my own son, and Whitbread had to take the part of the law. There was nothing to be said. It was no longer a question of trust. My son's life was in the balance. I would do anything to save him, even though I couldn't comprehend the charges brought against him. As Whitbread turned a stiff shoulder away from me, I knew there was nothing I could do but go home and face Stephen. We had to find a way to save our son. I set my jaw and allowed Fitz to usher me away.

As we climbed into Fitz's motor, I heard an exchange between Whitbread and the sharp-faced man. "No, leave it for now," Whitbread said. "We'll post a man to keep an eye on it. It's only a small part of what was stolen. We need to get the whole gang. I have an idea about that. Bring the overalls and the wrench." He took three steps to the side of our motorcar. "Fitzgibbons, keep your mouth shut about this. You're not to alert Mr. Frommer or anyone else. You understand?"

Fitz took a heavy breath. "All right, all right. As you say." He knocked on the divider and the driver took us away into the night.

THIRTY-TWO

I insisted Fitz leave me at the steps of our town house and I entered on my own, trying to pluck up the nerve to tell my family that Tommy had been arrested and to describe what was found at the garage. Before I could say anything, Stephen came to the door of his study.

"Emily, come in and sit down. There's some news I have to tell you."

He was so serious, my heart pounded. Something awful must have happened. What could be worse than Tommy's situation—in love with a dead girl and arrested for burglary? And those overalls stiff with blood. I'd spent the ride home trying to block out a picture in my mind of Tommy striking down Hazel with that bloody tool. What could be worse than that? Nonetheless, I held back my own news. It wasn't like my husband to be so dramatic. Stephen ushered me into the room, taking my coat and hat, and forcing me to sit beside him on the sofa. He took my hands in his as I watched him wide eyed, dreading what he would say. "It's Jack," he said. "He joined the university ambulance service. He told me today. He knew you'd object, but he said he had to do it. The university funded two ambulances with equipment and staff, and Jack signed up for one of them."

Jack. The one child I never had to worry about. He'd signed up for the battlefield so soon? "It'll be months before they do anything," I said, hoping I'd be able to change his mind before then.

Stephen grimaced. "I'm afraid not. It'll take months for them to send the army, of course—they'll have to register and draft the men, then train and transport them—but the ambulances will be sent to the Allies right away. I'm sorry, Emily, but he'll be leaving for France in a couple of weeks."

"No!" I cried, hammering a fist against Stephen's thigh. "No, no, no! Why did he do it? He's not war mad, is he?"

"Of course not. But any man of military age is going to feel obliged to serve. Jack just knows that he's most valuable as a medic."

"But he hasn't finished his training." I knew that the doctors and nurses worked close to the battlefields and were in no way completely protected from harm.

"Emily, you must respect his decision in this. That's why I had to tell you. He's not a child. We can't tell him what to do. The truth is, if I were his age, I'd do the same. As it is, I know they wouldn't take me. It's the young ones who'll go. There'll be a shortage of doctors, and I'll need to fill in back here at home." Stephen had given up medical practice years before to do pure research. But he'd never lost his skill in treating the living, or his devotion to curing illness. "You need to brace yourself, Emily. This is just the beginning. Even Tommy'll get called. I'm sorry, but it's true. His job in the city won't protect him in the long run."

"Tommy." I looked Stephen in the eye. "Tommy was arrested tonight…by Whitbread. For burglary. I think it's the safe burglaries that have been happening. He's in jail."

Stephen sighed. "I'm not surprised, Emily. I tried to tell you that he was going down a bad road. That foolish race car."

"But that's not all. They found bloody clothes in the garage, Stephen. I'm afraid they'll charge him with killing Hazel. And he couldn't have done that. He loved her."

Stephen took me by the shoulders. "Hazel? Tommy was in love with Hazel? And they think he killed her? No, I don't believe he'd sink to that. He's weak, but not evil. Whitbread arrested him?"

He pulled me to him in an embrace. "It's all right, Emily. I'll go to Darrow in the morning. He'll know what to do." He hugged me tighter. "Oh, Tommy, what have you done? Emily, I feel like I failed him. I could never get through to him."

"He didn't kill Hazel, I know he didn't," I kept repeating. I was thinking of George Spofford's face when he said he could imagine his brother going into a rage if there were another man. Tommy was that other man.

THIRTY-THREE

The next morning, Stephen left early to locate Clarence Darrow while I went to find Detective Whitbread. At the police station, Whitbread looked sad but determined. There was nothing to be said between us. We were back to where we'd left it eight years before. I had no choice, I had to try to defend my son any way I could, and Whitbread had to do his duty. I didn't need to justify my actions. I would do anything to save my son, no matter what Whitbread thought of it.

I was surprised when he invited me to be present during his interrogation of Tommy. But there was precedent. For many years before our break, I'd sat in on interrogations. I was his pupil and assistant. That experience might have provided a pretext for my presence but, more than that, Whitbread never allowed himself to be constrained by regulations. He did whatever he knew was best to get to the truth. He knew my son would be more pressed to speak and explain himself in my presence.

I didn't pretend to take notes, as I had so many times before. I just sat in stony silence, seeing the child I'd raised in the white-faced young man on the other side of the table. I wanted to reach out to him, but I withheld the gesture. This wasn't the place for it. I'd never felt a greater distance between us than I did when he sat across that table in the police station.

If he were a child who'd been kidnapped from me, he couldn't be further away.

"Mr. Chapman, you are charged with theft of the money found in your garage last night. We have ascertained that the bills and gold brick were stolen from the First Bank of Illinois the previous evening. Do you want to explain how they came to be hidden in your garage?"

"My husband is arranging for Mr. Darrow to represent my son," I cut in. Despite the fact that I was sitting on Whitbread's side of the table, I wasn't on the side of the police. Whitbread knew that. "Tommy, you don't have to talk until your father gets here with your attorney."

I expected Whitbread to throw me out then, but he didn't. He merely ruffled through some papers in front of him. Tommy showed no sign that he heard me. I wanted him to know his father would help, despite their differences. My son was so pained that I was seeing him in this disgraceful situation that he refused to look at me.

Whitbread didn't seem surprised by Tommy's silence. He continued. "We are aware that an organized gang has been responsible for a rash of burglaries in the past few months. They target a building, then blow the safes for multiple businesses on a single night. The Roanoke building was hit on March third, the Stanford building on April second. Most recently the Stewart building, including First Bank of Illinois, was hit the night before last. Did you drive one of the getaway cars? Was the money we found in the garage your split?"

Silence.

Whitbread consulted his notes. "We know there's a plan whereby you each receive a telephone call giving the time and place for the next hit. We've been able to tap the wire in your building and listen to the calls." This was the first time I'd heard of the possibility of someone listening in on other people's telephone transmissions. It seemed farfetched, but the detective was quite serious. Looking down at the notebook in front of him, Whitbread said, "The other evening you received a call in which the caller said only the following numbers—three, two, ten, two, thirteen, fourteen. What is the significance of the code? If you cooperate and tell me that, I may be able to advocate for some clemency in your sentence."

I looked at Whitbread. Could it be true? Was there hope for Tommy? Whitbread's willingness to negotiate was unexpected, and I was grateful for this generous offer. But when I looked at Tommy, I couldn't even be sure he heard what was being said to him. "Tommy, help Detective Whitbread. You must know what you've done is wrong."

He looked at me blankly.

Whitbread sighed. From a bag on the floor beside him he pulled the blood-stained overalls and the wrench. I gasped. Was that really Hazel's blood? Tommy's face drained of all color. Whitbread had his attention. "What of these? Did you kill Hazel Littleton, Mr. Chapman? Did she find out about your involvement in the burglaries and threaten to turn you in? Is that why you killed her?"

It was unbearable. Tommy looked at the overalls and the tool then up at Whitbread. "I loved her." He rubbed his face with his hands, whisking tears from his eyes. Then he sat up and faced Whitbread with a steady gaze. "I loved her. She found out about the burglaries, yes, but all she did was make me promise to give it up. I promised her, and she believed me. She was breaking it off with Spofford, because she believed me, and she knew I would give it up to be with her."

He reached out a trembling hand to touch the overalls, then shivered. "She was angry with him, anyways. She found him spying...that night. She had a row with him at his garage and ran away from him. We were just pulling in from the job when she saw us. She followed us in. She saw the money. She realized what we were doing, and she was heartbroken."

Poor Hazel. First, she found Fred spying at Hull House, and then, when she ran to Tommy for comfort, she found out his guilty secret. It must have crushed her.

Tommy pulled his hands back, hugging himself. "I saw how much it hurt her, and I couldn't bear it. I promised her I'd never do it again, never. I promised I'd leave it behind if she'd go with me. She believed me. She told me she'd run away with me." His mouth worked for a moment with no noise, as if he were too choked up to speak. He swallowed and said, "I was happy. We were going to go to California last week. Uncle Alden would help us." Tommy stared off into space.

I couldn't help speaking. "But Tommy, why were you running away? Why didn't you just tell us? Tommy, was Hazel going to have your child? Is that why you didn't turn to us for help?" I remembered how Hazel's mother feared that was why she ran away. I'd felt her anguish at the thought that she'd lost a grandchild as well as a daughter. Had *I* lost a grandchild with Hazel's death?

He glared at me. "No, of course not. Hazel wasn't running away because she was going to have a child. How can you say that? She only agreed to run away because I had to get out."

I caught my breath as I realized how we had underestimated poor Hazel. Lizzie was right while Hazel's mother and I had doubted the girl. I felt a rush of regret.

Tommy was indignant. "You don't know the kind of people we're working for. They wouldn't let me stop. Don't you understand? They'd kill me before they let me go. I *had* to run away if I wanted to stop and I promised Hazel. Then she was dead." He rocked back and forth with his eyes closed. "Fred must have found out. He must have followed her that night and heard us. He killed her because she was leaving him." He pounded the table with his fists, then dropped his head on his arms.

"Did you sabotage Mr. Spofford's racing car to punish him?" Whitbread asked.

"He deserved it."

Had Tommy really killed Fred? I knew he hadn't killed Hazel. I believed that he loved her, but if Fred killed the woman he loved, I could believe that Tommy wanted revenge. Still, to sneak around and sabotage the race car, was he capable of that? Was Stephen right? Had Tommy taken a road so far off course that he could carry out a deed of such treachery?

There was a commotion at the door. It was Stephen with Mr. Darrow and Mr. Mirkin. Whitbread allowed them to enter. Stephen put a hand on Tommy's shoulder, but our son cringed.

Darrow asked a quick series of questions to learn about the charges and Whitbread's offer of clemency in exchange for Tommy's cooperation. His hair fell in his eyes as he considered what to do next. "I'll need to confer with my client privately about your offer," he said, giving me some hope. No matter what doubts I had about Darrow, I knew that if anyone could save my son, it was this man. There was a hint of magic in the way he could get people to see things as he wanted them to. But who would save Tommy's soul if he'd killed two men in such a conniving fashion? It was one thing to strike out in anger but to plot death in cold fury was inexcusable. Nevertheless, he was our son and we had to do everything we could to try to save him, no matter the circumstances, no matter how badly Stephen and I had failed him. I couldn't help feeling we shared the guilt of our son.

Darrow asked us to clear the room so that he could talk to his client but, before anyone moved, Tommy sat up, looking grim. "I'll help you," he said to Whitbread. He stared at the blood-caked overalls still spread out on the table. "I can tell you what the code means."

Whitbread's eyes narrowed. "Clemency is offered only on the burglary charges. We are still investigating the deaths of Miss Littleton and Mr. Spofford and his mechanic. Any future charges in regard to those crimes would not be involved."

Darrow pursed his lips. "Well, I'm not sure we can agree to that. I'll have to—"

"No, that's right," Tommy said. He looked straight into Whitbread's eyes. "I *want* you to find out. Fred killed Hazel. *He* planted those overalls in the garage to get back at me, I'm sure of it."

Whitbread gave no indication as to whether he believed Tommy. Putting his hands together, he balanced his chin on his long fingers.

Darrow interrupted, standing up. "Gentlemen, Mrs. Chapman, I'll need to speak to my client privately before this can go any further. Please, I beg of you, allow me to consult with Tommy. Alone."

Whitbread gathered his papers and evidence and stomped from the room.

"Don't worry, Mrs. Chapman, we'll talk to the detective about cooperating. Please." Darrow held out a hand to usher me from the room. Stephen took my arm, leading me to a bench in the corridor.

"I know you have your doubts about Darrow, Emily. But he's the best criminal lawyer in the country. We must do what he asks. It's the only chance for Tommy."

"Stephen, they found bloody overalls and a bloody wrench in Tommy's garage. They think he killed Hazel. But he didn't. I know it."

"I know it, too, but there's nothing we can do but wait."

I wasn't good at waiting. I paced the floor while Stephen sat still. My mind was reeling with what I'd heard. I could believe Tommy was involved with the burglaries—such a foolish thing to do—but the bloody overalls would be given to Chief Kelly. Would he charge Tommy with Hazel's death?

Darrow's young associate, Mirkin, was also exiled to the corridor and I saw him receive a message from a young boy. After he straightened up to read it, he came over to us. "Mrs. Chapman, the other day, after our visit to Hull House, I conferred with my client."

"Mr. Hoffman?"

"Yes. I told him about Fred Spofford being exposed as a spy. He wasn't at that meeting, but he recognized Eric Langer, the name Spofford had been using. He was upset but wouldn't tell me why." Mirkin waved the sheet of paper in his hand. "He has just asked me to meet him. He says it's urgent. He's still at the Harrison Street station. Do you want to come with me? I appreciate your help at Hull House. I have no idea what this means, but it may be pertinent to Miss Littleton's death."

Stephen looked up from the bench. "Go, Emily. You'll go mad if you keep pacing like that. I'll stay and talk to Darrow when he comes out."

"I hate to leave Tommy."

"You can't do more than we've done. If Mr. Mirkin can help to find Hazel's real killer, won't that help Tommy more than staying here?"

I hoped so. Hoffman might only want to save his own neck but, even if the news implicated Tommy, the sooner I knew it the better. "I'll go."

THIRTY-FOUR

Mirkin and I took a trolley to Harrison Street. I was crushed into a seat with him hanging from a strap over me. As we got closer to the Loop, there were fewer passengers and, out the window, I could see chauffeured motorcars carrying pristinely dressed women to shop at Fields or other stores. It was like ascending a peak where the air got thinner the higher you went.

We jumped off and walked away from the civilized shopping district to the gloom of the Harrison Street station. Once there, we were shunted from one desk to another and made to wait on hard benches before Mirkin was allowed to talk to his client. I took a notepad and pencil from my bag, passing myself off as the attorney's clerk.

In a small, dank basement room, chipped green paint fell in flakes off the concrete walls to the scuffed floor. We were seated at a wooden table when Hoffman was brought in by a guard. He was a small man, and there were bruises on his face and bare arms, evidence of the struggle when he was arrested at the Blackstone. His eyes were sunk deep and he blinked at the light that hung from the ceiling.

"Mr. Hoffman, I've come at your request," Mirkin said. "What do you want to tell me?"

Hoffman frowned and pursed his lips. His eyes darted around the room but there was nothing to see. He looked down and started to mumble.

"Speak up, please, Mr. Hoffman. No one can hear you but us. Mrs. Chapman is here to take notes."

"You said yesterday that Eric Langer was a spy. Yes? You said he was from the American Protective people?"

"That is correct. We have found out his real name was Frederick Spofford and he was spying on the socialist group that meets at Hull House. He didn't work for the government. The American Protective League is a group of private citizens. But he was exposed by Miss Littleton at the meeting that you told me you didn't attend. Did you meet him at earlier meetings? Did you know him? Did you know he was an imposter?"

"No, I don't know that. I know Eric Langer."

"I see. You had met him." Mirkin looked puzzled. "Is there something you want to tell us about him?"

Hoffman hesitated, shifting in his seat. Then he looked directly at Mirkin. "If he was spy, why did he give the nitro?"

Mirkin was shocked. "He gave you nitroglycerin? Whatever for?"

Nitroglycerin? I knew it was highly dangerous and used in bomb making. Why on earth would Fred have given them nitro?

Hoffman expelled a breath and seemed to sink in the chair.

Mirkin's eyes opened wide. "Is it true? Were you working for Germany?"

"No, no. Langer heard them say there was no more money for dynamite. He said he could get them nitro."

"Do you mean your group was planning to make bombs?"

"Not the group, just Kurtz and some others."

"They were planning acts of sabotage? I thought your group was socialists. That sounds like anarchists to me." I could see Mirkin was trying to adjust his view of his client.

I stopped writing. If Kurtz's group were spies or saboteurs, as the APL suspected, and they found out Fred was an informer, they could have killed him and Hazel, too. She was the one who recognized Fred. What if they thought he'd told her of their plans?

Hoffman's eyes shifted around the room, anywhere but his lawyer's face. Mirkin was furious. I wondered if he was remembering the trouble his mentor, Darrow, had gotten into when he defended the bombers in Los Angeles. I didn't envy the young lawyer the job of representing a man who helped to plan bombings.

"I am socialist only. But some of the others in group start talking about bombing. We tell them to leave, not to meet at Hull House. I do not go to that meeting because I do not want to be part of that. But some of the other socialists were there and said that Kurtz and his friends came again and talked about bombs. Eric Langer was at that meeting."

"Why did they want dynamite?" I asked. "Were they working for the Germans?"

"No. You don't see. It was the waiters' strike, not Germans. Nothing to do with Germany."

"I don't understand," Mirkin said.

"It was waiters at Bismarck Garden. They are striking for a long time. They want to blow up Bismarck Garden."

"I know about that," I said. "The waiters began a strike there a couple of months ago. The owners of the Bismarck Garden café and a downtown hotel refuse to recognize the waiters' union, which is part of the Chicago Federation of Labor. The owners started their own organization, called the Hawthorne Club, and forced staff to join it. The older staff just did what they were told, but the waiters' union members went out on strike. They only make $1 a day, but they want $10 a week, and one day off each week."

Hoffman nodded his head. "It is going on for long time and union is running out of money. Some of them like Kurtz are desperate, want to force owners to recognize their own union and listen to their demands. They plan to put capsules of nitro into the sacks of coal at Bismarck Garden so when the coal goes in the furnace—boom. That would get the owners' attention!"

"That's awful," I said. "People in the restaurant would be hurt...or even killed."

"Kurtz got money from out of town unions to buy the nitro. But last month before they could do it, police caught them in a raid. Kurtz was not there. He got away but he was mad because all the nitro is gone and there's no more money. Langer heard Kurtz talk about that at a bar, after a meeting. Langer says he knows where to get nitro, for free."

"Did Langer—who was really Fred Spofford—know how they planned to use the nitro?" Mirkin asked.

"No. Kurtz didn't trust him that much."

I sat back in my chair. Fred had provided the nitro because he assumed Kurtz was working for Germany. He must have thought that if he provided the material the APL would have inside knowledge of when the attack was to take place and would be able to catch the conspirators in an act of sabotage. He didn't know it was for the waiters' strike and had nothing to do with the war. Did the local APL leaders even know what Fred was planning? When Fred was recognized by Hazel, Kurtz must have thought Fred was a police spy. The plot had already been thwarted once by a police raid. If the conspirators had killed Fred and Hazel to keep their plot a secret, I feared they would move ahead with the bombing as quickly as possible.

"When did they plan to put the nitro into the coal at the Bismarck?" I asked.

Hoffman looked at the ceiling. "I'm not sure. But it must be a trap if Langer was a spy. Why else would he give them the nitro? You need to tell them it's a trap."

"Surely they know that by now," Mirkin said.

Hoffman shook his head. "Kurtz is madman. He was angry they got money for nitro then lost it and six of his men got arrested. He wants revenge." He looked down at his hands spread out on the table. "Maybe you can stop him."

Mirkin fingered some papers in front of him and swallowed. "I'll see what I can do about having your cooperation taken into consideration by the authorities." He gathered the papers and stuffed them into a briefcase on the floor.

"I didn't hurt Miss Littleton," Hoffman said. "I didn't know her fiancé was a spy. I didn't know her at all. Please, you have to make them believe me. I didn't kill her."

I placed a hand on Mirkin's arm. "Mr. Mirkin, we must warn the authorities. Kurtz could plant that coal at any time." I looked at Hoffman. "Are you sure you don't know when they planned to do this?"

"I was glad when the police stopped them. I tried to tell Kurtz it was no good to do a bomb but he wants revenge. He told me if I told anyone he'd kill me."

"The police can protect you," Mirkin told him. "But only if you help us now by telling us when the bombing is to happen."

"What is today?" Hoffman asked.

When we told him the date, he said, "Then it is today. Tonight, when they are getting ready to serve dinner. The waiters will all leave and then...boom!"

"We have to warn the restaurant owners," I told Mirkin. "But I can't believe the union leaders know about this. It's clearly a secret action by extremists."

"This is so incredible," he replied. "If *I* find it hard to comprehend, I'm not sure the police will believe it."

"But, if it's true, people could be killed. We've got to tell Chief Kelly immediately."

"All right." He turned to his client. "It's good you told us, Mr. Hoffman. It certainly raises the question as to whether Kurtz or someone in his group attacked Miss Littleton." Mirkin called the guard and told him we needed to see Kelly immediately.

The guard grabbed Hoffman by the arm. "I'll have to take the prisoner back first."

"This is an emergency," I said. "There could be a bombing about to take place in the city, and we need to stop it."

"A bombing? Based on what this guy said?" He squeezed Hoffman's arm and lifted him to tip toes. "Yes, sure, ma'am, I'll tell the chief you want to see him as soon as I get this one back to his cell. Come on, you."

In the corridor, I paced. "I don't think he believed us. Do you think he'll actually tell Kelly anything?" It would take time to convince the authorities the threat was real. Meanwhile, the innocent customers of Bismarck Garden would be in danger. "They've got to let us talk to Kelly."

"They're not usually very happy to do anything I ask," Mirkin said.

"I'm afraid that, even if we get the police to listen, it'll take too long to convince them and for them to get organized to get up there," I said. "If somebody doesn't stop him, Kurtz will have plenty of time to plant the nitro-laced bags of coal. I'm going up there. I'll try to convince the owner to close the restaurant for tonight."

"There's no way to be sure they're planning the bombing for today," Mirkin said.

"We can't take the chance it's *not* today. You must tell Chief Kelly what's happening." I looked at the spectacled young man and despaired of Kelly paying any attention to him. "If you can't get Kelly to do anything, you have to promise me you'll contact Detective Whitbread and tell him. He'll believe you. Tell him I went up there." I was confident Whitbread would understand the seriousness of the situation. He wouldn't take a chance on people's lives.

THIRTY-FIVE

I was afraid the police would never take the word of a man like Hoffman. But the danger was real. When we were younger, Stephen and I were always able to act, to do *something* in a crisis. I felt like a horse whipped up to a frenzy but held back by the reins.

I took three trolleys to get to the corner of North Halsted and Grace Streets, fretting as I waited for each connection. On the way, I began to doubt myself. We only had Hoffman's word to go on. Perhaps Kurtz had abandoned his plan once he learned Fred was a spy. Or, perhaps he'd arranged for Fred's accident in order to carry out his plan. My head spun with the possibilities.

In any case, I had already sent Mirkin to alert the police. Whether or not the bombs were in place today, I needed to warn the owners of Bismarck Garden that the danger was real.

When I got off the last trolley, I stood for a moment looking across at the restaurant. It was a few minutes before three o'clock, and they'd just finished their luncheon service. I could see the staff setting the tables for dinner. I needed to act quickly.

From the corner of my eye, I noticed some figures disappear through a doorway in the shadows along the side of the restaurant building. Was that Kurtz and his gang, or was it my imagination?

I ran across the street and grabbed the arm of the nearest waiter. I pointed. "Where does that door lead?"

"That's the basement. Just storage. No place for a lady."

"I just saw some men go through there."

He shrugged and pulled his arm away. "Hiding from work most like, but I've got things to do myself." He walked away.

I listened, but there was no sign of the police yet. Should I have stayed at the police station to convince them to come? Mirkin had warned me they wouldn't believe him. But I'd told him to call Whitbread and I was confident my old friend wouldn't ignore the danger. They must be on their way even if it took longer than I expected.

But I knew there was no time to be wasted, if the plan Hoffman had told us about was true. I found the maître d' as he circulated around the dining room, checking that everything was in place for the dinner hour.

"Sir, excuse me. I've just come from the police station." I hoped that he wouldn't question my exact connection to the police department. "We've received word of a plot by some of the striking waiters to bomb your restaurant tonight. You must close for the evening or your guests will be in harm's way."

"Madam, I'll have to ask you to leave. What you're suggesting is preposterous. Our waiters are men of the highest caliber and would never dream of doing such a thing. Now, out. I have to prepare for our dinner hour. Out!"

As I'd feared, it was going to be difficult to convince the restaurant of the impending danger by myself, if I didn't have solid evidence of Kurtz's activities. I made my way to the basement door, through which I'd seen the shadowy figures enter. If the men I'd seen were indeed Kurtz and his gang, and I could hear what they were saying in the basement, I might find out if they had already planted the nitro. If I *knew* that was the case, then I could make a scene and force them to evacuate the restaurant. But I had to be sure. At the very least, I could keep an eye on Kurtz until the police arrived. If he tried to escape, I could tell Whitbread where he'd gone.

I entered through the door and stood listening carefully for sounds of activity below. Unable to hear anything, I crept down the stairs and along a dark corridor. There was light from a doorway on the left and another doorway further down. Between the two, in the corridor, I saw rough burlap bags leaning against the wall. That must be the coal. Perhaps they hadn't tampered with it yet. I felt a surge of hope that the explosives hadn't been delivered to the furnace room after all.

I heard men talking inside the nearest room. They were speaking German. I stayed still, pressed against the wall, listening carefully. I was desperate to get some clue as to what they were doing and what they had planned.

Suddenly, I heard the door above me bang against the wall. "Police!" I heard muffled sounds from above us, followed by whistles and pounding footsteps. "Police, everyone out of the building!"

Kurtz appeared in the doorway next to me, holding up a gun in one hand and a burlap bag in the other. Black coal dust hovered in the air, glittering in the light from the open door above us.

"Stop!" I yelled. "You don't want to do this. You'll hurt innocent people." I felt sweat on my forehead. "Please, the police are here." We could all hear the commotion above us. "Put it down."

I stood facing Kurtz. He was red and sweaty from his efforts, and his beard was streaked with coal dust. His eyes gleamed through greasy slits.

"Don't," I said softly. "There's no reason to die. It won't help anyone." It was difficult to breathe.

He pointed his gun at me. "Spies. They send spies to us. *They* give us the nitro, the ones who send the spies. We'll use it to blow them up." He raised the bag high. I guessed that the bag was full of coal already contaminated with nitroglycerin, and I held my breath. I should run, but he had the gun pointed at me. "They think the Kaiser will kill them. *We* will kill them. *We* will be heard." Too late, I saw there was no reasoning with him. He was giddy with his mad determination. He was ready to die by smashing that bag to the floor.

A scream welled up in my breast.

"*Run*," said a voice behind me.

Someone grabbed me by the waist and pulled me towards the stairs, just as a shot rang out. Stephen! It was Whitbread's long-barreled revolver that went off. The bag with nitro hit the floor. An explosion of dust, dirt, and pieces of coal flew out of the doorway, but Stephen was hunched over me. Another policeman had managed to duck behind the wall, too. My ears were ringing, and I coughed.

As Stephen staggered up, I saw Whitbread lying on the other side of the doorway. He groaned but rolled on his side and slowly got up as policemen pounded down the steps.

"Mrs. Chapman, are you all right?" Mirkin was by my side, propping me up.

Stephen was coughing and slapping himself to remove the dust. His face was grimy, and he grabbed me by the shoulders. "Emily, are you mad? What were you thinking?"

I leaned against the wall, taking in the view of my dusty husband, then I threw myself into his arms. "Thank you. I don't know what I was thinking. I just didn't feel like anyone else was taking the threat seriously enough. I wanted to find proof that I could take to the police...or at least get the restaurant owner to recognize the danger, so he could evacuate." He hugged me to him.

Whitbread coughed and blood ran from his nose, but he was all right. I suppressed an impulse to hug him as well. He turned away to direct some of his men.

Luckily, Kurtz hadn't planted nitro in the other bags of coal that were piled in the hallway, and thus they hadn't exploded. Turning to look back into the room, Stephen grimaced, then quickly led me away from the scene and back up the stairs. He didn't want me to see what was left of Kurtz's body.

We continued into the sunshine outside Bismarck Garden, still coughing. Across the street, we could see people at gawking. They were safe, unaware of the danger. Stephen hugged me to him.

As I'd hoped, any rumor of a German plot was quickly suppressed—after all, a German restaurant had been the target. So neither the American Protective League nor the bomber could receive any credit.

In an attempt to calm the public, the restaurant owners told the newspapers a lie. They said there'd been an electrical explosion. Of course, most of the papers didn't believe it and the story of a bomb was more dramatic. The next day's headlines read "Foil Plot to Blast Bismarck Garden."

In the torrent of terrible things raining down on us, it was a relief to know that we'd helped to avert this single catastrophe. I returned home still plagued by worry about the personal tragedies that we faced, but relieved that the only victim in this incident had been the bomber himself.

THIRTY-SIX

The next day we were a somber group as we helped Jack load a single chest with clothes and books. Worry about Tommy was like a throbbing toothache in the back of my mind. We had to wait for news from Darrow. At the same time, I bit my tongue, trying not to point out all the reasons why Jack's volunteering for the ambulance corps was a bad idea. In an uncharacteristic show of anger, Stephen had demanded that I respect the decision of our oldest son. Reluctantly, I had agreed to stop voicing my opposition. Completely unaware of my objections, my oldest son rushed around cheerily trading barbs with Lizzie about his belongings.

"You won't need this, surely," she said holding up a shirt of fine linen.

He grabbed it from her. "That's for Paris."

"Paris? You? I don't believe it. They won't be able to get you off the boat with all the junk you put in there. Binoculars? Really? You'll be in the hospital tent all the time, surely."

She and Jack exchanged a glance, not wanting to remind me of the filthy trenches and bloody hospital tents we all knew were his destination. "Those aren't binoculars, they're opera glasses. Hey, we'll be in New York before we leave. I might catch the orchestra while I'm there."

"You'll take a pretty young nurse, I suppose?" Lizzie teased. I could see her glance my way. She wanted to distract me from thoughts of Tommy or battlefields. I polished a pair of Jack's shoes before packing them.

Stephen came in with a heavy volume. "Here's *Gray's Anatomy*, for what it's worth."

"But, Father, that's yours."

"I expect you'll be hard pressed for a reference library where you're going," Stephen said. He was looking older, the lines engraved more deeply into his face, yet I could spot a hint of envy in his eye. He would have preferred to go in our son's place. It was exasperating to know our time for such things was over and there was nothing we could do about it. But I was fiercely glad he couldn't go.

"You're probably right," Jack said, tucking the book in among the clothes. He had no illusions. Many young men claimed they were anxious to get into the fight, even worried they would miss the "biggest thing" of their generation. But not Jack. He had no romantic dreams about the war. On the contrary, like his father, he would be one of the ones who would have to patch together men whose hopes and dreams, as well as their bodies, would be destroyed by their adventure.

Lizzie took the pile of folded pants from my hands. I knelt, poised over the trunk, lost in contemplation. "Mother, there's someone at the door. Perhaps you should see who it is."

It was Mr. Darrow and Mr. Mirkin. I led them into the parlor. Jack and Lizzie followed. I glanced at Stephen and he shrugged. They were no longer children. They knew Tommy was in trouble, and they were concerned about him. They had a right to know what was happening. He said all that with his shrug, and I couldn't disagree.

Darrow remained standing while the rest of us took seats. "We've come to an agreement with the authorities," he said. He put his hands in the pockets of his wrinkled suit and jiggled some coins. "In exchange for Tommy's cooperation, the charges against him will be reduced. It's up to Detective Whitbread to decide exactly how much but, in light of the risky actions involved, I'm pressing Whitbread to release him tomorrow."

"Risky actions?" I asked. This didn't sound good. I knew Darrow would try to make light of it, but Whitbread would demand a lot for any concessions. He certainly wouldn't do it for friendship.

Darrow paced in front of the fireplace. "It's dangerous, but Tommy insists he wants to do it. He promised the dead girl."

Hazel. He promised Hazel he would stop stealing. How could I have missed the affection between them? But, if I *had* suspected, I probably would have warned her off him, just as Lizzie had. My own son. Tommy had come to such a bad end. I was glad he finally wanted to turn his back on the gang and help to catch them, but I felt bitter knowing he'd gone against everything we'd taught him. Or that we thought we'd taught him. What bigger failure could I have than Tommy's crimes? He'd go to prison now. Feeling like I'd failed my son, I scorned my academic concerns, remembering long reports on prison conditions and rehabilitation theories that I read all the time. I'd never imagined my own son would be a person behind the statistics. Was Lizzie right to prefer the wealth and power of the Spoffords over my useless reform efforts and those of my friends? And yet Fred Spofford's fate was certainly no better than Tommy's. And if Fred killed Hazel, as Tommy believed, would Lizzie be safe with his brother?

Stephen and Jack asked Darrow about procedures during my lapse into this fugue of regret. Then Lizzie spoke up. "What about Hazel's killer? Who will they charge for that? Was it Hoffman? Or Fred?"

Darrow looked across at Mirkin who sat up in a straight-backed chair. "Mr. Hoffman is still in custody, but he's been given some credit for his cooperation in stopping the bombing. I've argued that Fred Spofford could have killed Miss Littleton in a fit of jealous rage. Chief Kelly hasn't accepted that, yet, but I'm hopeful."

Lizzie looked grim. "George and his father believe Hoffman, or one of the bombers, killed her and Fred, as revenge for his spying."

Mirkin shook his head and clasped his hands. "There's no proof of that. If Kurtz had lived, they might have gotten it out of him. I can tell you that Mr. Hoffman vehemently denies he ever even saw Miss Littleton that day."

"And you believe him?" I asked.

"He's my client. I have an obligation to defend him as best I can."

Lizzie stared at the young lawyer until he looked away. He didn't live up to her requirement to find the truth, and I was sorry for him, but more worried for her. And for Tommy. Mirkin was careful not to say it, but I knew the police would look at my son as a suspect in Hazel's death. I could tell by the look of anguish on Stephen's face that the same thoughts were running through his mind.

Darrow wasn't inclined to spare us. "What happens to Hoffman is irrelevant at the moment. The bloody overalls and the wrench found in Tommy's garage still have to be explained. It's possible a jealous man, Fred Spofford, put them there to implicate his rival. That's what we proposed to the police and with some luck they'll believe it. Especially after Tommy's cooperation tonight."

"Tonight?"

"Yes, there'll be a raid tonight to catch the safecracking ring, and Tommy'll be helping the police. Whitbread released him, so he could receive the message about where they'll hit, and he gave the police the code, so they know where they plan to hit. Tommy'll drive one of the getaway cars."

"The gang won't be happy if they suspect he ratted to the police," Jack said.

"That's why they let him go back to his normal schedule, and they left the money in his garage unguarded," Darrow said. He touched a china figurine on the mantel. "There's one thing

I should warn you about. Detective Whitbread was hesitant to release Tommy. He warned him that if he takes advantage of that freedom to run, he'll get no concessions for his cooperation. So, I'm warning all of you, if he tries to run—I don't expect him to do that—but, if he does, don't help him. There's no way for him to escape, and the consequences will be bad, very bad indeed, if he tries to escape and fails."

Tommy. All he's ever done in his life is run. That was what I thought and, looking across at Stephen shaking his head, I knew he was thinking the same thing. "I want to see him," I said.

Darrow waved his hands. "No, no, no. You must leave him alone. Detective Whitbread insists. I think he wants to forestall any action on your part, like you did when you got to the bombing before him. Please, Mrs. Chapman, for your son's sake, do what the detective asks."

"But he's my son. At least tell me where the raid will happen. I need to be thinking of him."

Darrow hesitated.

"You're his lawyer. They must have told you. I'm his mother. I have a right to know. He could be hurt in the raid. Please, Mr. Darrow, I promise I will do nothing with the information but to be ready in case something goes wrong. He's my son."

Darrow exchanged a look with Stephen, who shrugged. The lawyer didn't want to tell me, but he knew I wouldn't let him leave without knowing. "The Rookery," he said at last.

THIRTY-SEVEN

After we let Darrow and Mirkin out the front door, Stephen took my arm. "You must let Tommy do this, Emily," he said. "He wants to honor his promise to Hazel. You understand that, don't you?" He looked me in the eye. "Our sons aren't children anymore, Emily. They're men. You must let them do what they need to do. Both of them." He was very stern.

I swallowed. "I'm so worried for them, Stephen."

Relaxing, he hugged me to him. "I know."

At supper, I couldn't eat. I excused myself and went to lie down. I knew Stephen would retreat to his laboratory. He wouldn't want to disturb me, and it was his habit to return to his test tubes when he was bothered or worried. It was possible that Lizzie might look in at me, but she wouldn't disturb me if she thought I was resting. I had a picture in my mind of Tommy in the interrogation room at the Maxwell station. He'd been wild with grief for Hazel, I could see that in retrospect. He was wild when he insisted he would cooperate with the police no matter what Darrow said. He was wild in the same way he'd been wild as a boy, jumping from a tree. He didn't care about his own safety. Hazel was gone and there was no one to keep him from plummeting to his death. I feared that, when he went to this burglary, he would put himself in harm's way on purpose. Whitbread and the police wouldn't understand how desperate he was.

I honestly tried to do as I'd been instructed but, after an hour of tossing and turning, fretting over what might happen to Tommy, I couldn't resist the need to be nearby, in case there was something I could do to help him. I knew that I was being reckless, and that I'd be chastised later—by Stephen and Whitbread and Darrow—but I couldn't stop myself.

So, in the end, I did something I hadn't done since I was quite young. I built a dummy of myself with pillows beneath the covers, then snuck down the backstairs and out the kitchen door. I hoped that Stephen wouldn't discover my subterfuge until it was all over.

I took the late train into the city then a taxi to LaSalle Street. After dismissing the cab, I worked my way through shadows to a colonnade across from the Rookery. It was a fine building of red masonry where many prominent firms had their offices. When I heard a motor come to a stop nearby, I stepped back into the darkness. My plan was to be an observer, but my stomach roiled with anxiety, unsure what I could do if things went wrong. I just could not bear to wait miles away while my youngest son was in such a precarious position. I couldn't do it. My work with Whitbread over the years had brought me to places a woman of my background would never expect to be. Those experiences had bred in me the expectation that I could participate in action. I knew in my heart that if I'd been a man with as much knowledge of police practices, I'd have been allowed to be present one way or another.

"Mrs. Chapman."

I jumped. Behind me, Detective Whitbread put a hand on my shoulder. "I was afraid I would find you here. I rang your home and was told you were sleeping," he said quietly.

"I had to come. He's my son."

"Yes, well, I'm sure your son is as anxious as I am that you not destroy the plan we've spent considerable effort devising," he whispered. "Follow me. I don't want you giving it all away. Come along." He turned and slid from shadow to shadow until he reached an anonymous black motorcar with a hard top. Carefully opening the back door, he motioned me in.

"Thank you for at least giving Tommy the opportunity to make up for what he's done," I told Whitbread when we were settled in the back seat. "I know he'll have to pay for it, but his cooperation will count for something, won't it?" I was staring out the window at the Rookery across the street, not looking at Whitbread who was so tall he folded up like a grasshopper beside me. I spoke softly so that the driver and another man in the front wouldn't hear through the wall of glass between us.

Whitbread's long fingers grasped his knees. "I didn't tell Darrow or your son but, so far, I've let it be known that your son is working for me as a spy. As far as my men know, I recruited him, and placed him in the gang. I will vouch for him when it's over."

"Oh." I turned but, in the dark, I couldn't see his face. It was so much more than I'd hoped for. "I don't know how to thank you."

"He won't be charged for the burglaries, but I cannot speak for Chief Kelly. I don't know who he plans to charge for the murders of Miss Littleton and Mr. Spofford. I do know they discovered that Spofford was at a bar on the north side when Miss Littleton was killed, so it is certain he didn't do it. If Kurtz was the one, they'll have to get one of his co-conspirators to admit it."

At that moment, I wished Kurtz *had* survived the bombing. To my horror, I realized that, if *I* hadn't discovered him in that basement, he might still be alive and they might've gotten him to confess to Hazel's murder. Now we'd never know, and Tommy might pay for what Kurtz had done.

"Kelly might still take Hoffman to trial. I'm not privy to his plans," Whitbread said.

Or he could arrest Tommy for Hazel's death. I believed my son when he said he loved her. He was convinced that Fred had killed her in a fit of jealousy, but Whitbread was telling me that was impossible. If Fred hadn't put the bloody overalls in Tommy's garage to make him look guilty, who had? How would Kurtz know to do that? There must be a link we'd missed. The thought of George Spofford crossed my mind, but I shook my head to rid it of such a terrible suspicion.

"If they charge Tommy with Hazel's murder, we'll find a way to clear him," I said softly. I knew I could never stop until I found a way to do that. "I know he didn't do it. We'll save him. But, without your help, he'd go to prison for the burglaries. I'm so grateful."

The driver turned and pointed, as two motorcars slowly crept toward us.

"It's them," Whitbread said. When the cars reached the Rookery they stopped, and men from the burglary gang poured out silently, rushing up the steps. Whitbread leaned forward. "As soon as they're all in, we move." He turned to me. "Mrs. Chapman, stay in the motor. Promise me."

"Yes," I said. With all he was doing for Tommy, I would do anything he asked of me.

Moments later, men jumped out from several more vehicles, blowing whistles. Whitbread opened his door and was gone. Several police wagons barreled down the street. When they stopped, uniformed officers spilled out and ran to the doors. I watched, my face pressed against the window. I had been resigned to Tommy's conviction for the burglaries. I had expected he would get some leniency for his cooperation, but now Whitbread was going to spare him completely. A great weight lifted from my heart. Somehow, I would prove that Kurtz, or Hoffman, or one of their comrades killed Hazel. If I still worried that Tommy had caused Fred Spofford's crash, I buried the thought. I was convinced that the conspirators had killed Hazel as revenge for Fred's spying, then they killed him.

Shouts, whistles, clanking bells, and a few muffled gunshots made me flinch. As I watched I worried, yet my heart was lighter than it had been since Tommy's arrest. When I heard shots that were closer, I strained to see what was happening. A couple of officers were standing outside by the getaway cars but, since the robbers were blocked in by the police wagons, the men turned toward the building to watch for anyone trying to escape. Suddenly, I saw a door of one of the cars open slightly. A figure slipped out, crouching to the rear, then he loped away into the shadows, bent double.

"Oh, Tommy," I whispered. He'd been driving a getaway car. He must have been waiting in the car and ducked down at the sound of the whistles. I recognized his long driving coat and soft cap. It was just what Tommy always did. Run away. He didn't know that Whitbread was going to save him from prosecution! He'd spoil it all now, destroying himself again, always making the wrong choice. If I could reach him, I hoped I could get him to turn back before it was too late. There was no choice, I had to get to him.

I opened the door, then remembered my promise to Whitbread. He trusted me. But, if he found out Tommy had run, he'd never vouch for him. It seemed that we Chapmans were destined to break Whitbread's trust. Frustrated beyond endurance, I climbed from the car and hid in the shadows as I darted after my son.

THIRTY-EIGHT

I glimpsed Tommy far ahead, in front of the Board of Trade building. I couldn't yell but had to stay in the dark alcoves of a building across from the Rookery. The policemen guarding the motors were facing away from me. There were more gunshots. Hurrying to the end of the block, I saw my son far ahead, turning south onto Dearborn. If he caught the elevated train, I would lose any chance to bring him back.

Just as I reached Van Buren, Tommy turned, passing the steep stairs up to the elevated. Where was he going? I wanted to yell, but he was still too far ahead. I pictured the area and my heart sank. Dearborn Station was just south of us. That was where you could catch a train to Los Angeles. Tommy had wanted Hazel to run away to California with him. He wanted to escape by going to my brother Alden! How foolish.

At the last minute, he turned again. I breathed heavily, trying to follow. Was he going to the Twelfth Street station? Going home to Hyde Park? But there was nothing more we could do for him. He must know that. It was infuriating that Tommy didn't know he had the chance to go free, at least from the burglary charges. We would find out who killed Hazel, I knew we could. If only...

Out of the darkness a hand squeezed my arm and I abruptly slid to a stop. I tried to pull away, seeing the figure of my son loping on down the street, past the Strand Theater.

"Now there, pretty, whatcha doin' out so late?"

He was a stout man who reeked of whiskey. "Let go of me!" I cried, trying to turn from the fumes. He had a full beard with wet, pink lips pursed at me for a kiss. He staggered but wouldn't let go.

While he puckered up, I grabbed a hat pin from my straw boater with my free hand and stuck it in his arm. "Oww!" He let go and I gave a push to his beefy chest with the flat of my hand, which caused him to drop onto his well-padded haunches.

"Get away from me!" I hissed, dancing away to avoid the hand that tried to grab my ankle, and raced across the street. I wanted to scream but what good would it do? I'd only be stopped. I glanced around as I followed, realizing now where Tommy was heading.

I was back along Motor Row. He was going back to his garage. For the money? Of course. Whitbread had left it there to help bait his trap. I couldn't see Tommy, but I knew where he would be. All these metal monsters, so beloved of the young men who prided themselves on their vehicles. He was going to his motorcar.

It was a long trek through the Loop that night, and all the time I was trying to stay ahead of the doubts that pursued me. It couldn't be true. Tommy would never have hurt Hazel. I remembered the scene in the hotel stairway, the girl's eyes staring at the ceiling, the blood. I felt as if a knife had pierced a nerve in my own body and I wanted to scream. My son could not be responsible for that, could he? I tried to blank out the doubts, the memories of him breaking things, then running away. How would we ever face the truth if we discovered that he *had* killed Hazel? How could I face her parents? If he was going to retrieve the money so he could run away, how could I let him do that? But, as his mother, how could I let him hang?

I turned down an alley and saw light spilling from his garage. As I stopped with a hand on a brick wall, trying to catch my breath, I felt all the worries and suspicions I was running from engulf me. I didn't want to think those thoughts about Tommy. Whitbread said that Fred could not have killed Hazel. Who else would have killed her with such passion? Tommy said he loved her, and she'd agreed to run away with him. But when she found out about the burglaries, was it too much for her? It must have been. Was she going to betray Tommy, to turn him in? Had she only wanted to warn Lizzie before she did it? Had Tommy believed she was going to go back to Fred? Then, in his passion, had he killed her? And then Fred Spofford and his mechanic? Those deaths were so cold and calculated. What was my son becoming? I couldn't let him run away.

My mind swarmed with questions and I gulped back a sob. It was horrible to imagine him striking down the woman he loved and then killing two young men. I sagged against the wall. But he was still my son. There was nothing to be done. I had to face him.

I swallowed and forced myself to walk the rest of the way to the open door. I could hear scrounging as if a little animal were digging for food in there.

I straightened up and walked into the light. "Tommy."

He was foraging in the corner where the police found the money and the gold. He stood up.

"Lenny!"

THIRTY-NINE

A surge of relief mired with confusion flooded through my veins, rushing all the way to my feet. I staggered a bit.

"Mrs. Chapman, what are you doing here?" He wore a long driving coat and gloves. His discarded wool cap lay on the fender of the green race car. I saw a heavy revolver hanging from his right hand.

"Lenny, you're running from the police. You were driving the other car, weren't you? You've got to give yourself up. It's all over now. I'll talk to Detective Whitbread. We'll help you. But you must stop and give yourself up." Blood pounded in my ears, but my heart was light. It wasn't Tommy who was trying to get away.

Lenny's light brown hair fell in his eyes as he strained to look behind me for the police. He looked like a small boy quivering with fear. His right hand came up with the gun. I put my hands up in protest. "No, Lenny, please. I'm alone. I know you and Tommy were part of the gang. You drove the getaway cars when they robbed the safes. But they've caught up to you now and it'll be much better for you if you give yourself up."

Poor Lenny. What chance did he have? I blamed his father for abandoning him by committing suicide. I blamed his mother for being unable to cope with it, and Fitz for not taking better care of the fatherless boy. He stood up, blinking in the light of the oil lamps.

"You got too caught up in the racing, both of you," I said. "I understand. You were competing with other young men who had money."

"It's not fair," he said. "We could've won the Vanderbilt Cup. They canceled it. Did you know that? After all we did, they canceled it because of this stupid war."

Lenny and Tommy were so foolish…and so young.

Lenny frowned and raised the gun higher. "Tommy squealed, didn't he?" Keeping his gun and his eyes on me, he hunched over a crate.

I was going to tell him not to be ridiculous when I realized what he was doing. The gold brick and money had already spilled to the floor near my feet, beside an open burlap sack. That wasn't what he was looking for. I remembered what else the police had found. My hands were clammy with sweat. "They're not here," I said.

He glanced down, then back up and moved to the next box.

"The bloody overalls and the wrench aren't there. Whitbread found them already."

Lenny stopped and stood up, aiming the heavy revolver unsteadily. He reached up with his left hand to support the gun. The black hole of the muzzle was pointed at me from only a few feet away.

"You killed Hazel, didn't you? Then you hid the overalls here. Lenny, why did you have to kill her?"

His eyes darted around the space, finally resting on me again. "She was going to ruin everything. She saw us that night. She had some fight with Spofford and ran to Tommy. I came back for my cut after I got rid of the car and she was already here. She knew about the burglaries! I heard her. She made him promise he'd stop."

I tried to step backwards.

"Don't move!" He jumped forward and grabbed my sleeve with his left hand. I could smell his sweat. Beads of it rolled down from under the loose thatch of his hair. They might have been tears, but his eyes were wide open and dry. His neat little mustache gleamed. He clutched the fabric of my sleeve and the gun wavered in his right hand.

"How could you do that to Hazel?" How could the affable, joking young man turn so violent? He'd killed the girl just to keep her quiet.

"She wouldn't listen." He pulled at my arm. "I had to keep her from talking. She was going to tell Lizzie about the burglaries." His head went up and he looked around quickly, as if he heard something, but then he pulled me close again.

"I heard her tell Tommy she'd run away with him, but she was going to tell Lizzie first. So, I followed her home. I stayed all night," he complained. He seemed indignant at the inconvenience. "I had to wait till morning to find out what she would do. She went to the Blackstone. I knew that meant she was going to tell Lizzie. I followed her in."

His eyes darted around. He didn't want to tell me the next part, but he wanted to excuse himself. "I tried to talk to her," he told me earnestly, his forehead creased. "She wouldn't *listen* to me. I couldn't let her tell." He shook his head and looked off into the darkness. "I put my hand over her mouth...she kept trying to scream. I had the wrench in my pocket. I had to stop her. I only meant to stop her from talking. But she dropped, like a doll, and she was bleeding all over the place. I didn't mean to do it. I'm sorry, but I couldn't let her tell." The whites of his eyes were showing, like a horse rearing up.

My heart jolted in my breast. "Would you have killed Lizzie, too, if she'd been there with Hazel?"

He was so far gone I was sure he would have killed Lizzie without blinking. He wasn't going to let me go either. Afraid to set him off, I held my breath and didn't speak. I prayed Stephen would forgive me. He would be so angry when he found out I left home after promising him I'd stay away from the Rookery.

"Sorry, Mrs. Chapman. But I *have* to get away. Tommy gave us up. I see that now." He frowned and raised the revolver to point at my forehead. I trembled wildly. I closed my eyes and heard him cock the gun.

An explosion ripped through the air. I felt something strike my left shoulder. Was I hit? I opened my eyes in time to see Lenny's eyes turn up in their sockets. Then he crumpled to my feet as I jumped back, screaming.

"Mother, are you all right?" Rushing from behind a pile of barrels beside us, Tommy dropped a gun onto a packing case and took me in his arms.

"Tommy." He'd crept up along the right-hand wall to get close to us while Lenny was confessing.

"I'm so sorry," Tommy repeated several times until I pushed him away, looking over his shoulder. No one else was there.

"You ran away," I said.

"I saw Lenny run. I was going to stay at the Rookery, like I promised, but then I saw someone follow him. I didn't know it was you until I got here. He was going to shoot you." He hung his head. The gun sat on the box and Lenny lay on the floor.

Tommy had heard what Lenny said before he died. He and I could testify to Lenny's confession that he killed Hazel, but who would believe us? My son would get no reprieve now. Whitbread couldn't help him. Tommy stared at his friend's body in horror.

I'd shot a man once, when I wasn't much older than Tommy. It was during the Pullman strike. The man had killed before and he would have killed me if he could. I shot him dead, but another man claimed the deed, so no one ever knew—except Stephen. And I think Whitbread guessed.

My son stood with his hands over his face. He wasn't ruined, as I feared. He was foolish, but not evil. "Did Lenny kill Fred?" I asked.

He nodded. "He loosened the axle. He didn't tell me till after. He said Fred killed Hazel and he did it for me. For revenge.

I didn't know..." He looked down at the friend he'd shot. "He killed Hazel. And he was afraid that she'd told Fred about us."

I reached out and took up the gun Tommy had cast aside. I nearly dropped it from the weight. "Run!"

"Mother..."

"Run, Tommy." I could hear the clanking of a police wagon bell. "Now."

Doubt flashed in his eyes. He took a final look at Lenny's crumpled body, turned, and fled into the night.

FORTY

That night, Whitbread sent me home in the custody of two uniformed officers with instructions to deliver me to the Harrison Street station in the morning. I told my family everything and we all spent a fitful night. Rather than angry, Stephen was morose.

By the time I was ready to leave the next morning, Stephen had rousted Darrow from his bed and arranged for a hurried conference in the kitchen.

Darrow was sure the police would believe I shot Lenny in self-defense although he looked worried. We all crammed into the police car and, when we arrived, we were taken to the seventh-floor room reserved for interviews with prominent citizens. Darrow assured us it was a good sign. I was too tired and heart sore to care.

Finally, Whitbread marched in followed by Fitz. I was surprised to see the City Hall operative, but I was mildly gratified that he was concerned enough about me to attend. I knew Whitbread would resent any attempt by City Hall to influence him.

It turned out Fitz had not arrived purely to support me.

"Mrs. Chapman," Whitbread said, holding a piece of paper in his hand. "Before you give a statement about the events of last night, I want you to hear what Mr. Fitzgibbons has to say." Whitbread had never liked Fitz and he appeared to be holding back his hostile feelings.

Fitz cleared his throat. "Your son, Thomas, came to me last night," he said, pausing to look over his shoulder at Whitbread. "He told me what happened. He said he followed you and Lenny— Leonard Frommer—to the garage last night. He witnessed Mr. Frommer pointing a gun at you, Mrs. Chapman." He turned toward Whitbread. "To save his mother's life, he fired a pistol, killing Mr. Frommer." Fitz heaved a big sigh for the young men who had spent a year working for him. There were tears in the politician's eyes. "He said that his mother took the gun from his hand and told him to run, and he regretted that he'd done it. That's why he came to me. He was afraid his mother would try to take the blame for Lenny's death, and he couldn't let her do that."

I closed my eyes against tears. How many times I had regretted Tommy's instinct to run away from his problems but, this time, when I wanted him to run away, he refused. "Oh my God," I said. "Was he arrested?"

"No. Mr. Fitzgibbons failed to call the police in time. He escaped," Whitbread said.

I opened my eyes and took a huge breath. At least he got away. I ought to be angry at him, but I couldn't be. He had no chance if he stayed.

"Did he tell you that Lenny killed Hazel and why?" I asked.

Whitbread stepped forward. "Mr. Fitzgibbons did find the time to have your son write down what he says Mr. Frommer confessed about the murder of Miss Littleton and the sabotaging of Mr. Fred Spofford's race car."

"I heard Lenny admit to killing Hazel as well. He told me last night just before he was going to shoot me."

Whitbread gave me a weighty stare. "Your testimony will be taken. However, until we arrest your son, we won't be able to verify those claims. I must warn all of you that Thomas Chapman is a fugitive and if you assist him you risk prosecution yourselves.

"It is regrettable that Mr. Fitzgibbons was *unable* to restrain him but, as City Hall vouches for Fitzgibbons, he probably won't suffer from his failure to prevent Mr. Chapman from escaping. Mr. Fitzgibbons insisted that you hear what he had to tell us *before* you give testimony concerning your own actions last night and I have allowed it. There is no need for you to perjure yourself to take the blame for your son."

I realized that both Fitz and Whitbread believed I would have confessed to shooting Lenny to save my son. They were right. I felt Stephen squeeze my hand.

"That certainly won't happen," Darrow said. "As Mrs. Chapman's attorney I'll make sure her testimony supports that of her son." I could tell the lawyer was greatly relieved. He knew I had lied to him that morning when I claimed that I was the one who shot Lenny. But he showed no surprise at this outcome.

I spent the rest of the day at the police station giving my statement. It grieved me that my son had to run away once again and that this time I had to approve. There was no other way to keep him safe.

FORTY-ONE

Two weeks after the events that caused my son to flee, I attended a peace rally at the Strand with that small minority of people who clung to the tattered hope that conditions for peace could still be proposed.

Stephen had declined to participate. He shook his head and said, "It's no good, Emily. The country is committed now, and we have to see it through. There'll be no peace without military victory. I know you don't want to believe that, but it's true. Once men's passions have been raised to spill blood, there's nothing to do but ride the wave of violence till it's sufficiently smashed down one side in defeat. It mustn't be our side that is crushed." He never objected to my activities, but he was entrenched in his own beliefs.

Jack had left the previous Saturday and I balanced on a brink of foreboding, waiting for news of him. I never even told Lizzie about the peace rally. As far as I knew, she was steadfast in her engagement to George Spofford. Registration for the draft was due to begin within a month and they would marry before that. My grief at Tommy's disappearance and disgrace spared me from participation in the planning of their wedding. I had no idea where my youngest son was, and the Spoffords couldn't bear the mention of his name.

It was a sunny day for such dark thoughts. Looking down the street I saw crowds converging at the door of the Strand. It was the place where we'd heard the Four Minute Men speech with the Spoffords. There were the usual somberly dressed people arriving in a timely fashion for the meeting. A professor from the university would preside, with speeches from representatives of churches, unions, and socialist groups. A crowd of young men in brown uniforms had gathered at one side, along with a few people carrying signs calling us traitors and Kaiser lovers. With so many young men about to be pulled from their families to be sent overseas, all the fear and anxiety people felt was being turned against German Americans and anyone who objected to any aspect of American participation in the war.

As I hurried toward the theater, I saw a motorcar stop in front of the Blackstone. It was George's touring car. I halted to watch as his parents and Lizzie stepped to the curb. A porter drove the car away and the Spoffords looked down the street toward the Strand.

Lizzie was quite beautiful in a pale blue walking suit with creamy lace trim and a stylish hat. She seemed neither happy nor sad as she contemplated the mix of people in front of the theater. Lizzie had told me the Spoffords were deeply pained to hear the sordid story that surrounded the deaths of Fred and Hazel. It shocked them to discover their firm belief that their son was killed by German sympathizers was untrue. They didn't want to believe it. They also wanted to reject the explanation that the bombing was part of a waiters' strike rather than a German plot. They refused to believe the reports that Fred had provided the bombers with the nitro. Richard Spofford was vehemently adamant that the American Protective League would never have gone to such lengths to uncover saboteurs.

"George and his father have to believe Fred died to protect the country," Lizzie told me. "It's too soon for them to accept what really happened. They're afraid. They lost one son and they can't bear the thought that George could be drafted, yet they fear being called out as cowards, too. They want to do something patriotic. They want Fred's death to have been for a patriotic cause." She took a big breath. "Poor George. He so wanted to give me that big wedding. But everything has changed now."

I remembered when my mother died and how I felt as if the kaleidoscope of my life had turned, the old pattern suddenly gone and a completely new pattern of my life in Chicago begun. The pattern was changing for Lizzie now…for all of us.

I stood for a moment on Seventh Street. Watching them from afar, I caught Lizzie's eye. I knew she didn't begrudge me my persistence in the peace movement, which most people thought so useless. And I understood her determination to stand by her fiancé during this crisis. She smiled, but Regina Spofford looked at me with anger, muttered something, and stalked into the hotel followed by her husband. As George reached out for Lizzie, I turned away.

I saw a disturbance at the theater and hurried toward it. Several young men in brown uniforms were stopped at the door by two of the organizers.

"We're interested," said the bulky youngster in the lead. "We want to ask what it's all about."

"We don't want any disturbance," one of our men said.

"Who are you, young man?" I asked. "Where are you from?" If they were here to cause trouble, it would help to be able to track them down afterward.

Four of them shifted on their feet in front of me, looking at each other. Then the leader looked back at the corner and waved to a larger group to come over. "We're from the training camp at Fort Sheridan." He grinned. The closer the larger group got, the more confident he was.

One of my committee ushered a few of our real audience through the door behind us.

"We just want to come in and hear what you've got to say," the young man said.

"Yeah, it's a free country, isn't it?" another one said. The larger group arrived and was filling in the space around us, elbowing out some of the rally participants who stepped back in confusion. They didn't want any trouble, but they wanted to get through the door.

I frowned. "What is your name?" I asked. This was turning into a confrontation. I was quite sure our side, filled with middle-aged academics and progressives, was bound to lose against so much youth and vigor. Someone would get hurt.

"Here, now, you don't need to know that." The young leader took a step forward to loom over me.

"Step back!" one of my fellow pacifists demanded, but the young trainee just smiled.

Gritting my teeth, I prepared to push back when there was movement behind the young man and a gloved hand tapped the tall shoulder. He frowned and turned sideways.

Lizzie stood there smiling politely. The young man was immediately flustered by her beauty. He stared, open mouthed.

"Surely you can tell my mother your name," she said, her eyebrows raised in feigned surprise. "I'm Lizzie Chapman, and this is my mother." She held out her gloved hand.

"Your mother?" He ignored her hand.

"That's right. Now, *we've* got a meeting to attend. I'm sure it would be very boring for you and your friends, so why don't you let these people through and be on your way?" She waved the group through as the young men looked uncertain. People brushed past them, rolling their eyes at the rudeness of youth.

The brash young leader snapped his mouth closed and frowned. "We came to attend the meeting, too, and we mean to do it."

This time another hand clapped harshly onto his shoulder, turning him around. "Time to get back to your training station," Detective Whitbread said.

The young man faced the tall, gangly detective. Over his shoulder, I saw uniformed officers spread through the crowd, separating wheat from chaff as they let rally participants through to the door and pushed back the young men in uniform.

"Hey, you can't do that," one of them said, and some began pushing back at the policemen.

Whitbread blew a whistle and held up a hand. "All right. Pay attention all of you. If you've come here to try to disrupt this meeting, we won't allow it."

"They're supporting the Kaiser!" someone yelled.

"Traitors! We're going to fight and they're supporting the enemy!"

There was more pushing and shoving against the line of policemen protecting people pouring into the theater. Whitbread blew his whistle again. When he had relative silence, he shouted, "Every legitimate right of free speech and assemblage will be protected. If you men start any trouble you'll be arrested, and we'll call in your superiors from Fort Sheridan to deal with you, so keep that in mind."

There was grumbling and whispered insults, but the young men were reluctant to get in trouble with their superior officers. Whitbread had convinced them and, as they drifted away, I thanked him.

"Tempers are up," he said. "But we've a duty to keep the peace. I can't say I agree with your committee in there, but they've a right to meet." He started to turn away, then stopped. "I know it's been hard for you with your son gone, Emily," he said quietly. "You know if he shows up, I'll do everything I can to arrest him. But there's no need for us to quarrel. Gracie says she'll be in touch." He tipped his hat and moved out to direct his men.

I was touched. At least that wound of broken trust between us might heal now. I turned to thank Lizzie and send her back to the Blackstone.

"No, Mother, I'm going in with you." She nodded toward the door and took my elbow to lead me forward.

"But George?" I said. I was afraid George's parents would be furious with her over this. I wanted to spare her the heartache.

"It's all right, Mother." She stopped, glancing around. We were in the lobby. They were just closing the doors as the speakers began. "It's over between George and me."

"The engagement?"

"It's off. I broke it." She sighed. "He wasn't surprised. I was determined to tell him today, and when I saw you it gave me the courage to speak as soon as we got inside the Blackstone. I told George I couldn't go through with it. With Jack gone and Tommy who knows where—I can't leave you and Father alone. George understands. He has to think of his own parents. With Fred gone they're petrified that George will have to fight. I had to break if off now, while there's still time for George to find someone else. Don't worry. There are plenty of girls in our set who'd love to marry him and rescue him from the draft." She gave a little laugh. "You'd be surprised. It's the thing to do these days—marry a young man and save him from the war."

EPILOGUE

Lizzie didn't marry George. George married another young woman and got the marriage exemption from the draft. Then, when his father died suddenly of a stroke, George took over the advertising agency. Their work for the government propaganda efforts made him indispensable. Over the next years I sat on a number of local defense committees with George Spofford or his wife. They were always very cordial, though he seemed a bit sad.

Lizzie resolutely refused to be drawn into any war work. She took up studies at the Art Institute, painting and even apprenticing to a sculptor. Later, she worked at a company that designed masks and artificial limbs for men who returned from the war disfigured by burns or as amputees. But that's another story.

Jack was posted near the front and, when injured by shrapnel, he came home for a month, long enough to spend many evenings in Stephen's study with his father and a whiskey bottle. Then he went back. I hated to see him go. But at least he returned after the armistice. Like many men, he was changed by the experience and suffered from it. But we had him home. Alex Mirkin's number came up in the first draft, but it wasn't till much later that he was listed among the dead at Belleau Wood.

Fitz sent me a newspaper clipping with a picture of Thomas Chapman, a pilot with the Lafayette Group. It seemed that he was one of the young men who got help from Mr. Insull to go through

Canada and enlist in France. In January 1918, we received a letter from his commanding officer reporting his valor in combat before his death in a crash. As was the custom, each man left a letter for their family in case of their death. Tommy's was enclosed:

Dear Mother,

If you're reading this, I'm gone. I know it will make you sad but at least I've done something with my life. The men I serve with are more than I deserve, and we look out for each other. I'm so sorry I caused you and Father so much pain. I know I broke my word to Detective Whitbread and Mr. Darrow when I ran away, but I couldn't bear it. I loved Hazel, and to find out it was my fault she was killed destroyed me. I wanted to die but at least I've spent what's left of my life doing something useful. We've saved men with our flights over the enemy.

I love flying. You've no idea how wonderful it is to soar above it all. It's the only place where I can feel whole again, and where I almost feel I can talk to Hazel. Think of me as being with her now, I hope for it.

Tell Father and Jack and Lizzie how very sorry I am to have caused so much grief. Remember me from before all that, please.

Your loving son,
Tommy

AFTERWORD

Since the Emily Cabot Mysteries are set against the backdrop of important historical events in Chicago, I always intended to have at least one story take place during World War I. Chicago is a quintessential American city, and that war was a critical turning point for the country. With the old civilizations of Europe locked in a stalemate, the United States finally, reluctantly, entered the war, and the importance of this new world power was stamped into history. It's a challenge to imagine what it was like at the start of a huge conflict like this, when the people described have no idea how the story will end. We look back now knowing the results, but they were looking ahead, unable to see where the path was leading.

So, thinking about what Chicago was like in the spring of 1917 was an interesting exercise. As usual, when I started researching in contemporary sources, I discovered many things I hadn't known. For instance, the fact that President Wilson ran for reelection boasting that he had kept the United States out of the bloody conflict. And yet the following spring he would lead the country into the war. We don't remember how strong the sentiment was against getting involved in that war, so the fact that the popular song of the year before was "I Didn't Raise My Son to be a Soldier" was a surprise. I think the way public sentiment seemed to turn on a dime away from isolationism toward a patriotism that was fueled by war madness, was shocking yet totally believable.

I grew up during the Vietnam War, when there was deep dissension in the country. It's useful to realize that what may have seemed like straightforward support for wars of an earlier time was really much more strained, difficult, and uncertain. Of course, with Emily's background working at Hull House, Jane Addams's efforts to find peace had to be included. In the preface to her book *Peace and Bread in Time of War* (1922), Jane Addams mentions how many people objected to her stance as a pacifist. She writes, "Our portion was the odium accorded those who, because they are not allowed to state their own cause, suffer constantly from inimical misrepresentation and are often placed in the position of seeming to defend what is a mere travesty of their convictions. We realize, therefore, that even the kindest of readers must perforce still look at our group through the distorting spectacles he was made to wear during the long period of war propaganda." It was not until 1931, long after World War I ended, that she received the Nobel Peace Prize.

The fictional character Hazel was inspired by the real Women's Peace Parade of August 29, 1914. That solemn march down Fifth Avenue right after war was declared in Europe was the beginning of peace activism that included public demonstrations. The Woman's Peace Party was formed soon after, and it became the American arm of the Women's International League for Peace and Freedom after the 1915 conference that Hazel attended. A report about that conference and the visits to warring countries afterwards was published as *Women at the Hague: The International Congress of Women and its Results*. https://archive.org/details/womenathagueinte00adda/

Another surprising set of events were the sharp confrontations between labor and capital at the time. There were many bombings that had nothing to do with spies or the war and everything to do with labor disputes. The aborted bombing of the Bismarck Garden café was a real incident described in newspaper reports of the time.

I also learned that the German American ethnic group in Chicago never really recovered from the bad feelings of that era. The renaming of places and things, while sometimes ridiculous, was a symptom of the intense hatred of all things German. It's interesting to note that the Bismarck Garden was renamed Marigold Garden in December 1917. But anglicizing names was a comparatively mild reaction. The most draconian anti-espionage laws in our history were passed at that time. They have been used to indict people who released classified data on the Internet in recent years. It's best not to forget what we've done in the past; sometimes we suffer amnesia when it comes to earlier conflicts.

Some of the sources I used included *Chicago Transformed: World War I and the Windy City* by Joseph Gustaitis (2016). Also, Augie Aleksy at Centuries and Sleuths bookstore in Forest Park, IL, suggested *Intimate Voices from the First World War* (2004) edited by Svetlana Palmer and Sarah Wallis, which was helpful in presenting the points of view of real people at the time.

Clarence Darrow seemed like someone Emily Cabot Chapman would have known, and it was interesting to learn where he was in his career in the spring of 1917. Biographies I consulted included *Story of My Life* by Clarence Darrow (1932), *Clarence Darrow: Attorney for the Damned* by John A. Farrell (2011), and *Clarence Darrow for the Defense* by Irving Stone (1941).

Discovering the Four Minute Men was fascinating. Advertising was already important early in the twentieth century, and the use of advertising men, with their strategies to turn the tide of public opinion in favor of the war, was a much more organized activity than I had ever imagined. The fact that this effort was begun by men in Chicago meant it had to be a part of my story.

The history of the American Protective League was another eye-opener for me. The idea of amateur spy hunters watching and informing on their neighbors reminded me of stories of Chinese communism later in the century. I had no idea we'd indulged in such "spy on your neighbor" activities. I consulted online versions of the reports from the league, available through HathiTrust, and also a number of secondary sources on the APL. Soon after the time of this story they began trying to identify "slackers," men who failed to register for the draft. They also hounded some German Americans with accusations of spying. The story of my fictional character Fred Spofford being an agent provocateur who gives the strikers bomb materials is not based on any real incident. It was intended to demonstrate how labor movements like strikes were confused with anti-American activities like spying during this time.

Of course, the rise of the motorcar is such an important American story in this era that I had to include it. The book *Blood and Smoke: A True Tale of Mystery, Mayhem, and the Birth of the Indy 500* by Charles Leerhsen (2011) provided useful information about racing motorcars during this time period. For more information on the South Loop area designated as Motor Row, I consulted https://chicagology.com/motorrow/. Additional materials are available from when that area was designated a historic district.

As always, contemporary newspaper stories were most helpful. I learned that Chicago police detectives whose appointment predated the civil service exams were being demoted at this time. Also, information about Mayor Thompson's opposition to the war and attempts to defend his German American voters was a surprise. Things are never as straightforward as we want to believe. I think it's fascinating that the mayor of a major city was so outspoken in his disagreement with the country's entrance into the war. The book *Big Bill of Chicago* by Lloyd Wendt and Herman Kogan (1953) provides more detail about Thompson, one of the many colorful mayors of the Windy City.

Newspaper reports of the spring of 1917 were also the source for the subplot about the burglaries. An organized gang was blowing safes in buildings, and they used a code similar to the one described. I was very surprised to learn the police were already doing wiretapping at that time to catch criminals.

The description of the bakers' strike and the meeting at which District Attorney Clyne threatened the bakers with internment in camps was also from newspaper articles. Internment camps were established in Utah and Georgia. At first, they were used for Germans, especially the crews of German ships caught in the United States at the time of the declaration of war. Later, they were used for non-citizens who were accused of sympathy for Germany, including many classical musicians, such as Boston Symphony Orchestra conductor Frederick Stock.

Society pages in the papers also describe the enthusiasm of young women who jumped in to do war work and the desire of many young men to get married to avoid the draft. It was a point I only touched on in passing, but I was fascinated to learn that the draft, as we knew it in World War II and Vietnam, was actually first instituted in 1917. Also, I hadn't realized that the ROTC was started in preparation for World War I and that it was active at the University of Chicago. Nor did I know that the income tax was first proposed around this time.

I skipped many years of Emily Cabot's life to bring the story to this point. My intention is to have the next book follow much sooner. It will be set in the fall of 1918. Thank you to the readers who ask for when the next book will be out. It's an inspiration to know someone is waiting to hear more about the characters. I hope the new books don't disappoint.

ACKNOWLEDGMENTS

T hank you to my new critique group in Cambridge, which includes Leslie Wheeler, Mark Ammons, Cheryl Marceau, and Katherine Fast; and also my old critique group from Chicago, The Complete Unknowns—Anne Sharfman, Nancy Braun, and Emily Victorson. We've scattered a bit to the winds, but I appreciate their willingness to continue to be beta readers for the series, along with Stuart Miller and Roz Hoey. Special thanks to editor and publisher Emily Victorson of Allium Press of Chicago.

ALSO PUBLISHED BY ALLIUM PRESS OF CHICAGO

Fiction with a Chicago Connection

Visit our website for more information:
www.alliumpress.com

THE EMILY CABOT MYSTERIES
Frances McNamara

Death at the Fair

The 1893 World's Columbian Exposition provides a vibrant backdrop for the first book in the series. Emily Cabot, one of the first women graduate students at the University of Chicago, is eager to prove herself in the emerging field of sociology. While she is busy exploring the Exposition with her family and friends, her colleague, Dr. Stephen Chapman, is accused of murder. Emily sets out to search for the truth behind the crime, but is thwarted by the gamblers, thieves, and corrupt politicians who are ever-present in Chicago. A lynching that occurred in the dead man's past leads Emily to seek the assistance of the black activist Ida B. Wells.

◆

Death at Hull House

After Emily Cabot is expelled from the University of Chicago, she finds work at Hull House, the famous settlement established by Jane Addams. There she quickly becomes involved in the political and social problems of the immigrant community. But, when a man who works for a sweatshop owner is murdered in the Hull House parlor, Emily must determine whether one of her colleagues is responsible, or whether the real reason for the murder is revenge for a past tragedy in her own family. As a smallpox epidemic spreads through the impoverished west side of Chicago, the very existence of the settlement is threatened and Emily finds herself in jeopardy from both the deadly disease and a killer.

◆

Death at Pullman

A model town at war with itself . . . George Pullman created an ideal community for his railroad car workers, complete with every amenity they could want or need. But when hard economic times hit in 1894, lay-offs follow and the workers can no longer pay their rent or buy food at the company store. Starving and desperate, they turn against their once benevolent employer. Emily Cabot and her friend Dr. Stephen Chapman bring much needed food and medical supplies to the town, hoping they can meet the immediate needs of the workers and keep them from resorting to violence. But when one young worker—suspected of being a spy—is murdered, and a bomb plot comes to light, Emily must race to discover the truth behind a tangled web of family and company alliances.

◆

Death at Woods Hole

Exhausted after the tumult of the Pullman Strike of 1894, Emily Cabot is looking forward to a restful summer visit to Cape Cod. She has plans to collect "beasties" for the Marine Biological Laboratory, alongside other visiting scientists from the University of Chicago. She also hopes to enjoy romantic clambakes with Dr. Stephen Chapman, although they must keep an important secret from their friends. But her summer takes a dramatic turn when she finds a dead man floating in a fish tank. In order to solve his murder she must first deal with dueling scientists, a testy local sheriff, the theft of a fortune, and uncooperative weather.

◆

Death at Chinatown

In the summer of 1896, amateur sleuth Emily Cabot meets two young Chinese women who have recently received medical degrees. She is inspired to make an important decision about her own life when she learns about the difficult choices they have made in order to pursue their careers. When one of the women is accused of poisoning a Chinese herbalist, Emily once again finds herself in the midst of a murder investigation. But, before the case can be solved, she must first settle a serious quarrel with her husband, help quell a political uprising, and overcome threats against her family. Timeless issues, such as restrictions on immigration, the conflict between Western and Eastern medicine, and women's struggle to balance family and work, are woven seamlessly throughout this mystery set in Chicago's original Chinatown.

Death at the Paris Exposition

In the sixth Emily Cabot Mystery, the intrepid amateur sleuth's journey once again takes her to a world's fair—the Paris Exposition of 1900. Chicago socialite Bertha Palmer has been named the only female U. S. commissioner to the Exposition and she enlists Emily's services as her social secretary. Their visit to the House of Worth for the fitting of a couture gown is interrupted by the theft of Mrs. Palmer's famous pearl necklace. Before that crime can be solved, several young women meet untimely deaths and a member of the Palmers' inner circle is accused of the crimes. As Emily races to clear the family name she encounters jealous society ladies, American heiresses seeking titled European husbands, and more luscious gowns and priceless jewels. Along the way, she takes refuge from the tumult at the country estate of Impressionist painter Mary Cassatt. In between her work and sleuthing, she is able to share the Art Nouveau delights of the Exposition, and the enduring pleasures of the City of Light, with her husband and their young children.

◆

Death at the Selig Studios

The early summer of 1909 finds Emily Cabot eagerly anticipating a relaxing vacation with her family. Before they can depart, however, she receives news that her brother, Alden, has been involved in a shooting death at the Selig Polyscope silent movie studios on Chicago's northwest side. She races to investigate, along with her friend Detective Henry Whitbread. There they discover a sprawling backlot, complete with ferocious jungle animals and the celluloid cowboys Tom Mix and Broncho Billy. As they dig deeper into the situation, they uncover furtive romantic liaisons between budding movie stars and an attempt by Thomas Edison to maintain his stranglehold over the emerging film industry. Before the intrepid amateur sleuth can clear her brother's name she faces a serious break with the detective; a struggle with her adolescent daughter, who is obsessed with the filming of the original Wizard of Oz movie; and threats upon her own life.

THE HANLEY & RIVKA MYSTERIES
D. M. Pirrone

Shall We Not Revenge

In the harsh early winter months of 1872, while Chicago is still smoldering from the Great Fire, Irish Catholic detective Frank Hanley is assigned the case of a murdered Orthodox Jewish rabbi. His investigation proves difficult when the neighborhood's Yiddish-speaking residents, wary of outsiders, are reluctant to talk. But when the rabbi's headstrong daughter, Rivka, unexpectedly offers to help Hanley find her father's killer, the detective receives much more than the break he was looking for. Their pursuit of the truth draws Rivka and Hanley closer together and leads them to a relief organization run by the city's wealthy movers and shakers. Along the way, they uncover a web of political corruption, crooked cops, and well-buried ties to two notorious Irish thugs from Hanley's checkered past. Even after he is kicked off the case, stripped of his badge, and thrown in jail, Hanley refuses to quit. With a personal vendetta to settle for an innocent life lost, he is determined to expose a complicated criminal scheme, not only for his own sake, but for Rivka's as well.

For You Were Strangers

On a spring morning in 1872, former Civil War officer Ben Champion is discovered dead in his Chicago bedroom—a bayonet protruding from his back. What starts as a routine case for Detective Frank Hanley soon becomes anything but, as his investigation into Champion's life turns up hidden truths best left buried. Meanwhile, Rivka Kelmansky's long-lost brother, Aaron, arrives on her doorstep, along with his mulatto wife and son. Fugitives from an attack by night riders, Aaron and his family know too much about past actions that still threaten powerful men—defective guns provided to Union soldiers, and an 1864 conspiracy to establish Chicago as the capital of a Northwest Confederacy. Champion had his own connection to that conspiracy, along with ties to a former slave now passing as white and an escaped Confederate guerrilla bent on vengeance, any of which might have led to his death. Hanley and Rivka must untangle this web of circumstances, amid simmering hostilities still present seven years after the end of the Civil War, as they race against time to solve the murder, before the secrets of bygone days claim more victims.

Promises to the Dead

As Chicago recovers from the Great Fire of 1871, the Civil War continues to haunt its residents. What begins for Detective Frank Hanley as the simple case of a missing railroad clerk quickly escalates into something much more complex. Ezra Hayes, who has made a daring escape from forced servitude on a Louisiana sugar plantation, brings to Chicago proof of nefarious doings in the South. His information implicates the missing clerk's employer, a major shipper of sugar. As Hanley struggles to untangle the web of circumstances surrounding the railroad's role in the clerk's disappearance, Rivka Kelmansky faces her own personal struggle. Her brother is pressuring her to marry a young man from her tight-knit Jewish community, but she still dreams of forging a new life with Hanley. When her mulatto sister-in-law is wrongfully accused of murder, Rivka turns to Hanley for help. Facing opposition on multiple fronts, they must race against time to save Ada's life and uncover the shocking truth.

Honor Above All
J. Bard-Collins

Pinkerton agent Garrett Lyons arrives in Chicago in 1882, close on the trail of the person who murdered his partner. He encounters a vibrant city that is striving ever upwards, full of plans to construct new buildings that will "scrape the sky." In his quest for the truth Garrett stumbles across a complex plot involving counterfeit government bonds, fierce architectural competition, and painful reminders of his military past. Along the way he seeks the support and companionship of his friends—elegant Charlotte, who runs an upscale poker game for the city's elite, and up-and-coming architect Louis Sullivan. Rich with historical details that bring early 1880s Chicago to life, this novel will appeal equally to mystery fans, history buffs, and architecture enthusiasts.

◆

The Reason for Time
Mary Burns

On a hot, humid Monday afternoon in July 1919, Maeve Curragh watches as a blimp plunges from the sky and smashes into a downtown Chicago bank building. It is the first of ten extraordinary days in Chicago history that will forever change the course of her life. Racial tensions mount as soldiers return from the battlefields of Europe and the Great Migration brings new faces to the city, culminating in violent race riots. Each day the young Irish immigrant, a catalogue order clerk for the Chicago Magic Company, devours the news of a metropolis where cultural pressures are every bit as febrile as the weather. But her interest in the headlines wanes when she catches the eye of a charming streetcar conductor. Maeve's singular voice captures the spirit of a young woman living through one of Chicago's most turbulent periods. Seamlessly blending fact with fiction, Mary Burns weaves an evocative tale of how an ordinary life can become inextricably linked with history.

Where My Body Ends and the World Begins
Tony Romano

On December 1, 1958, a devastating blaze at Our Lady of the Angels School in Chicago took the lives of ninety-two children, shattering a close-knit Italian neighborhood. In this eloquent novel, set nearly a decade later, twenty-year-old Anthony Lazzeri struggles with survivor's guilt, which is manifested through conflicted feelings about his own body. Complicating his life is a retired detective's dogged belief that Anthony was involved in the setting of the fire. Tony Romano's delicate handling of Anthony's journey is deeply moving, exploring the complex psychological toll such an event has on those involved, including families...and an entire community. This multi-faceted tale follows Anthony's struggles to come to terms with how the events of that day continue to affect him and those around him. Aided by a sometime girlfriend, a former teacher, and later his parents—after long buried family secrets are brought into the open—he attempts to piece together a life for himself as an adult.

◆

Sync

K. P. Kyle

Every day we each make thousands of decisions. Sometimes it's the big ones that change our lives, sometimes it's the tiny ones. What if all the choices not made led to billions of alternate realities where different versions of our lives unwind? On a cold and rainy night in New England, the paths of two strangers collide—a young man fleeing from his past, and a forty-something woman dreading what her future holds. When his past catches up to him, the two of them embark on a journey of danger, adventure, and self-discovery. Ultimately, they each need to face the question, How far would you go to help someone in need? K. P. Kyle's debut novel is a riveting technothriller/road trip/ parallel universes combo with a healthy dollop of romance. It will keep you hooked until the very end and make you ponder the choices you've made in your own life.

FOR YOUNGER READERS

Her Mother's Secret
Barbara Garland Polikoff

Fifteen-year-old Sarah, the daughter of Jewish immigrants, wants nothing more than to become an artist. But as she spreads her wings she must come to terms with the secrets that her family is only beginning to share with her. Replete with historical details that vividly evoke the Chicago of the 1890s, this moving coming-of-age story is set against the backdrop of a vibrant, turbulent city. Sarah moves between two very different worlds—the colorful immigrant neighborhood surrounding Hull House and the sophisticated, elegant World's Columbian Exposition. This novel eloquently captures the struggles of a young girl as she experiences the timeless emotions of friendship, family turmoil, loss...and first love.

A companion guide to *Her Mother's Secret*
is available at www.alliumpress.com. In the guide you will find
resources for further exploration of Sarah's time and place.

◆

City of Grit and Gold
Maud Macrory Powell

The streets of Chicago in 1886 are full of turmoil. Striking workers clash with police...illness and injury lurk around every corner...and twelve-year-old Addie must find her way through it all. Torn between her gruff Papa—who owns a hat shop and thinks the workers should be content with their American lives—and her beloved Uncle Chaim—who is active in the protests for the eight-hour day—Addie struggles to understand her topsy-turvy world, while keeping her family intact. Set in a Jewish neighborhood of Chicago during the days surrounding the Haymarket Affair, this novel vividly portrays one immigrant family's experience, while also eloquently depicting the timeless conflict between the haves and the have-nots.

A companion guide to *City of Grit and Gold*
is available at www.alliumpress.com. In the guide you will find
resources for further exploration of Addie's time and place.

OUTLIER BOOKS

Novels without a Chicago connection that will appeal to those who've enjoyed other Allium Press books.

◆

Never Walk Back
Adam J. Shafer

All Ruth Casper wants is to make her mark on the world, but in the post-Civil War South she's considered a person of no consequence. After witnessing a speeding locomotive massacre a herd of wild elk, she conjures up the design for an improved railroad brake. It's based on an invention that her husband, Henry, a tinkerer and a dreamer, has been unable to bring to reality. Ruth encourages him to construct the brake, and the two of them undergo a perilous trip north to Washington to have it patented. There they encounter Augustus Windom, the man-child heir to his father's railroad empire, who's obsessed with establishing his own legacy. When he decides that he'd rather steal Henry's creation than pay for it honestly, the three of them set upon a collision course with each other that has far-reaching consequences. Rich in historical details, this novel will appeal equally to railroad enthusiasts and readers who enjoy stories about women who chase their dreams with boldness and grit.